THE
JOY
DIVISIONS

SCOTT DIMOVITZ

TAILWINDS PRESS

Text copyright © 2023 by Scott Dimovitz

Tailwinds Press
P.O. Box 2283, Radio City Station
New York, NY 10101-2283
www.tailwindspress.com

Published in the United States of America
ISBN: 979-8-9886903-0-6
1st ed. 2023

The
Joy Divisions

For Lara, Quentin, and Beckett.
Interdum vita bona est.

PART I
PHILADELPHIA
1990

CHAPTER ONE
PHILADELPHIA, MAY 11, 1990

"I'm telling you, Ed. Tod's got plans, man—*The* Plan," the voice squealed greasy over the diner din and the power-chord chomp of Tony Iomi's guitar and Ozzy Osbourne's plaintive howl that blared through the restaurant's sound system. "Jesus, I can't believe it's only been nine months since you left. It's totally different now. It's just *different*. Allentown's getting this vibe. Everyone's up in arms. Literally, with the kids. Allen High's got real cops, now. You get that? *Real* fucking cops. Not just the rent-a-cops from when we were there. *Real* cops."

"Real cops, Eddie," said Kevin.

"Actually, Serge," said Ed, "I was at Central Catholic."

"That just it, man. You just don't know. The kids are carrying

AK-47s in gym bags. That's how you can tell—when the bag's weighed down. My kid brother's still there, man. AK-47s? Shit. What'd we have? Huh? Couple-three knife fights at worst. At worst. They're even talking about putting metal detectors in and getting ID badges. I-fucking-D."

"IDs, Eddie," said Kevin. "Not even egos or superegos. *I-Ds.*"

"Exactly!" Serge Cieco glimmered with what he thought was a union of souls—a perfect understanding between himself and Kevin, who nodded empathically, making eye contact without waver. Serge met this occasionally, in between glances around the room as if looking out for someone or something.

Ed Pullman sat erect, staring at this shifting gnome of a human specimen, trying to remember Serge, a shade of his former self, whom, despite his uterine estimate, Ed had not seen in over a year. It was around Christmas break when Serge, Freak Ferguson, and Tim the Enchanter were graduating to bigger and better Produce—opium and acid, to be precise. The grad school of Produce Studies, Ed supposed, before moving on to post-doc work in angel dust and smack. In the year-and-a-half it had been since Ed last saw him, Serge had metamorphosed from a prostrate slacker, prone to impromptu disquisitions about the similarity between the veins in a leaf to the veins in his hand, to this bobbing homunculus, expletive-heavy, fraternal-minded, with an apocalyptic, glassy-red stare, as if he had been to the desert and didn't fare as well with the Evil One as some more famous colleagues from the past.

Serge had taken Ed by surprise. He had heard from Freak over the break that Serge OD'd on tainted crank and was laid-up unconscious at Sacred Heart Hospital. He must have lost about forty pounds since Ed saw him last. As Ed and Kevin had entered the South Street Diner, he had heard Serge's voice call across the room.

"Dude!"

Oh, yes. It was like that. "Dude" was precisely the type of greeting Serge Cieco would use on just about any occasion—phone calls, job interviews, weddings, funerals. It was the anachronistic Dead Head's all-purpose "Aloha"—a sort of shibboleth for Those-Who-Carry to distinguish themselves from Those-Who-Don't. Ed had not been a Carrier in over a year, since his ex-girlfriend Dana's punk was strictly straight edge. But since their break-up, he was increasingly tempted to remember how he could get baked and eat half a Salvatore's pizza by himself in one sitting, a consistent weekend activity his junior year when supplies weren't being shut off from some sting or other from wherever they got it from. Back in Allentown, he had got to know Dolphin Street over on the East Side as well as his own—the down-sloping road off Hanover Avenue where the motorcade of Acuras, Lexuses, and BMWs cabal-cruised in clutched neutral, waiting for the walkie-talkie strapped Harrison-Morton Middle School kids to get to them like some surreal drive-in diner out of *Happy Days* or *Grease*. In retrospect, Ed found it hard to believe that the police didn't know about this setup, yet some sanguine standard allowed the passover for his poor-ass self when he drove with his rich West End friends.

"It's a fuckin' race war," Serge said. "We see it coming, Eddie. I *see* it. Tod says the brothers have been down for too long. Black over white. Shit, you know what it's like, man. The Compton brothers get more and more people at every one of their parties. All in their swastikas and shit. And we got it coming, Eddie. You *know* we do. I can *see* it. It shall come to blood."

Ed tilted his head like a dog hearing a whistle in the distance and let his dyed-black hair flop back to its normal dangle over his left eye. The "shall" hung in the air, prophetic and weirdly out of place. Serge was quoting. But from whom? And for what purpose?

"What are you doing in Philly?" Ed asked.

"That's what I'm *talking* about. Everything's cut-off. There's crackdowns everywhere. Dave Gusterson was sent up last summer. They got both Fluties over Christmas break. Shit, even Tim got busted. This time he was a voter and KidsPeace wouldn't consider him 'cause he tested over 70. I have to take over his route till he gets out. But they're in Camden, and they won't talk to a non-brother. Some racist code, man. And they are so full of shit. I know what they're packin', and all they've got is a bunch of poppers and some third-rate Adam."

"Adam?" Ed said.

"MDMA," said Kevin. "Ecstasy."

"Fucking designer jean, ravin', Tide-box-purse-carrying *bullshit.*"

Ed looked at Kevin.

"Club kids," said Kevin. "You know. Tristan Tzara without the depth."

"Fucking *A.* Which is great if you wanna screw your mommy-clone or whatever. But it fucking sucks if you're an *explorer.*"

For an instant, Ed was actually moved by the sight of Serge's slack-jawed sincerity. The freeze-frame lasted only a second or two, but in that moment, Ed sensed a level of wide-eyed commitment he hadn't experienced in non-architecture school students for a long while. Not the teeniest irony. Not the tiniest smirk. Ed felt a movement within him, a sort of pulsion to aid Serge as a Boy Scout might go in quest of an elderly woman to help her across an intersection so he could turn his pin right-side up for the day. And now that he had planned to drop out of college this morning, he couldn't find a reason not to.

"We'll help," said Kevin.

Serge started yet seemed dubious. He searched Ed and Kevin's faces.

"How?" he said, lowering his voice. "You know some brothers?"

"You're looking at him," said Ed.

Serge looked at Kevin, then at Ed, then back at Kevin. He blinked and tried to focus his eyes as if Kevin were a long way across a valley. He turned to Ed, brow furrowed.

"You shittin' me?"

"I don't shit," said Ed, looking at Kevin. Serge blushed and stammered.

"I-I am *sorry*, dude." Blink. "I di-didn't mean." Blink. "Y-you know you don't look African-American."

"I'm not," said Kevin. "I'm Canadian."

Serge looked at Ed as if for a translation. Ed looked back, following this script in his mind as he went along. Serge blinked and smiled. Kevin smiled back and poured an unmeasured pile of sugar into his cup, stirring counterclockwise. Ed considered his friend's shadowless face and earthen eyes—smooth, serene. Hair slicked back with Studio Gel. Kevin was the product of Yippies on the run to Winnipeg nine months after Seymour Hersh horrified the nation by breaking the news about the My Lai Massacre. The Canucks were also far more accepting of a mixed-race marriage, and even though his mother was very fair-skinned from another mixing back in the day, she still felt tensions after the 1969 race riots in York, Pennsylvania. They returned to Pennsylvania in 1974, homeschooling him on Abbie Hoffman and Mao Tse-tung. Little Red Textbook.

"Great . . . great. Oh, *man*. I'll owe you big time. People got me in a . . . I've got responsi*bili*ties to certain people. I'll hook you up. I'm good for it. Ask your cousin."

"By marriage," said Ed. Awkward pause.

"Hey, Ed," Serge said. "You're almost done, aren't you? When you getting back to Allentown?"

"I don't think I am. I'm checking out a couple of leads for a summer job tomorrow, I think."

"Why?" asked Serge. "Aren't you finishing the semester?"

Ed closed his open sketchbook and looked at the black vinyl cover, worn, dog-eared, words carved down to the cardboard with an X-ACTO blade and filled in with colored pencil—*The Cure*, *The Smiths*, and *XTC* written in Wite-Out across the front and back. He fanned his fingers across the smooth, lusterless, woodgrain Formica surface of the table in front of him and watched his veins rise up between the flexed tendons under his anemic olive skin, fingers tremulous. His fingers cast a bleary penumbra from the faux Tiffany stained-glass fixture hanging over

9

the table like a cheap pool hall lamp.

"He just found out his mom's dying," said Kevin. "Stage four lung cancer. Inoperable."

A silent clairvoyance passed between them. The ticking clock on the wall next to them pulsed below the labyrinthine metered counterpoint of Bach's *Brandenburg Concertos*, which bleated through the diner's warbling Soundesign speakers. Ed had read that the concertos were among the first messages to whomever or whatever in space might receive them, wedged among Leonardo Da Vinci's *Vitruvian Man* and Beethoven's Fifth on a gold-plated copper record aboard the Voyager spacecraft, which was sent out in 1977 as a desperate plea that we are not guilty of our history, that we should not be judged by our sins, that the violence and the lust and the blood shared between us are an unfortunate consequence of fate, a mere byproduct of our humanity, not to be confused with the continuing upward trajectory of our destiny—a melodramatic accident in our consonant diatonic harmony.

Muraled across the diner's chalky-white west wall, a map of Greece faded away into Albania on the left and Turkey on the right; *Athens, Stromboli,* and *Patras* in black boldface. Crete was eclipsed by a lone customer, a leather-jacketed Odysseus with black hair, black eyes, and a glossy rayon shirt, crouching over a dog-eared paperback of Aristotle's *Nicomachean Ethics*, his right foot anchored between the straps of a black nylon Eastpak backpack on the floor. Blue, blocked letters arched across the top of the wall:

SOUTH STREET *DINER*
"A SOUTH STREET TRADITION SINCE 1890"
"2ND BEST DINER IN PHILLY"

Ed turned and looked through the arched windows of the brick-faced north wall onto South Street, which would be crawling in just a few hours with goths, punks, postpunk alternativos, and weekend wannabes, hair gelled into rainbows of antigravity caprice, some smiling, some scowling at the amused stares from passersby. To see and to be seen, Ed thought. Looping a gothic circuit from second to tenth. The Alienation Association. A legacy of violence and repressed origins. My only brotherhood.

"Sorry, man," Serge finally managed. "That sucks." Brightening. "Well, whenever you get back, I'll hook you *up*. Okay. Cool. You know the place?"

"Under the water tower next to the old Campbell's factory," said Kevin.

Ed turned to him.

"Give me a break. What'd you expect? I'm an art major. If I were at the music school, I'd know the best coke outlets. It's Marcus's gang. He was catering a party a couple of months back, and we . . . shared some hors d'oeuvres. A bit rough, but I know the password primeval."

"Oh, this rocks. This *rocks*. Okay. Let's go."

"Hold on. They get a little nervous with too many people. Let's meet up later. You have the C.O.D.?" Serge tapped a crumbled copy of the *Philadelphia Inquirer* against Kevin's leg. "Good. What time do you have?"

"5:45."

"Okay. We'll see you at Zipperhead at 8:00. Don't be late. And don't even *think* of flaking. I'm not carrying that shit around all night."

"No, no. Of course. Zipperhead. 8:00. Of course."

Serge beamed grinning on his way out of the diner. Ed watched him bounce-tripping along South Street.

Ed looked at his friend.

"I don't vouch for him."

"He's cool," said Kevin. "Ish. Too much of a weasel to go anywhere. Besides, it'll give us something to do until tonight."

"What's tonight?"

"Megan's having her showcase tonight. You remember. Costume party. All the pretension you can fit in one art gallery-owning father-financed flat."

"Oh, crap," said Ed. "That's tonight? What time?"

"Also 8:00. Don't worry. I think Brian's got a set of tweeds in the trunk. You can go as a Penn student."

"I am just completely absent-minded lately."

"Hey, you don't have to be Freud to see you're about off the charts on the stress Richter scale. First Dana. Now this."

Don't let it come, Ed thought, warding off Kevin's tendency to temper his inept empathy with half-baked theories he picked up from his father's primal scream therapy books. Ed wondered what the primal pater's practice must look like. Home office near Rittenhouse Square. Akhenaten bust and dark oak paneling. Requisite couch for the type-minded tykes. Lights down low to stimulate the pain. Screams through the August night, insulated against lawsuits and laughter.

"Don't worry. We'll get your friend's package. We'll have some fun. We'll booze. We'll schmooze. Not to worry. There should be plenty of those anemic undertaker tomboys you like so much. It'll be good to get your mind off things for a while."

"I suppose. What's the showcase? Senior project?"

"Nah. Something top secret, she says. Been working on it under wraps for a year or so."

"Doesn't she do the blindfold paint-splatter thing?"

"That was last year. Her pop freaked when he saw how much paint wasn't making it to the canvas. Now she's into neo-hyperrealism, or some such."

"Ah. I didn't realize it was neo already."

"All I'm thinking is free wine and nibbles. Megan's a flake, but she's threatened to host as Salome. And you know what a sucker I am for dancing."

"You doing the Marquis de Sade again?"

"Uh-uh. Nope. This year is a surprise. That's why I have to hit Zipperhead. Got to finish the costume."

Kevin picked up the check, sensing Ed was short again, and Ed turned away guilty. As Kevin paid at the register, Ed turned and watched the young waitress, listening to Love and Rockets' "Mirror

People" skipping on the diner speakers. *Because I could. Could.* A Babel of despair. Groove slicing backwards, backwards, backwards. *Should. Should.* Dusty needle hops popping.

> *nothing at all*
> *nothing at all*
> *nothing at—*

CHAPTER TWO

Six giant black ants crawled over the facade of 407 South Street, a Dalí painting come to life. Zipperhead was a store unlike any back in Allentown, and even before he started college, Ed and his girlfriend would make monthly pilgrimages sixty-five miles south in his gold 1977 Pontiac Sunbird to the goth-punk accessories store that the Dead Milkmen's "Punk Rock Girl" ironically immortalized the year before. Zipperhead crystallized everything Ed loved about South Street's goth-punk scene. The front of the store sported a three-story zipper, halfway open with one of the ant statues scuttling from the spreading teeth. Two Photostat norms flanked the iconic sign, each face impassive, even though its brain was in the process of being exposed. The store opened in

1980, its shelves crammed with all the equipment necessary to uniform the abused and depressed, the outcast and dispossessed. Doc Martens and dog collars; bondage bracelets with locks and latches; leather jackets and pleather pants, patched with studs, spikes, and buckles in sometimes apparently random patterns; real leather whips for only $10; Manic Panic hair dye in kaleidoscopic colors—Atomic Turquoise, Bad Boy Blue, Purple Haze; white face paint and black lipstick to complete the nineteenth-century cadaver fetish, half in love with easeful death; hand-screened shirts with logos and messages to amuse and offend the masses, with an almost obsessive repetition of Charles Manson and David Berkowitz images; posters and T-shirts advertising the bands that rarely made it to K-Rock—the Misfits, the Dead Kennedys, The Damned. Then there were the postpunk goth and alternative bands, less hardcore but still within the realm of acceptable marginalization: The Cure, The Church, Camper Van Beethoven. This world shat from the excesses of prog rock and the triviality of disco, fermented as the alternative to Reagan's "Morning in America" of pastel Lacoste polos and Members Only jackets, Tiffany's "I Think We're Alone Now," and Poison's "Every Rose Has Its Thorn." This world where Ed felt most at home.

"I won't take long," Kevin said. "You can stock up on eyeliner and Aqua Net, if you need it." Ed didn't know what Kevin could have wanted, since Kevin was not in the scene himself, and he never tired of teasing Ed about his grandiose Experiments in Self, even when he was most vulnerable. But at least it seemed to be done with affection. Ed followed him into the zipper.

From the loudspeakers, Ian Curtis's melancholic baritone announced their arrival like a soundtrack to their lives. *Love, love will tear us apart . . . again.* Ten years earlier, Curtis had taken his life, hanging himself with a kitchen washing line after fighting with his wife—a viciously ironic domestic denouement. Ed always felt a strong connection to Joy Division's lyrics, and he wondered vaguely if he liked the lyrics because of his own tendencies or if the music reinforced his own bleakening worldview. Did we seek out the art that reinforced our beliefs, or were artists really the unacknowledged legislators of the world? Did art reflect reality, or did it create it?

Ed had struggled with this question for years in his double-period high school AP art classes and in the oil painting classes he had taken at the Baum School back home. All of his teachers up to now reinforced a strict formalism. It didn't matter what the works depicted. Did it do it *well?* *Triumph of the Will* was equal to *Casablanca*; *Piss Christ* was on the same plane as the *Mona Lisa*. Still life exercises were important, as were figure drawings, since the thing represented was just an excuse for the formal experiment. Whatever it took to practice chiaroscuro or gouache techniques. Content would come later. But now his teachers kept asking him to *explain* his art choices, and he could not hide behind his formalism or arch demands to let the work speak for itself. Even abstraction, for his professors, was a negation of representation— an aesthetic and political gesture, even in denial. Ed feared that everything he felt he had to say came out either obvious or pretentious, and his current professors, not to mention the brutally competitive upperclassmen, seemed so far unimpressed.

Lost in his reflection, Ed found himself staring at a display of novelty sex toys of not-so mimetic forms: rotting zombie dildos, triple-holed Pocket Pussies, baby Jesus butt plugs. What circle of hell, he wondered, for the creator of a baby Jesus butt plug? Ed blushed and spun around to see if anyone was watching, and he clamped his gaze at a display of talking Beetlejuice dolls. He heard Kevin at the back of the store, in an invisible exchange.

"Dude!"

"What-up, Nigga?"

Kevin said this last in his best ironic N.W.A.-Dr. Dre cadences, and it always unnerved Ed to hear him switch back and forth between the two speech patterns. Kevin got his complexion from his white father, not his mother, and he was so light-skinned that to hear him speak in gangsta slang felt to Ed like the aural equivalent of blackface. He had just done the same with the dealers in Camden, except without the ironic twist, but because they knew him, they seemed to take it in stride. Ed could not tell if Kevin was still in that mode or if he was just doing it to mess with Serge. Ed could never tell which was the real Kevin. Or were they all performances? What would it mean if Kevin were always playing a role to accommodate him and the other mostly white kids at Spring Garden College? And what did it mean that Ed never thought of his own speech that way?

To pick up Serge's package, Ed and Kevin had taken a cab across the Ben Franklin Bridge and found the spot under the great tower. While Kevin checked his beeper, Ed unfixed his eyes and stared out at the Delaware River between the riveted beams of the bridge. He tried to imagine this sordid little score as something more heroic, something not quite so ugly, to prove that the contemporary quotidian could be grander than it seemed. But nothing worked. It was all just so tawdry, and it made him paranoid. This was not his world.

"Cheer up, Edward," Kevin said.

"You chew some Adam, and you're going to have a great time." Ed flinched. "What?"

Anthropophagy. Transubstantiation: the meaning of the ritual. Do this in remembrance of me.

"You will get annoyingly touchy, though. Fair warning. You'll want to be careful. There's heroin-based, speed-based, and meth-based MDMA. You don't need the smacky stuff in your state."

"I heard the heroin thing was a myth."

"Can't be too careful," said Kevin.

The forlorn hopers. Donner Parties probably not so fun.

"I don't know, Kevin. Not really my thing."

"I'm not big into it, either. But you could use it. Get outside yourself for once."

"Maybe."

Ed made it through the transaction, standing as far back as he could while still acting like backup, though everyone could see that he would be useless if things went wrong. They got back to

South Street just as the alternativos started to fill the sidewalks. They scoffed past the Benetton, browsed briefly through Blaxx clothing store, and date-checked the posters for the upcoming Robyn Hitchcock concert at the Theatre of the Living Arts, touring for the *Eye* record. Ed and Kevin had seen him last year for the *Queen Elvis* tour, and Ed remembered loving all of the fretless electric bass and surreal lyrical juxtapositions:

> *Superman, Superman. Crunchy little Superman*
> *Found you in a Corn Flakes box*
> *Nourished you in privacy*
> *Touched the parts you couldn't reach*
> *You improved immediately*

Ed didn't know what it meant, but that seemed . . . well, just larger to him, somehow. Bigger than the obvious world of Top 40 radio. He wondered how Robyn Hitchcock would handle his art professors: *Well you see, Superman is crunchy because . . .* The motley sea of people flowed by them as they steered up to Tower Records so Ed could pick up Hitchcock's *Eye* cassette before meeting back with Serge. Outside the Tower, a wizened old Bangladeshi woman swayed side to side in accompaniment to herself playing "America" on a plastic kazoo, eyes squinting in a rapturous trance; a fierce mohawked woman in her thirties glared at her while she finished her cigarette. Mohawk had two full sleeves of tattoos with intricate etching. Ed couldn't make out the pattern, but from a distance, the brown splotches looked like she was encased in tree bark.

By the time they got to Zipperhead, Megan's party was starting, and Ed wanted to get through this night as fast as possible. Serge and Kevin finished in the back of the store, and Ed saw someone he recognized from the Music Composition department—an incongruently glamorous six-foot-tall Amazon who, unlike every other student, always wore full makeup and her own blend of grown-up clothes and alternativo wear, depending on the day and her mood. Ed approached the counter, where she was making a decision.

"Hey, Eva."

She looked up, smiling, and took long enough to recognize Ed to deflate him.

"Oh, hey," she bluffed. "So, what do you think? 'The Kiss of Death' or 'Hot Hot Hot'?"

Ed paused. What code was she using? Was "Hot Hot Hot" a Cure reference? Was she offering physical connection or something more?

"Lipstick," she said.

Ed looked at the case. Eva smiled.

"You can never have too many options," she purred.

"Hm. 'The Kiss of Death' is nice, I suppose. I'm partial to Raven."

Eva smiled. "Of course, you are," she said. "Kiss of Death, it is." She headed toward the counter to pay, Ed trailing. "So, what brings you down to our lovely neighborhood?" she asked.

"Megan's party tonight," he said. "You going?"

"Of course," she said. "We have so many priors." Ed allowed his gaze to look down Eva's body, which he normally studiously avoided doing.

"You need a costume, I think," he said. Eva made a comic pout.

"Oh, Eddie," she said. "I'm always in costume." She smiled again, turning. "See you there," she lilted, leaving the store.

Kevin came up with a large bag, iconic exposed cranium on the front. "Ready to head out?" he asked.

"What the heck you have in there?"

"Oh, you'll see."

They emptied out into the sea, Ed scanning everyone's face for recognition, for consolation, for desire. To see and be seen.

CHAPTER THREE

Megan Dee was born in the Upper East Side of Manhattan as Megan Dorschowski, but she legally rechristened herself at sixteen after she learned that the performance artist Orlan had changed her name from Mireille Suzanne Francette Porte. Megan's father was infuriated, and he thought that it was revenge on him for leaving her and her mother two years before. He was only partially correct, since Megan was convinced that no one named Dorschowski would ever become a famous artist, and she knew by twelve that that was what she would become. Not that she had any particular love of art. In fact, from an early age, as her parents dragged her from gallery to gallery, she began to loathe the entire art world. Her father, Samuel, whom she called by his first name, was an art dealer, and after she saw the raw reality of the commodification of what she had thought of as True Art, her cynicism widened. Samuel specialized in Dubuffets, which all looked the same to her, and she remembered being perplexed when she learned that her father kept many of them in storage to keep the prices up on the few he displayed. Anything more would flood the market, he explained, and the value had to be kept artificially high. Megan did not understand what her father meant by "value," since she had always thought that art had an intrinsic value, and weren't all those paintings in the Met there because art should be a public good? Her father smiled and explained that she would understand better one day. Her mother was irrelevant.

Megan had not anticipated just how much more liberated she would feel without the patronym, as though without her father, she could become her own greatest creation. She saw her life and her entire self as a great confidence trick on the rest of the world, which for some reason had not understood this basic truth. Her closest friends never knew exactly which of those shifting selves she would show on any given day. This was not multiple personality disorder; this was art, and her friends would have to accept that if they wanted to stay in her inner circle. Most of her friends could not articulate why exactly they wanted to stay "in her inner circle," but they knew it had something to do with power, with pride, with an authentic performance. Even her body was an extension of her work—the tattoos, the piercings, the cutting, the emaciation—and she saw her sexual encounters as performance art, whether her lovers, male or female, knew it or not. She had a tattoo of Aphrodite from *The Judgment of Paris* by Ivo Saliger, the National Socialist painter, etched across her lower back; she luxuriated in every level of irony this implied, especially when taken from behind, *especially* from someone who was Jewish. The main space of her loft off South Street was overlooked by a fifteen-foot-wide print of Orlan's photograph, *Orlan accouche d'elle m'aime*, in which the artist gives birth to "herself" as an androgynous mannequin. The original was the only print and Orlan had destroyed the negative. Megan, however, had taken a picture of the picture when her father had Orlan's attention, and Orlan did not notice such a small camera. Megan thought that Orlan might really appreciate what she did if she thought about it the right way. Obviously, she was excited to hear that Orlan was beginning a plastic surgery performance art piece, *The Reincarnation of Saint-ORLAN*, in which she would fight against the innate, the natural, and the God-given by undergoing a series of plastic surgeries, transforming her own body into what she wanted it to be. This was what it meant to be transcendent. This was the Apollonian. This was what Megan wanted.

Going to Megan's loft intrigued Ed as much as it annoyed him.

He thought of himself as an introvert, but there were times when he wanted to see his friends and colleagues, to feel the press of bodies and the white noise din of fifty voices at once. It was the same with coffee shops and diners, where he did his best thinking. The more general the chaos of others, the more he could be himself. But Megan was problematic. Whenever she deigned to talk with Ed, which was rare, it always seemed like she was in on a joke that Ed had not heard. At most schools, this would not be a problem, as seniors might not even come into contact with the freshmen; but Spring Garden was "different," as the brochures desperately tried to underscore—so small that you could not hide, and the upperclassmen were encouraged to think of themselves as mentors, so Ed could not really escape her neglectful paternalism.

The sweetly pungent odor of oil paints and varnish hung in the air in the loft, a smell that always made Ed feel somehow at home. Ed and Kevin stood in the entry of the loft, taking in the space for the first time. The forty-foot by fifty-foot space had exposed brick walls with twenty-foot ceilings and twelve-foot windows, casements flaked with dull lead paint chips. The loft used to house a recently closed carpet firm, J&J Weaving, which had been in operation since Millard Fillmore was president. A fading and apparently authentic booster sign declaring that "Philadelphia is the Workshop of the World" in chipped stenciled lettering faced the naked Orlan, declaring the space to be part of Philadelphia's long history of manufacturing. But what manufacturing was this, if not industrial? Ed thought of the Lower Trenton Bridge, and its southerly boast:

And thought of his own parents, who met and worked at Phoenix Clothes in Allentown back in the mid-60s, long before it was bought out by Genesco and became Greif Industries, a name that everyone initially read as "Grief." A couple of kids, he realized in retrospect. His father worked swing shift on the line, and his mother worked in the steno pool, taking night school classes in photography at the newly opened Lehigh County Community College back in the old Courthouse. She now worked on the cutting floor with the other union workers, and she did photography on the weekends to make ends meet and send her son to college. She said she loved her jobs.

Below the sign, Megan's immaculate six-foot oak easel propped up a two-and-a-half-foot-tall canvas covered in cloth. Undoubtedly, this was the centerpiece of the whole unveiling, though Ed couldn't see why it needed to sit at the foot of manufacturing. This bothered him for some subterranean reason he could not piece together. Ed was tempted to unveil it, strip it bare, and wondered what that immediate impulse implied.

The room throbbed with people, most dressed in some kind of costume, although it being Megan's party, few of the costumes were conventional. In fact, there was no particular reason why this had to be a costume party. Megan used any excuse to get people to dress up, because, she said, that was the only way to get to our true selves. Near the entrance, Ed saw Jason of the Argonauts chatting up a woman dressed as a man in Elizabethan garb, and he couldn't tell if it was supposed to be Orlando or some kind of reverse Shakespearean drag king. Ed thought of the strange eroticism of women in drag. The doubling of desire. Marlene Dietrich in *Blue Angel*: Rathful rage sprung from spurned yearning. Othello's fantasy.

"Kevin," said a young Salvador Dalí, who lived in Kevin's wing, "I don't know what that shit is you are working on for your final, but I'm sure it is going to be great." Dalí was not using slang. Kevin's medium was his own excrement on six-foot-high canvases, and he was about to be evicted from the dorms for his senior thesis,

"The Messianic Eclogue"—an explosion of zigzagging tracks and radiant blotches. Dalí looked hopefully at Kevin from behind a pomaded mustache, twined into curvilinear lines—the most serious part of his personality.

"Thanks, man," Kevin said. "You really grow that mustache for this party?"

"Oh, yeah. Part of my Greek heritage. I can grow this in a few days. You should see my family during the holidays. *Grape Ape. Grape Ape.*"

Kevin looked, impassive.

"Heh . . . Yeah . . . Excuse us," said Kevin, steering Ed by his elbow past Dalí, who still seemed to be talking to him.

"Is it racist when the person says it himself?" Ed whispered.

"Depends on the context," said Kevin, "like everything else." The phrase hung portentous between the two. It sounded important. But how far did that go? "His big freshman Bambi eyes unnerve me. Every time I look at him, I either want to pop him in the kisser like Shemp, or I just want to squash his hopes and tell him he doesn't have a future in art."

"You think?"

"Not really. Who knows? It's not like we have a truckload of Cosimo de' Medicis just hanging around, distributing cash. He's just so damn earnest."

"And earnest is so bad?"

"Well, Edward," he looked Ed in the eyes and then down at his wrists. "One can be a bit too earnest, don't you think?" He looked back at the crowd. "Besides, look at history. Pope Innocent IV. Mussolini. Hitler. Ronald *fucking* Reagan. The only people hard to take are the ones who believe in shit."

Ed touched Kevin's forearm and deadpanned, "I believe in your artwork, Kevin. I guess I'm guilty."

Kevin smiled. They headed back to the wine table, which was tended by a slender man in a bowler hat and what looked like some kind of milkman's outfit, except for a prominent cream-colored codpiece. He leaned towards the pair, and chanted in a terrible cockney accent, "Welly, welly, welly, welly, welly, welly, well. Welcome to Korova. To what do I owe the extreme pleasure of this surprising visit, my brothers? Can I offer you some Moloko plus?"

Kevin seemed to get the joke, so Ed acted like he knew what was going on.

"You must be bezoomny, mate," a suddenly cockneyed Kevin returned. "Not this early. Besides, I have to get on me costume, if I hope to score a bit of the old in and out."

The man seemed to approve. Ed gave a chuckle and avoided the codpiece's eyes, hoping he wouldn't keep up the game. Kevin headed off to the bathroom to change. Ed asked for some of the pinot noir, and as he waited, he listened to snippets of conversation float by in a strange pastiche of words. The Pardoner from *The Canterbury Tales* explained his new artwork, in which a crucifix served as a toothpick for a rotting McDonald's quarter pounder with cheese, to the Wicked Witch of the East, dressed in authentic silver shoes, whom Ed recognized as their friend, Glenda, who actually was a practicing Wiccan. A Penn-looking kid in a Brooks Brothers suit introduced himself as someone named Drexel Burnham Lambert to a guy who was a dead ringer for Michael Milken, impressively committed to the costume with a curly-haired wig over pattern-bald scalp, which he seemed to have shaved himself. Ed saw a couple of architecture majors he recognized from the 3am studio sessions, dressed like two jovial friars, talking with a character out of *Jesus Christ Superstar*. One of the friars was Luis Gondry, who seemed to have an endless supply of anticlerical jokes to make Ed squirm. *"A prostitute?" says the nun. "Oh, thank God. I thought you said you wanted to be a Protestant!"* How is a priest like a Christmas tree? Ed didn't know what he believed anymore, but he wasn't ready for such deliberate sacrilege, and he flinched Pavlovianly, like whenever he passed a stained-glass window, which in his Eastern European Croatian version of Catholicism always connoted some Boschian vision of eternal damnation.

In the cordoned-off bedroom area next to the wine table, he

saw a few smiling guests listening to Al Capone playing a Martin acoustic, which looked like he had lifted it from Scott's room. Capone was a philosophy major who liked to call himself a Hegelian, usually after first meeting someone. Ed wasn't really sure what that meant, nor was he sure that Capone knew either, although he did have a heavily highlighted copy of *The Phenomenology of Spirit* ostentatiously positioned on his desk so anyone could see it.

"For my next song," Capone intoned, "I'd like to do a little number I call 'Lady Philosophy.'" He bent over the guitar and started strumming a manic version of the opening piano line from the Beatles' "Lady Madonna." He sang in Paul McCartney's mock Fats Domino intonation:

> *Lady Philos'phy*
> *Debates ontology*
> *Wonder why she'll never just let it be*
>
> *Lady Philos'phy*
> *Epistemology*
> *Have you read the latest pure sophistry?*
>
> *Jacques L's ideas are really low-rent Sartre*
> *Michel ball-gagged distortions into form*
> *Jacques-y D ran out of thoughts in six-eight*
> *Gee, how they're wrong*
>
> *Lady Philos'phy*
> *Axiology*
> *Ethics are a farce, but only relatively.*

He finished with a flourish, mock-Pete Townsend style, and Ed thought about the little ironic joke statue he left behind in his dorm room of a green guitar-slinging termite, right arm sprawled in a mock Townsend windmill. A circular path frozen in time. It was the final gift from his girlfriend, Dana, now two months his ex-girlfriend, whom he had sincerely thought of and referred to as his fiancée from their ringless pillow-talk promises for the indeterminate future. Ed pictured the whole of the abandoned dorm, resembling the aftermath of a tornado strike, and saw, as if for the first time, the constructed chaos of his life. It was not as though his room was more cluttered than the average architecture student's. It was just that he had never imagined that the meticulous demands of structural design would have had such an inverse relation to the environment of the creator. Sprawling stacks of curling velum draped across every free surface of the floor and furniture, the sharp-ruled graphite lines still clear from the workable fixative, titles marked in free-hand lettering so tight as to appear stenciled. Almost two semesters of Ed and his roommate's three-dimensional model projects had embedded fine foam core shards into every rigid fiber of the puce industrial carpeting, both within the room and in the hall outside. The furniture itself reminded Ed of the disordered jumble in the pictures of Tutankhamen's tomb from his art history book. In the center of the room, Ed's freshman year final project, a six-foot papier-mâché column in the shape of a feather, imposed its unfinished, grotesque, wireframe-exposed glory as a sort of mute testimony to the limits of the medium. Beside it lay two weeks' worth of the *Philadelphia Inquirer* in a shredded heap next to a bucket filled with flour and water, which now, a week after he had begun, gave off the sweet and pungent smell of decay.

Ed felt a slow squeeze on his upper arm. He turned, and his eyes met Eva's, directly gazing at him with her makeup dramatically swept in Eye of Horus curls around her left eye. The effect was striking, making her eyes seem much larger than normal, and he thought he could see himself reflected and contained in her pupils, although that was not really possible in the dim light. She was dressed as Siouxsie Sioux, and Ed thought of his own poster of Siouxsie in concert, cat-eyed, ferocious, crawling on her hands and knees in full BDSM regalia.

"You went with Raven," Ed said. She smiled.

"I *bought* the Kiss of Death. I just happened to have Raven already."

"You wear it well."

"I know," she said. Eva's eyes took in the room like she owned the space, devouring every detail of the costumes, savoring this moment. Everyone here was her guest, it seemed. Ed marveled how some people seemed to go through life owning their space, even if it was not theirs, whereas he rarely felt comfortable unless alone or safely under the cover of large numbers of anonymous strangers.

"So, I hear that your column is made out of feathers," Eva said.

Ed started, his mind racing to process this information. Was she really asking about his work? Did she overhear something from someone, and so that's why she thought it was made of feathers instead of a statue of a feather? Or was she just batting him around again? Dripping in self-deprecating tones, his only real mode of talking about himself, Ed explained the "gentle irony" he intended, saying it as though it meant to modify some other kind. He told the long story of his slow realization over the year that he was not cut out for architecture; how he used to love to paint and draw until the school had slowly ground the love of creativity out of him. The mixture of Communication Arts, Design, and Drawing classes desiccated him, he explained, as he had never seen his projects as products to crank out like some aesthetic assembly line. How ridiculous he felt when it finally dawned on him that an architecture firm does not have time for hothouse artistes, or whatever it was he thought he was. How he had a mild panic attack when he heard the final assignment. He had just wanted to finish the semester, and everyone seemed so cocksure about what they were doing. But he had nothing left. Nothing. He wanted something gentle in the midst of this strength. Even if it wasn't really gentle, it could at least have that appearance. At least that much. And now there was no point, since he was never going to finish.

Eva gazed over the party a long time. She turned to him and touched his upper arm.

"I'm sorry to hear about your mom."

Ed looked at her again, and she smiled. Gently.

"I'll be back," she said. Ed watched her move back towards the bathroom, where a death-clad figure was exiting.

Ed turned to observe the festivities. As he watched the room, he eavesdropped on a conversation next to him. Ed thought they were philosophy majors, since they were always hanging around Capone, and they always seemed to be bickering about things using their private vocabulary so that Ed usually had no idea what they were talking about. One had a bushy mustache and glaring stare of post-horsewhipping Nietzsche; the other was dressed like a slick French intellectual: dashing suit, gray hair, and one too many shirt buttons open.

Ed sipped his wine, wondering where Kevin was. He watched Megan talking with a few people by her canvas, and he anticipated the coming unveiling. Ed headed over in her direction and tried to make out her costume. Breastless body, nipples poking their eyes through the form-fitting mod mini dress; smooth hair surgically parted from left to right; the blue contact lens irises and triple layers of false eyelashes; the sensuous pout, lips natural. Makeup pancaked to look like a Warhol screen print and knee-high boots that were clearly made for walking. Twiggy, of course. Sweet Cockney accent. Successor to Jean Shrimpton, like that Smithereens song. Ed felt guilty, as he usually did, when observing a woman's body. He was enough of a feminist that he could never see himself in a strip club, but as an artist, he was meant to mark the visual. Not that he wanted to reduce a person to their body parts like poor Petrarch's chopped-up Laura. He just loved to luxuriate in the details of bodies, to celebrate their uniqueness, to sharpen his observation and appreciation of the real. Figure-drawing class was enough to change his entire perspective about the body. Countless hours, gazing at the flesh of naked models, male and female, some splayed back across a fainting couch, Botticelli style, their rolls of fat draped like Elgin marble cloth; some resembling the manic dancer who modeled for extra cash, contorting his body into Cirque du Soleil forms and holding it perfectly still until told to switch position again, dick dangling to the point that the only reason it mattered was that you wanted to get it right. But what was desire without the gaze, he wondered? Especially when he so rarely felt the touch of another.

Glenda the Good Wiccan approached, smiling.

"Ed, you surprise me," Glenda teased in an impressed tone. "Pretty open-minded for a Catholic. What *will* Father So-and-So say?"

Ed blinked, frowning.

"What do you mean?"

"I saw you talking over there. So weird to see you flirting. Who knew you were so transparent? I just always fingered you for a hetero-repression-fest. Not that I disagree. I say, go for it. She's worth it."

For the umpteenth time that day, Ed felt that he was missing some private language that he was not meant to understand.

"What? Eva? I'm not sure she knows who I am half the time."

"Read the body language, Ed. Don't be a simp."

"Well, what's the problem?"

"No problem at all," Glenda said. "You have great taste. I just never thought you'd be that open to embrace. . . well, you know . . . "

Ed's mouth opened, and he revolved his gaze around to meet the Eye of Horus, which stood over by the wine table, watching. Something came into focus, and Ed wondered what it meant. He looked back to Glenda, but she had already started to turn away to the festivities.

From the back room, Al Capone came up to Megan and turned off the stereo. Ed thought about Robert De Niro's Capone, from Brian De Palma's *The Untouchables* a few years back: *I want you to get this fuck where he breathes! I want him DEAD! I want his family DEAD! I want his house burned to the GROUND! I wanna go there in the middle of the night and I wanna PISS ON HIS ASHES!*

"So, what do you think?"

Ed turned and looked into Kevin's now heavily eyelinered gaze.

His head was covered with a black wig, teased up and Aqua Netted into a fern-like spray. A Salem Light dangled from lips smeared red like Robert Smith in concert. A thick layer of white pancake face paint covered every inch of his already white skin as if he were some demented mime. An untucked black mandarin shirt drooped over black Levis tucked into sloppily laced ten-hole Doc Martens. On top of it all, he wore a ratty black pea coat, bought earlier, no doubt, at the Salvation Army.

Ed felt nauseous. "I don't—"

Kevin smiled. Nothing. Pause.

"I'm you."

Capone tapped a fork against his glass, silencing the room.

Megan Dee radiated, her poise erect. "Ladies and Gentlemen, friends and foes. Thank you so much for coming tonight to witness my latest work, which has been a long time in the making— twenty-two years, to be exact. Most of you have observed my journey, and while none of my works have been bad, none have quite matched this new phase, which I assume will be my last. With my customary humility that you all have come to know and love, I can truly say that I think that this work will set the terms for the next wave. The only art possible, and the only one we deserve." She paused, smiling at some internal script. "I look forward to seeing it on the walls of my father's gallery."

Megan signaled to the Pardoner, who pulled off the cloth to reveal an exact reproduction of Leonardo da Vinci's *Mona Lisa.* The guests gasped and applauded, and Megan took it in like she expected nothing less. Ed stood confused. Of all the things he anticipated, this would not have been on the list. He moved a little closer to examine the painting. This was not like Duchamp's *L.H.O.O.Q.* This was a stroke-for-stroke recreation of Leonardo's work. The off-center part in the hair; the broad simpleton forehead and freakishly plucked brows; the bored sfumato eyes; the mild smirk; the buxom teats; the awkwardly draped right hand; the sensuously fleshy figure in front of the stark, incongruous back-ground with no single or stable vanishing point, serpentine paths, bridges to nowhere over an exhausted riverbed, all ending in an icy mountain range, void of humanity. Ed thought back to Walter Pater's ekphrastic riff in *The Renaissance*: *She is older than the rocks among which she sits; like the vampire, she has been dead many times, and learned the secrets of the grave* . . . Everyone pushed past Ed to talk to the artist. Ed turned to Kevin, who smiled mildly back at Ed.

Megan Dee exulted.

PART II
ALLENTOWN
DECEMBER 31, 1992

There are over 100,000 stories in this naked city.
Many of which need heavy revisions.

- "Allentown," *Pennsylvania: An Individual Vision*

CHAPTER ONE
OVERTURE

"The nearest coffee shop," Philos King repeats.

The old woman peers at the leather-jacketed man, squints her eyes in concentration, cranes her head closer to his, spins consternation across her face. A map of Allentown: a network of lines leading nowhere but back to the beginning. He proffers the city map, fresh from the Sixth Street Terminal, a one-room ticket counter with perpetual transients. The woman's eye floats behind a cataract, failing to focus on the figure before her. The sun through streaking clouds of acid rain. His eyes pierce her swimming gaze as she bobbins the Hess's Department store bag closer to her body. *It's starting*, she thinks. *New York or Philly, I don't know. But it's starting. Can't keep them on the East Side forever. What's he want? The map. No eye contact. They hate it. No sudden movements. No nothing. A coffee shop? Say it. Say*

"A coffee shop?" she says too harshly, flinching, the words redoubling, amplified in the sometime hollow chamber of dusking small town streets, like voices—parting, maudlin, echoing—in a recently vacated house or long-abandoned church. The man smiles. Kill her with kindness.

"I've been on the road a long time. Have to hook up the caffeine IV, you know?" No smile. Something behind the cloud that's beyond contempt, beyond mere prejudice. Yellow, withering hair like draughted corn. Slight hunch; hands tremble: autumnal fields. That's it. Not me, my six-foot frame. The notion beyond that frame. She fears the solitary reaper, my words only the foreign language of an other. But what are words worth?

The man's smile widens at his inner joke. The old woman trembles, spindly hairs leaping to attention in the primordial desire to seem larger than one is. Go. *Go.*

"Twenty-third and . . . no, wait. Nineteenth. Nineteenth and Allen is the new one." Pale sweat. The name. The Beginning? No: Origin. Yes. "Origin's Hava Java." Yes. "I think."

"Oh, great. And which way's—"

"I have to go. Thank you. It's almost . . . " Voice trailing. An antique caboose across a Breadbelt plain. The man follows the woman's trembling gait with a squint and a smile. Welcome to Allentown. City of Trees. City of Averages.

The leather-jacketed man backpacks his map and surveys his choices. Sixth Street: past sooted redbrick row homes, asphalt streets, quarter-an-hour meters, Symphony Hall, the *Morning Call*, its adjacent garage, lots, language centers, and corner stores displaying fading Marlboro, Goya, and Yoohoo placards. Or Hamilton Street: through the ghosted, ten-block, downtown shopping district that peaked, it seemed, around World War II; past chipped and unlit neon not-flashing from Titlow's Music's display window where half-sized acoustic guitars, clarinet reeds, and Kingston Trio sheet music quietly decompose into the dust that covers them; between multiple Five and Tens whose sole Indonesian supplier specializes in American plastic pop culture icons; past the Liberty Bell Shrine's authentic fake replica of the monument that probably never really came; under the half-cylinder glass canopies covering the pavement from Sixth to Tenth, raised in the seventies to simulate a mall by blocking the sun in an attempt to provide a shelter that never would be. He chooses Hamilton.

Foot after foot, the young man steps in tune to an inner song, remembering that septum-pierced punk's Walkman, projecting Pantera over the rattle and hum of the bus—

Spread the word throughout the land
They say the bad guys wear black

The melody transformed. The tempo, upbeat. Swing it, jazz it. Slow it down. Orchestrated in the transcendental unity of apperception. He passes the Liberty Bell Shrine in the basement of Zion's Reform Church. Founded AD 1762. I.H.S. *Waiting for thee O God in Zion.* Still waiting after all these years. Not my style. Prefer the traipse through the diaspora. Legacy of the Indo-European side: the polytropos. Immobility breeds irrefutable limits.

Seventh Street. Center square. Two miles north, before it turns into Seventh Street, Route 145 slopes down from the City View Diner, revealing the Soldiers and Sailors Monument at the intersection of Hamilton and Seventh before the gridded streets break down, winding around the retirement home toward the south side. Bronzed Goddess of Liberty atop the phallustal, flanked by bas-reliefed reunification of the States and Philippoteaux's review of the First Defenders of Pennsylvania *the valor and patriotism of the soldiers and sailors of the county of Lehigh and the war of 1861-1865.* Abraham's monolith, anointed with oils. October 19, 1899. Ninety-three years ago, liberty replaced the bull. This statue was once the center of town, but it was not what he saw coming into the city. PP&L: Pennsylvania Power and Light building: Allentown's only skyscraper. Focal lines decentered.

Light changes. Across the intersection, Philos King gazes up at the silhouette of the Goddess of Liberty, in relief against the sky. Dusk's fading light upon the flag. She faces East. Nostalgia. All kingdoms: fabled, lost. Harappa or the Indus Valley. Or land of the Rising Sun. The world is too much with us, Ozymandias. When will the end come? Perhaps the millennium? Wheels within wheels.

Foot after foot. Methuselah on a wooden bench. Charlie Brown skull and toothless gape, fingering a beltless loop of his unpressed polyester pants in metered strokes. He waits for the bus, eyes focused on eternity. His version, at least. This place of waiting. Neatly bound donut box at his side: Egypt Star Bakery. Bethlehem next door and Nazareth down the road. Perhaps a tad overkill on the Levantine christening, juxtaposed against the Pennsylvania towns named after the tribes that were moved or massacred:

Susquehanna, Catasauqua, Tamaqua.

Ninth Street. Base of the Tower Building. The top floors of Pennsylvania Power and Light flame with a scarlet, incandescent glow. Twenty-four stories, three times the size of Liberty. Must have dug deep to get through the limestone. Out front, a small table: Palm and Tarot Readings by Dormin. Squat Dominican, shawled, beaded, and bandannaed, looms over three bleary children. Pitching staccato screams. Christmas special: two dollars a hand. Jesus was a Capricorn. Not bad, I suppose. More in New York. Authentic psychics so hard to come by these days.

"No, no," the medium cries, "*Usted tiene que hacerlo. Es necesario. Absolutamente necesario.*" Smirking scatter under Dormin's arms, flailing. "*¡Ahora mismo!*"

Shops long closed. Christmas decorations droop. Up till the second week of January, no doubt. Sadder then. Downtown BID ringing in the new year with contour-line kids on pennants with dangling crepe. Orange-fiery lingam, gently twisting beneath the breeze, plucking the air for an absence. Hindus sure knew their symbolism. Like that time in Benares. Temple jungle. Yugging their way to transcendence. Upstream, flamed and soused, corpse flotsam made its way again to the great mother who vomits it back in a fevered pitch. Not good to drink the dead. So long ago, now, he thinks. The duality of temporal perception: last week and ten years past, depending on a second's shift.

Tenth and Hamilton. The glass canopies give way to cadaver-white streetlights and blurry stars. Venus ascending. Unmarked office buildings mix with shops so long fixtures as to appear invisible. To the right, two decommissioned Mark 81 "Firecracker" bombs with decorative painting guard the entrance to the Great War Store. Paling Stars and Stripes backdrop a sign: *We buy and sell all military items from all nations: pistols, rifles, shells, swords, daggers, knives, uniforms, insignias, flags, trench art, souvenirs.* Memento mori without the angst. Nostalgia for the coming Armageddon.

Twelfth street. A hunkered man clings to the wall of the Brass Rail Restaurant and Bar, willing stability. Early twilight festivities.

Ordinary boys belch exhaust from howling metallic-blue Novas and midnight Monte Carlos to make the light. Rubber tires burn. Acrid tears well. Morrissey moaning Manchester strains:

> *But you were so different*
> *You had to say no . . .*

Perhaps not that different, though. A little, of course. My Attic foundation. Not to be repressed. The cars turn left around the angular, redbrick, bleeding-mortared Allentown Public Library, fountain dry with patches of charcoal snow, and make their way around to pass again. The Circuit, they used to call it. Probably here, too. Lots of Circuits strewn across North America at sundown. Industrial peacocks. *Beschauen und beschaut werden.* To see and to be scene.

He continues west. On his right, tinted, unfixed faces stare out of the lobby window, waiting for their rides. Overtime shades insured with a blue cross and blue shield. Staff of Asclepius on the aegis: undertones of the Kundalini. Ida and Pingala wending their way to the wings of science. Only one snake here though. Variation of Ningishzida. That syncretism lost.

Past Thirteenth Street, foliage thickens as the houses spread apart. Doctors, dentists, and the occasional chiropractor intersperse between curtained homes and corner stores. Fashions by Anne, Haircuts Galore, and Family Eyecare. Front lawns more like patches of green hair. Nature inverted. Less rust on the parallel parked cars here. Packs of extracurriculars continue to stream past in opposition from somewhere up ahead. Voices smiling, strutting.

A young girl catches his eye. Eats his gaze. Antigone in a red dress. Shit-colored flats. Pursed lips pouting, steeled against the late-December chill. Paraffin eyes, unfixed, stoic. Sallow-cheeked; unfurrowed brow. Dreamless. An adolescent Ruth. Friends satellite her indifference, chattering tales of teachers, keggers, and Harlequin love. Who'll watch whom at tonight's bonfire. Wish-fulfillments of working-class youth. She walks an invisible line across the manicured patches and moss-cracked sidewalks. Psychology of the Archimedean point. Twelve paces behind, quadruplet William Allen High School Wrestling jackets follow in time. Cursive names above left breasts. Militia-cropped pates and staring eyes. Furtive dreams. Silent.

Fifteenth Street. Knotted birches along the block. Hary's Bar under the Traylor Inn. Open-mic New Year's celebration. A gaggle of deviated-septumed James Taylors huddle smoking, bantering the tense camaraderie of co-conspirators. Palm-soldered acoustic guitar cases. They debate the merits of D'Addario ten-gauge strings and clip capos. Charging displays for Alpha Folk Singer. Coffee-cup tales of unrequited love, lonely nights, and dime-store philosophy. Drowning in their lyrical reflections. From Fifteenth Street, a stilettoed Amazon turns the corner and sachets up the walkway. Foundation thick over slight Adam's apple. Guitar case with white stenciled letters: Queen Eva. The James Taylors red sea to let her pass. They say nothing. Everyman is open-minded. The dark Danes: the illusion of depth beneath a crystalline shell. But Humpty falls. He's always already falling.

Yet I have buried my dead.

Sixteenth Street.

And so does he. A tall specter in a crumpled trench, forever tugging at the too-short sleeves, from which limp two delicate, dangled wrists, like floating doves with broken necks. Shiny black pants in ten-hole Docs. Either a freedom fighter or a South Street anachronism. Occasional stout men crowd the specter's path, palms pumping crisp consolation. Weber Funeral Home, Inc. Lorel Leh Pullman. Services 4:00. Plantation porches and Doric columns. Victorian firmament: shades of the afterworld better suited to shuttered wood than Plexiglas and steel.

Philos watches the specter watch the casket. Pallbearers stare ahead vacantly, not-focusing on his presence. They rehearse the face of sallow tears. There, but for the grace of God, they think. Frosting sweat. Dull thud on the hearse's tailgate. Penultimate insertion for poor Lorel Leh. Carved oak quality for the final happy land. Into the gouffre.

A dewdrop young woman approaches, face compressed with carnal caring. Black stockings under lilac print skirt. Patchouli patina and Birkenstocks. Dawn of the hippie mourning.

"Ed," she whispers. The specter winces slowly. Rapid eye fantasy: away or within. Swaying under the fluorescent torch. Her arms steal a steady caress. The specter embraces her. Breathing erratic.

"It's okay. Everything's going to be okay. My dad says you can stay with us for a while. We'll clean out the attic and put his stuff in the garage."

"But—"

"No buts. It's all arranged. You just come with me later. Okay?"

Ed nods absently, eyes fixed on the brass-handled box in front of him. He squints against absent tears, follows her parting smile, and lurches toward the midnight train. He sees me. The look of the other. Reflective cogito. I. Haven't we met? Slight widening of the lid and arching brows. I think so. Was it? No, I've never been. Perhaps? No, I don't know her. Well, familiar anyhow. Yes. Strange. Yes. It's the glassy green-brown eyes. So distinct. Yes, I've heard. Well, I must be going. Good luck with the toss-in. Thanks, gotta run. Oh, yeah, didn't you hear? The world needs people who cry at their mothers' funerals.

Engines rev. A plaintive chorus. Wheels within wheels.

Gone now. The motorcade of dissolution. Reflections upon the catafalque. Reflections upon the guillotine. Camus. The only serious philosophical question. He had the marks. Saw it when he checked the time. Left Bank resistance: homeland exile. Must have been nice to have had such a clear personification of evil. My parents met there. Angelo and Olah King. 82nd Airborne and the WACs. Dancing under the eyes and ears of the world. Tiger, Tiger, rolling blight. I'm the king of Kings, he'd quip. Smell of Aqua Velva and Lucky Strike. How long gone now? Ten years, even. Jesus.

Philos King turns the corner and follows the path of the motorcade down 17th Street and William Allen High School, the source of the extracurriculars. Central Ionic edifice with lightless, flightless wings. Annex to the side: *Erected AD MCMXXIX*. Right before the Crash. Random silver air conditioners fleck the building's facade. Christmas recess. Students chat excitedly about the bonfire preparations. On the corner of Seventeenth and Turner, a small group encircle a forty-foot maple, too old for high school. One with his back to the tree, left side of his head shaved, the right side long. Half Mephistos, half Nazarene. A fervent rant. Hands animated. *Ringaroundthe*—Mesmer without props. Again, the feeling of recognition. *Pocketfullof*—

"It's the coming together." Forefingers touching. "Like that, you see? The point's not where we are on the chain, but how we understand it. There are energies you can't possibly fathom. Duality is an illusion. Most people live lives of quiet desperation, believing they are separate from the world. The average person can never understand. It's the release from all those illusions—from family, from church, from society, from the things that *divide* us. *There* is freedom. It's all a progression. And yet, motionless. Like Hegel, you know? Thesis, antithesis." Dramatic pause. "Synthesis. See what I mean?"

Or something like that. Ashes. Ashes. So the wrong ones won't be saved. They seem to see. Or see to seem? Can't be sure with the doe-eyed stare of the converted. Tattoos on each right hand: parallel lines across eternity. A symbol. Of what? Ancient practice, of course. The shapersons. One stands off to the left, pyramid-patched with radiant eye, leaning against a flagpole. Self-possessed smirk of a nihilist or the footman of the Second Coming. Watches me cross against the light.

Foot after foot. Seventeenth and Chew Street. Allentown Hospital across from the Allentown Fairgrounds. Where's the Allentown Store and the Allentown Morgue? Orange brick entrance. Twenty-four-hour banking on the corner. He stops for a moment and peers through the Fairgrounds' gates to the other side. Walk around or cut through? The shortest distance between two points. He cuts between the steelrail road demarcation and the barbwire fence and walks his invisible path across the wide Fairgrounds parking lot. The stands would be here in the summer.

The Midway over there. Local fairs all the same: corn dogs, cotton candy, bingo tents, and rides with names like The Zephyr, The Hellhole, and The Whiplash. And here the Ferris wheel. *La Machine Infernale.* The Dionysian horde. Communal exile. Serves a purpose, I suppose. But I found too many actors there.

The main building of the Allentown Fairgrounds Farmers' Market: redbrick fortress with covered stalls where carriages used to enter. He looks across the signs that cover the main building and the smaller structures to the side. Ritz Barbecue: Our Famous Ice Cream. Double coupons. Utz Potato Chips (Farmers' Market Fresh). An Amish horse-and-buggy outline on the annex's wall. Little girl nibbling her bread. One Great Baker. Dutchy manna. Telephone wires and power lines web an industrial canopy across the lot. Sooted, bulldozed snow piles bulge from the asphalt, fused into smooth, perpetual landscape features. Teats of the Glacier at the angle of repose. Back in a time made simple by. Sled tracks carved from southeast to northwest. Around the largest mound, four prepubescents race to knock a fifth from his stance. King of the hill. Fending off the quaternity. Two girls among them. Different when I was young. The loss of detail. Burned, dissolved, and broken off. Probably better this way. As much aggression in them as us. Alpha hermaphrodite. The oldest of the two grins as one of the boys clips the king from behind, flipping him backwards off the pile and onto his head four feet below with a thwack. Hollow echo across the lot.

"Gog," he grunts. Flat on back. Pause. Giggles. He's okay. Stop. Still among his peers, smiling. Teasing laughter from three. He gets up again, swaying. Clears his eyes of clotting blood and gets back into position.

Amazing what they can withstand. More than me now. Look back once again. The youngest of the two stands atop the mound, fists on hips, like the appearance of Superwoman. Only thing missing is the cape. Taunting derision. Daring laughter at her four companions. Hex sign nimbus from the wall behind. The Colossus. Sadness in her eyes, though.

Lost sight around the corner, between the Farmer's Market and Agricultural Hall. Stop sign cemented in a red-painted barrel. Back to the path. Clean breeze across the lot. A hint of cinnamon and faintly pungent apples. Really need that coffee now. He looks to the left between the slats of Ag Hall's adjacent horse stalls and sees the funeral procession in the cemetery beyond. To his right, the racetrack and bleachers behind the market, where the bands must play during the summer. So desolate now.

Northern gates. Empties onto Lafayette Street, one block past Nineteenth. He turns right and makes his way back along the chain-link fence. Ritz Ice Cream: Made on the Premises for over 50 years. There it is, halfway down the block, across from the Nineteenth Street Theatre's bulb-bordered marquee, wedged between the lightless fronts of Stella's Peace Emporium and the Crystal Waterfall. An island of the blessed. Small wooden sign hanging from a wrought-iron bar: Origen's Hava Java. Must have heard it wrong. Pretentious in its unpretentiousness. Should have *Ye Olde* in front of it. A soft light from the bay window. Voices muffled from inside. Inviting.

He looks through the window at the small front room within. Fairly crowded for New Year's Eve. Second home of the dispossessed. Packs of individuals cradle mugs around marble-topped tables. Walls decorated like a postmodern Diego Rivera: patchwork frames mixing high with low. A browning, fifties Coca-Cola ad against a *Starry Night* print, an autographed picture of George Takei, and an anonymous lithograph of Tiresias sticking his staff between a pair of spinning snakes. Harmonic, somehow. From a shelf high in a back corner, a glowing plastic Pietà overlooks the scene with a sign tacked underneath:

> *I don't care if it rains or freezes*
> *As long as I got my plastic Jesus*
> *Riding on the dashboard of my car*

Every chair a different style: paneled straightbacks, corduroy armchairs, wooden stools, and three different sizes of deacon's benches along the walls amalgamate into a motley, earth-toned display. Cobalt glass jars, antique coffee makers, white stucco walls, and four woodblade ceiling fans, quietly pulsing their circular path. Soothing sensory overload. From the ceiling, hundreds of cups, mugs, and steins from around the world hang on small brass hooks. Homey effect.

He enters. Voices hush. Observance of the new. Cautious; tribal. The eyes of the world upon me. He meets their stares with a disarming gaze until he feels accommodation. From two corner-mounted speakers, the syncopated riffs of a Coltrane tune bleat over the silence. He approaches the counter, slings his backpack onto a stool, and reads the rainbow-chalked menu. Cursive scrawl.

A wan epicene young woman, gray thrift store T-shirt draping over untorn Wrangler jeans, unsquats from behind the counter, brushes her unpolished hands against her hips, crooks her head to an inquisitive angle, and smiles at the dark figure before her. Horn-rimmed glasses: my whole reflection from her eyes. Unsettling distortion. Christmas Eve when I was ten, sitting under the tree, staring at the featureless round red ball on the lowest branch. Waiting for them to return. Lights all out to let the tree glow. Popping electric Tyco spinning its eternal circle around the base of the plastic pine. Doppler effect. Aunt Sarah by the menorah. Listening for the key, watching the clock. *Too late for another*, he had said. Steel smooth voice of authority. *Very risky at your age.* The brother I never. My entire body in the red ball. Enormous eyes; diminishing feet. But all there. That's *I* too. Shifting my head from left to right, watching ear eye nose eye ear fisheye to prominence, then recede. And now in her eyes. Far on the ringing plains. Jet black hair, beardless face. Leather jacket down below the waist.

"What do you need?" she asks. Voice soft. Unwavering. Tapered fingers resting against the counter. A piano player's. Short brown hair. Eyes observant behind the glass. Appraising.

"Large house, please." Her smile broadens as she turns. The room returns to a muffled din. Conversations resume. But not for me. Temporary stations: U-Haul Manor. Good enough, good enough. He places a dollar onto the counter while the young woman draws his drink. I will drink coffee to the lees.

"Is there a restroom I could use?"

"Oh, of course. It's back to the right. Second door."

"Thanks. Would you mind watching my bag?"

"Not at all. Just leave it there."

Tap closes as he rounds the corner. She follows his path with her eyes, places the glass mug on the counter, and looks at the bag. One of those Eastpaks that are everywhere on campus. Trademark name over minimalist earth. Nylon, oversized. Couldn't have been hiking. Not enough dirt. Worn, though. She reaches over and lifts a strap. Leather patch on the back.

She drops the strap, gathers a fistful of sugar-encrusted mugs, and starts to scrub them at the sink. Strange name. Greek, probably. A little Jewish? Striking features. Sculpted brows. Angular cheekbones. Those large, piercing eyes, black all over like they're all pupil. Looks right into. Something about a person that looks right at you. Usually violent or sexual. Here's hoping for the latter. Busy at the glass. Last mug steadied in the plastic strainer. The door. Bootsteps on the linoleum. Not from around here, I don't think. Definitely the coffee shop type. Would've been here before. Maybe Ed knows him, or Tod. They'll be in later, no doubt. After the funeral. Should be over soon. He'll be a wreck. Could get him back to school finally. Or somewhere. Three years working the graveyard shift at that hospice in Philly hasn't exactly been the best thing for him. Can't do it forever. Maybe it prepared him somehow. Nice to have him back, though.

From around the corner, fresh from the facilities, face scrubbed, ruddied, and refreshed, eyes black upon her, Philos King returns.

CHAPTER TWO

In the back room of Origen's Hava Java, Philos King opened his ledger to a page entitled "Allentown, PA" and scanned down the signatures until he found the name he recognized: Lorel Leh Pullman. With his fine Pentel pen, he lightly drew a line through her, writing "(D)" after the entry. He noted the child's name scribbled below it, counted up the number of names listed in the Allentown section, and closed the yellowing pages softly. He looked at its aging maroon cover. The ledger was the size of a midsized city's phone book, and it contained thousands of signatures from all across the country and even down into Mexico. There was even one abortive page that said "Benares," but listed only twelve names. On the cover in elegant custom calligraphy read the single word:

Conversions

Philos frowned at the word, thinking of the possible doubled truth contained within, a pun he had lived with for almost twenty years now. He restrung the elastic band around the cracked cover, spine fractured and always threatening to fall apart, and stashed it back in his backpack. He took out another notebook and a highlighted copy of *Allentown: A Pictorial History* and began reading silently, making notes from time to time. A middle-aged man sat nearby, reading the *Morning Call.*

The back room of Origen's was smaller, more rundown, and

more intimate than the front room, with three large oak tables and four smaller, more idiosyncratic ones, everything exhaling the smell of stale cigarette smoke and cloves. The walls were decorated with a similar pastiche of images and icons as the larger front room, some ironic, some sincere: a framed copy of R. Crumb's illustration of Big Brother and the Holding Company's *Cheap Thrills*; dried flowers bunched and hung upside down from a nonfunctional antique gas lamp; a black-and-white photo of a Popemobiled John Paul II from his 1987 visit to San Francisco. Someone's amateurish, yet still unnerving, life-size recreation of Hans Bellmer's *Die Puppe* stared at the guests from a dark corner like some uncanny mummy excavated from a Guanajuato tomb. The flaxen pages of an old copy of Jonathan Swift's *Gulliver's Travels* wallpapered an entire wall, glued side to side with occasional highlights and underlines, which invited the guests to see what someone else found important and to mark their own favorites. Some went for the ethically-minded quotes: *But great allowances should be given to a king, who lives wholly secluded from the rest of the world, and must therefore be altogether unacquainted with the manners and customs that most prevail in other nations;* some liked the self-consciously playful: *I hope the gentle reader will excuse me for dwelling on these and the like particulars, which, however insignificant they may appear to groveling vulgar minds, yet will certainly help a philosopher to enlarge his thoughts and imagination;* some went for the sardonically provocative: *. . . a wife should be always a reasonable and agreeable companion, because she cannot always be young;* while others were unclear whether they were sarcastic or really revealing some pathology: *I must confess no object ever disgusted me so much as the sight of her monstrous breast.* Nothing could be learned from these highlights, as there was no single person making the selections, and the intent could only be guessed. But what, thought Philos, might you learn about someone just by looking at her books and highlights?

After a quarter of an hour, Philos noticed Ed Pullman's slouching gait entering the room, followed by the young woman he had been talking to at the funeral. Ed noticed him and made a slight double take, giving a nod of recognition. They sat around a small handmade table with the surface constructed from an old movie reel at the end farthest away from Philos, who always liked to sit in a corner to observe the motions of others. Ed had coffee; Ester tea. The table was in the corner against the wall shared with the main room, and there was a small retracting partition between the areas to deliver orders. Ed slumped a little in his chair, still wearing his black trench coat. Ester watched him; he stared at the table.

"They did a really nice service," Ester said. "The turnout was great, too, don't you think? It's hard to imagine that your mom even knew that many people. She didn't really go out a whole lot, especially at the end. But everyone loved her, you know? Whenever she'd meet people, they'd love her right away."

Ed stirred the contents of eight sugar packets into his coffee.

"Father Anteil was nice to come," she continued, "even though she was out at that Evangelical church for so long."

"Hm."

Ester dipped her tea bag into her cup.

"Where'd your friend disappear to? She didn't come to the cemetery."

"Eva? She ended up going to an open mic over at Hary's. She couldn't do graveside. She has a phobia she picked up after her own mom's death. Had a kind of vertigo as they lowered the casket into the ground. She was absolutely sure that she was going to fall or jump into the hole. She didn't, luckily. But ever since, she can't be around cemeteries."

"Yikes."

"I know. I started to feel the same thing a little over at Greenwood, like the hole had some kind of gravitational pull. Freaked me out. I probably wouldn't have felt that if she hadn't told me that story."

Ester sipped her tea. "So, how long have you two been roommates?"

"Since I left college. She graduated and has been working on her music career. Did pretty well on her first CD. She's starting to get a buzz around Philly, playing the coffee shop and small bar circuit." Ed smiled. "Captain Dropout here hasn't been nearly as ambitious."

"You'll get there, Ed. Everyone's on their own timeline, you know?"

"I'm not sure where I'll get to. Three years at the hospice, and no clue what to do now. Again."

Ester shivered.

"Why in the world did you ever take that job, anyway?"

Ed shifted in his chair.

"I don't know. It's a little hard to explain. It was like, after I heard my mom's cancer diagnosis, I realized that I didn't know anything about life. I was just a kid, you know? I used to screw around with fantasies of suicide, like I'd ever really have the nerve to go through with it."

Ester thought back to the night when Ed was fifteen, when he had come over with the bandages on his left wrist, saying he had had an accident with an X-ACTO blade. The blood had started to seep through the top of the bandage, which took up the first few inches of wrist. She didn't buy it then, and she wasn't buying it now. If that wasn't "nerve," she didn't know what was.

"So, I took the orderly job, I think, to try to figure out what dying was all about. The way I approach everything, right? Read about it. Control it. Try to conquer death by knowing about it. The graveyard shift gave me a lot of free time, and I spent most of it reading comparative religion, psychology, Elisabeth Kübler-Ross, that sort of thing. She's the 'five stages of grief' woman; calls herself a *thanatologist*, which, let's face it, is unbelievably cool. In the mornings I sometimes talked to the patients. I tried to learn from them, you know? Turns out that there was very little wisdom at that stage, or things you probably could have figured out after thinking about life for ten uninterrupted minutes. I just felt like such a spiritual vampire sometimes, and I think the patients felt it too." Ed sighed. "The overturn was so fast. It was just brutal at times. Those nurses are goddam saints."

"Did it help?"

Ed sipped, thinking. "I couldn't save her, could I?"

Ester got up and gave Ed an awkward hug while he still sat, their faces almost equal because of his height, and then she sat back down.

Ester wiped a tear Ed couldn't see in the light.

"Do you really think she wanted saving?"

Ed shrugged, uncommitted.

A silence descended. Ester paused and looked around the room, checking the door.

"So, does Eva dress like that . . . all the time?"

Ed looked at Ester, anticipating every coming question, as usual. "Yep."

"Huh," she said. "Even around the apartment?"

"Pretty much."

"So, is she a transsexual?"

"Nope. Just a transvestite."

"H— . . . She . . . still has everything?"

"From what I've seen."

Ester's eyes widened slightly. "Damn," she said. "She's beautiful."

"True fact."

"Do most people buy it?"

"You'd be surprised."

"No. I did at first, too. I only figured it out after she made a joke about it, like I already knew. She spends so much time trying to pass, but then she just tells people anyway?"

"I know."

Ester sipped at her tea, looking down at the table. "So, have you two ever . . . ?"

"Nope."

Ester hissed. "Why not? I'd be tempted to."

"Mostly because I'm a coward, no doubt," said Ed. "She's doing just fine in that department, anyway. Besides, it isn't like you just choose those things, is it?"

"Oh, please," Ester snapped. "Don't give me that. We're children of the seventies. David Bowie and Phil Donahue."

"No, I meant the other person's desire," Ed said. "Doesn't matter." He stirred his coffee some more. "You know, I didn't even get the 'Sheehy' pun."

"That's not her last name?"

"No, Eva Sheehy isn't her birth name. It's the one she gave herself as part of her self-rechristening."

"Wow."

"I know," said Ed. "She's amazing."

"So, have you been dating anyone?"

"Not since Dana."

"Not since *Dana*?"

"Nope."

"Ed, that was four years ago."

"True fact."

"That's crazy."

"Well, have you, since the . . . ?"

"The stillbirth?" Ed looked down. "You can say the word, Ed. The only way to deal with trauma is head on. Use the right words for the right things."

Ed tilted his head.

"Okay, point taken. Well?"

"Well, no. But I'd say that's a little different, wouldn't you? We're talking about a healthy young man, not even trying." She smirked. "Well, healthy-esque." She shook her head in mock exhaustion. "You could use some red meat, dude."

"Says the lacto-ovo-pescatarian," Ed teased. "Different in details, maybe. But it's been three years for you, right? And you still hang out with him, too."

Ester twitched her head side to side, losing her composure for the first time since he had returned last week.

"Tod's different, Ed. You'll see." Eye contact, pleading. "It just didn't work out for us romantically. I still *believe* in him . . . "

As Ed tried to read this tone, a large stocky figure at the doorway eclipsed the light from the main room. A man in his late forties entered. His slightly wrinkled khakis slung low under his prodigious pot belly, over which draped a simple black tie. His face was pocked with rosacea across his nose and cheeks, and his hair cut tight against his pattern-bald head. He looked around the room, recognized Ed, and approached.

"Hey, Ed. I don't know if you remember me, but my name's Eugene Stanislavski. Everyone calls me Stan. I was looking to talk to you after the ceremony. I'm so sorry for your loss, kid. I worked down at the mill with your mom; your dad, too, back when he was still alive. You probably don't remember, but your dad and me used to run around the 6th ward back in the day when we were a couple of hellions, looking for trouble. We used to ditch school and hop the line up to the quarry." He laughed. "Your grandma couldn't be bothered with twelve other kids around, but she would've beat him senseless if she found out. It was the times. I know you didn't know your old man, Ed, but he was a hell of guy."

"Thanks," said Ed.

"Even when they offered him a management position, he stayed with the union. I always wonder what he would've said when they made me the shop steward. Oh, man, he'd've busted balls on that one."

Stan turned to Ester. "Your old man, Richie, used to be around too, until he quit to do that doll stuff."

"Oh, yes. I think that's right," said Ester, shifting in her seat.

"Yeah, we had some good times. Way back in the sixties, your folks and Billy and Betty Gebitch, and me and my wife, Sheila, we'd all go up to the Lake Wallenpaupack in the Poconos and just swim and drink and laugh and have the best time. Your mom was so funny back then, before Teddy died. You wouldn't know it, but she could tell a filthy joke out of nowhere, and we'd all just die laughing because she was usually so straight, you know?"

Ed listened, trying to take this information in.

"We used to rent a whole house for just $125 a week, if you

can believe it," Stan said. "Those days are over. Heh."

Ed watched his private reverie.

"And, you know, I know your mom got a lot more conservative after your pop died and tried to drop out of the union and all, but she was still a great lady. I can't believe she was only forty-nine. Too soon, Ed. Way too soon."

Ed and Ester nodded.

"So listen, kid, if you need anything, you let me know, okay? I go way back with your parents, and I'll help however I can."

Ed considered a few seconds, thinking that Stan was serious.

"You have any jobs down at the plant?" Ed asked.

Stan glanced at Ed's hair, which now just dangled over his left eye a little.

"At the mill? I don't know. I thought your mom did all that overtime to send you to college. She even sold the house and got that apartment."

Ed looked down. "It didn't work out exactly as planned," he said.

"Oh, she hadn't really said," said Stan. "Well, let me think. We've had a slowdown in hiring because of all the management disputes and the downturn. Recession's got us by the balls, and they're using it to keep the union on the ropes. Our plant lost ninety workers back in May. Thank you, Mr. Bush, for trickling down on us, if you know what I mean. Anyhow, you can't really do line work, since you probably don't have any experience. Your pop was a cutter back when that was still done by hand all the time. I can't say we really need anyone. Maybe I can put you in for something in cleaning department or maintenance. It isn't fancy, but it is union."

Ed looked at him like the word meant nothing to him.

"Perfect," said Ed.

"Okay, kid. Let me check on it on Monday, and I'll get back to you. Where can I get in touch?"

Ed gave him Ester's home number.

"Thanks, Stan," said Ed. "I really appreciate it."

"Alright, Ed. I'll call you when I know."

Stan headed out as Eva walked through the door, and Stan did a little bow of his head as she passed.

"Holy shit, Ed," said Eva, after he was gone. "You're a full-on blue-collar textile worker, just like dear ol', dear ol'." She put her guitar case against the wall, kissed Ed on the cheek, nodded to Ester, and sat between them. "Long way from architecture school."

Ed pushed her gently.

"It'll pay the bills for a while," Ed said. "Besides, I'm tired of being in my head all the time. I need some physical labor for once."

"Besides," said Ester, "Change is always good."

They talked briefly about the cemetery, and Ed told Eva about the hole. He asked her about her set list. She loved opening her sets with a cover of Lou Reed's "Walk on the Wild Side" or The Kinks' "Lola," just to own the stage before she launched into her own songs. Ester turned the conversation around again.

"It is amazing how little you seem to ask of life these days," said Ester.

"It's not that," said Ed. "Life gives plenty. Asks too much, maybe. I just don't want to commit to anything anymore. I need to be free, you know?"

Eva sang out in vaudeville Janis Joplin, "Freedom's just another word for nothing left to lose."

Ester looked at her, impressed. Ed chuckled.

"Maybe so," he said. "Maybe so. Back at school, my girlfriend was everything until she dumped me; architecture school was everything until that fell apart."

"Dumped by architecture school," said Eva, "without even a Dear John. What a bitch."

Ed rolled his eyes.

"Well," said Eva, "Spring Garden still closed after the bankruptcy. You would've had to have left the next year, anyway."

"I know," said Ed. "But everything I thought was a choice was just part of another system. Everything I thought had defined myself was just an empty charade. What's the point of saddling myself with some more nonsense? As soon as you commit to anything, it defines you, and you're done."

"There's still God, Ed," said Ester. "He's always there for you."

Ed sighed. "I don't know, Es. Don't tell your parents or anything, but that's the biggest prop of all that I lost."

Ester gaped. "But you practically wanted to be a priest!"

"I did, I know," Ed sighed, not really wanting to get into this conversation now, but knowing that it was inevitable. "After I left school, I decided to finish reading the whole Bible, cover to cover. Let's just say that I barely made it out of Leviticus before that was about done for me. The New Testament was a little better, I suppose, but have you actually read *Revelation*? I don't know. I just lost it. Everything."

Eva listened quietly to Ed talking. She had watched this entire transformation over the last three years, and it had been tough to witness, not nearly this condensed flippant version. Eva herself had gleefully jettisoned any faith back when her father kicked her out of the house when she was thirteen after she came out as "a full-time tranny," as he put it. But she knew how important it had been to Ed, so she listened to him tell it again.

"Oh, Ed," said Ester. "Wait until you meet Tod. He'll make you see things differently."

"What, that women really are filthy when they menstruate?"

"No, no. Nothing like that. You're just looking at religion all wrong. He can explain it better. He's doing such good work. You'll see."

"Does that have anything to do with the tattoos?" Eva asked, pointing at the parallel lines across eternity. Philos looked up from the back of the room. "You all have that tat on your hand, don't you?"

"Oh, yeah. You'll see."

The tattoos were Tod's idea after they lost Eternity, the name they gave their stillborn child. They never said if it was a girl or a boy; they only referred to it as "their child." Soon after, Tod told her that he could no longer be with her romantically—that his path was on a different, but parallel, trajectory; they would always be together, and they would always be connected by their child. Ester had wept when he suggested it, not thinking twice about what a tattoo between the right thumb and index finger might mean for her future job prospects. After the stillbirth, she got a part-time position in a Crisis Pregnancy Center, counseling young women who thought that they were going to an abortion clinic for help. Her job was to "witness" her story, as she said, using the word in the correct, but awkward way of born-again Christians. With her story, she tried to convince the women not to go through with it. She was not the one responsible for telling the women about the "studies" linking abortion to breast cancer or claiming that they would likely become sterile. Ester was not exactly happy with those lies, but, as she told her friends, she was committed to promoting a "culture of life" so that "no other babies needed to die." Anything she could do to help encourage that was fine by her. Most listeners at this point would feel uncomfortable at the reference to her stillborn fetus, and they rushed to change the subject.

When other people started to join the group and move in, they all saw the tattoo as an auspicious augury, and they each got the same marking in the same location. Tod never required it; they volunteered freely. They were not always sure what it meant, but they all had their own version of the ambiguous symbol, and they felt that having this individual meaning in the context of their group dynamic was a beautiful metaphor.

Tod Griffon finally arrived, and when he came in, everyone did a different kind of double take. The left side of his head was shaved completely, while the right side cascaded its tow-colored locks to his shoulders. He walked immediately up to Ester, kissed her on the cheek, and met her smiling look while they each held the other's forearms. Tod had an intensity to his eyes that was the inverse of Ed's swimming gaze, and he had a way of locking onto whomever he was talking to at the moment, as if he or she were the only person in the room.

"And you must be Ed," Tod said, turning his attention fully

to him. He offered his hand and shook it earnestly. "I am so sorry for your loss, Ed. I was hoping to come to the funeral to offer my condolences, but your cousin told me to wait until it was over. What everyone says is true: Losing your mother is just as horrible as you fear, and worse than you can imagine."

Ed paused, uncomfortable at this level of immediate intimacy. "Thanks, Tod," he said. "I appreciate it."

"And who might you be, my dear?" said Tod.

"Eva Sheehy, my love. And I was just heading out." Eva put her white leather jacket back on and gathered her guitar. "Ed, I have to head back to Philly. Are you sure you're going to be okay?"

Ed reassured her, and they parted with a long hug goodbye. "I'll call you when I get back. Bye, all. Nice to meet you, although I wish it were under better circumstances."

Tod moved into Eva's seat, took a deep breath, and looked at them both, smiling.

"So," Tod said. "Ester tells me that you might be interested in the Plan."

Ed was in no mood to counter and had no other topic of conversation to offer, so Tod began his story. He had gone to Muhlenberg College, graduating in 1982 with a degree in psychology and a degree in marketing, the last of which to make his parents happy. He was the first in his family to go to college since the nineteenth century, when, he was told, his family had lost all their money and never fully recovered. He was most fascinated by "the mind," as he put it, and preferred the older psychological ideas of Freud, Adler, and Jung. He especially liked Jung, who really helped him organize all of his ideas. The psych department, however, was largely empirically- and cognitively-based psychology, so it was mostly a lot of Skinner and Piaget derivatives, zapping rats and running mazes. What he found in his two majors, however, was that they told a similar story about our humanity, and he started to get a sense of what was the problem that was affecting the world today.

In 1982, another recession was in full swing under Lego-haired

Reagan, who also had just busted up the air traffic controller strike; England was in the process of trouncing Argentina in the Falklands War, that pathetic, slow-motion simulation of the real imperial power they used to wield. Israel invaded Lebanon, hunting the PLO. Hinckley was tried for shooting Reagan. The Equal Rights Amendment finally died an inglorious death, just three states shy. It just felt like everything was falling apart. So much strife. And for what, ultimately?

For a few years after he graduated, Tod felt despair at the millenarian thrust to contemporary politics, and he turned towards using his marketing degree to make a living. He was immediately recruited by a company called Mystic Cuts, which specialized in selling knives, door-to-door. During the orientation and informa-tion meeting, Chad, the group leader, told the twenty young men and women that they should not be offended if he paused his presentation and asked them to leave. There was nothing personal; he was just highly trained in being able to spot people who were going to make great knife sales representatives. Tod knew exactly what Chad wanted and made his face blur into a blissful smile showing that he was absolutely captivated by what these mystic knives from Japan could do. As Chad started to deliver his pitch, the attendees were picked off one by one for even the slightest raised eyebrow, the tiniest break from rapturous fascination. By the end, only five of the elect remained, and they all felt as if they had been chosen for some great purpose. They should be proud, Chad assured them. Very few people made it this far. All they would have to do before they would begin their intense training would be to invest in their demonstration set, which included fifteen varieties of knives and a simulation leather case, for only $1200. Everyone but Tod broke their rapture, only momentarily, and Chad allowed these infractions to pass and even broadened his smile. As the group queued to sign up and set up their payment plans, since none of them would have been here if they were not already unemployed, Tod leaned down and whispered in Chad's ear, "You're good, man. Really good. I'm better, but you are good."

Chad continued to smile at Tod as if he had no idea what he was saying, and he turned his attention back to the new converts.

As he left, Tod swore to himself that he would never fall for someone else's scheme, and he went into sales for himself. Over the next eight years, he developed his own system of door-to-door sales, importing a variety of products that seemed to have nothing to do with one another—dish detergent, energy bars, vitamins, and disposable cameras—and branded them around a lifestyle mantra: AWAKE! The mantra was vague enough that everyone could project their needs into it, and they saw their purchases as inspirations for aspirations. The products leaned towards items that would have to be renewed in perpetuity, and Tod created a mailing list of repeat customers that he kept adding to. Wake Industries did very well, and after seven years, he was able to pay cash for an old Victorian behind the post office off 5th and Hamilton towards the end of 1989.

Ever since he had graduated from high school, Tod took pride in the fact that he had never owned a TV. When he was growing up, his parents left the television playing all day long. Even when they would sit down to talk about a serious issue, his father would pause the conversation to make sure that the TV was playing, but then he had the decency to put it on mute. Tod would never follow in his parents' footsteps. When he was bored, he could read a book or at least a *New Yorker*. But the woman he was dating at the time liked watching *Baywatch*, god help him, so he decided to get cable installed; and since Bethlehem's Service Electric claimed to be the oldest cable company in the country, it was pretty cheap. Besides, he rationalized, CNN would be useful to keep up with the basics. It was November 10, 1989, a year that inaugurated George H. W. Bush, who seemed to reignite the apocalyptic. The U.S. shot two Libyan fighters over the Mediterranean; the Ayatollah Khomeini had issued his fatwa against Salman Rushdie for *The Satanic Verses*; the Chinese had just squashed the student protests in Tiananmen Square, even if that one guy stood up to the tanks. Tod was already feeling that unease from 1982, and he was wondering how much longer he could still do AWAKE! and live with himself. As the Service Electric installer ran the wires from the pole, the television brought the first of many signs he would come to rely upon in his new phase. The first image Tod saw when he fired up CNN was the channel's twenty-four-hour coverage of jubilant men and women of all ages destroying the Berlin Wall. The "wall woodpeckers," as they were nicknamed, smashed chunks of this ultimate symbol of the Iron Curtain for posterity, and Tod had the first of many epiphanies.

Tod was born into the Cold War. Since he was a kid, he grew up absolutely certain that humanity was doomed, and the general fear of our global annihilation played in the background soundtrack throughout his life. Stanley Kubrick's grimly hilarious *Dr. Strangelove* orchestrated the overture at a very early age. In the 1980s, after Reagan pulled his adolescent prick out and declared that the Soviet Union was an "evil empire," which he would fight with "Star Wars," there seemed to be an endless stream of inevitable destruction fantasies dreamed up by Hollywood: *The Day After*, when the entire country seemed to have seen the horrific montage of nuclear blasts for the first time, and everyone shambled along the next few days, trying to process it; *Threads*, the BBC's even bleaker answer to that film; *War Games*, where Matthew Broderick's hacker fuckup almost ignites complete global destruction; and even that devastating British cartoon with the Roger Waters music, *When the Wind Blows*, with the cute little tweedy couple slowly dying of radiation poisoning. Most of the world seemed paralyzed by a metaphysical version of smoker's gallows humor, joking about cigarettes being "coffin nails" because there seemed to be no escape. And now here was history unfolding before him, and the ultimate divider that separated us was coming down. Tod had to be a part of that. He had his revised vision, and so the Kin were born.

What Tod came to realize was that the problem with the world, especially in the West, was this: Ever since we were born, we've been trained to see the world in terms of contraries, binary tensions set in opposition. We're not to blame for this way of thinking, he assured; it stretched back at least as far as the Zoroastrians, four thousand years ago. At the simplest level, the minor conceptual linkages were merely heuristic organizations: light versus dark; men versus women; up versus down. This tendency to organize the world, he argued, grew out of a kind of Kantian logical capacity, an innate tendency to carve the world up this way. As babies, every time we learned a new concept—*banana*, for example, or *man*, or *God*—our brains were capable of constructing its opposite—*not-banana, not-man, not-God*. On this level, the organization is simple enough; we have the pure logical possibility of negation: *not-X*. No other animals have this particular logical function, Tod maintained. The most they can do is act on instinct, to undo a state that they find unsatisfactory: Hunger? Want food. Tired? Want sleep. Pain? Want relief. Animals, however, only desire a different state of being; they do not conceive of what this means. They act on pure instinct, and for that, they are the purest beings and already saved.

This last word suspended in the air between them as though it had an actual dimensionality.

The difficulties get going when they start to link other concepts to the "not-X" formulas, which then get locked into this strife. So *woman*, for example, becomes the *not-man*. Therefore, she is deficient man, and she is always defined in this opposition, rather than just on her own terms. There is no reason why *woman* should not have come first, with man being *not-woman*; it was just an accident of history, patriarchy, and power. And that's bad enough on the gender relations. What about entire societies? The powerful versus the powerless. Us versus them. Insiders versus Outsiders. The chosen versus the goyim. All racism, all xenophobia, all violence, was a function of this one logical fallacy—the linking up of otherness into this primal negation. This human capacity for negation is the beginning of our Fall.

"The not-Garden?"

"Exactly. And without this negativity," Tod explained, "we

would see the world as the animals see it: as pure being. There is no good and evil. There is no distinction between races. There is no distinction between nations."

"And religions?" Ed asked.

"No!" Tod tapped a knuckle on the table. "All religions are one!"

"Tell that to the Israelis and Palestinians. The Irish Catholics and the English Protestants."

"And that's the problem. That's *exactly* the problem. The apocalyptic prophecies of the Old Testament codified tribal warfare as an absolute and unchanging tension. Going back as far as Isaiah, the apocalypse was a simple matter of wiping out everyone who was not in the tribe. Ezekiel sets up the ultimate paranoid fantasy of us versus them, when he prophesies a leader of Magog named Gog, who will gather all the nations of the world against Israel. Guess how that turns out? Mountains destroyed. Fire and ice. Everyone annihilated except the Chosen, and the enemy corpses become food for the wild animals. It is the ultimate fantasy of retribution, and once you have that in place, you'll never have peace. And you wonder why there are Iron Curtains everywhere you look?"

"What about activism? A lot of oppressed people dedicate themselves to causes to make the world a better place."

"Sure, for them. Are you kidding? No activist wants his cause's antithesis to perish. He needs the antithesis to function. To be. And more than needs: the activist *loves* his antithesis. Do you really believe that Gloria Steinem wants equality of the sexes? That's preposterous. If she wanted equality, she would want her own annihilation. No, she desires strife, constant strife. And when there is no visible strife, she looks for more. It could probably be argued that she chose such a profession—and activism is, first and foremost, a profession, an identity—that she chose such a profession because she knew that there never would be equality, that the male-female dynamic was an eternal conflict, older than Zoroaster's opposition of good and evil—which can't be excised with spiritual castration, sensitivity training, dime-store mysticism, or whatever therapy-of-the-month talk shows are offering as a path to the sexes' mutual annihilation into a metaphysical melting pot."

Tod was getting going. Ester looked at him with a beatific gaze that watched something beyond that half-shaved head that Ed could not see.

"Activism is a dead end," Tod continued. "It only perpetuates the othering of people by segmenting the world into problems and solutions. Do you think the Buddha did not see the strife in the world around him? Of course! There have always been poverty, famine, war. The problem is trying to believe that you could change this. To reach transcendence, to reach nirvana, you have to let go of those illusions. The world *is*. And whatever *is*, is right—is holy." He paused, drinking some of his espresso.

"So, you're a Buddhist."

"Not quite, no. But as I said, all religions are one."

"Maybe," said Ed. "But the world still seems pretty shitty most of the time."

"Look, in philosophy, how do you determine something's value? How do you know if a thing is good or not? What makes 'a good fork'?"

"Um, not not-fork?"

"Ha. Very good. No, a 'good fork' is one that functions the way it is supposed to. It lives up to its dictionary definition. *A small tool with two or more pointed parts used for picking up and eating food.* Once it ceases to have those characteristics, it is no longer a good fork. It is, as you say, a *not-fork*."

"But *fork* has other definitions, like 'a fork in the road'; 'a move in chess'; 'a forked tongue.'"

A forked tongue, indeed, thought someone in the room.

"Metaphors, and not the point. Now, how do you know if the world is good? Well, how do we define the world? Look up all the words in the dictionary—justice, beauty, kindness, but also war, strife, bigotry—and they are all a part of our world. And all the religions of the world, and all the different belief systems and ideologies. Everything that can be said about it, is what the world is. Therefore, the world is good, as it is, and it can't not be."

"So, nothing changes. The only problem is thinking you can change things. We should do nothing to help suffering?"

"I'm not talking about suffering. I'm talking about inner peace. The apocalypticists were right about one thing: the end times are coming. You can feel it in the approaching millennium. You can feel the despair and the energy. But we have a choice of what that means. If we maintain differences, then we will surely destroy ourselves. Either some despot will get his hands on a nuclear bomb, or some hacker kid will unleash the hounds of hell, but something will take us down."

Saved . . . Holy . . . Apocalypse . . . Hell, Ed thought. *It's like stepping on wasps . . .*

"But how do you stop that if you don't believe in activism? What's the point of your—group?"

"You stop it by changing our perceptions. By changing our very assumptions about how we organize our lives. If divisions are illusionary, and they are only held in place by what William Blake called our 'mind-forg'd manacles,' then we have to be shown that the manacles are not really there, even if we don't want to see that. If there is one thing I learned from marketing, it was that you have to create desire in people if you want them to buy what you are selling. My haircut is kind of like those buttons you see people wearing: 'Make money working from home. Ask me how.' Most people would just go along in their lives, hating the other and seeing the world in the fractured little bits of beliefs and prejudices that they picked up from their parents. Once we get people to realize the innate holiness of the world, once they can transcend the limited Manichean binary thinking, we will finally transcend that trajectory and avert the apocalypse. It is the only way."

Tod explained how the Plan operated. The people working on the Plan called themselves the Kin, or, more playfully, the Kinfolk. They liked the contradiction implied by that name in the etymology of the term, suggesting that they were blood relations, even though they were not, and that they were a tribe or nation, as it meant in Old English, even though they had selected their own affiliations, their own nation. Most of them had other jobs, but most of them were living in Tod's rundown old Victorian. They each had their own small space, and they spent most of their free time in a communal rec room-cum-library in a first-floor annex to the main house that was added without much long-term planning back in the 1950s. The walls were covered with hand-made bookshelves, and they were stuffed with an eclectic variety of Tod's passions and the Kinfolk's own additions. They read, worked on art projects, wrote poetry, and studied various systems of religion, politics, and philosophy, always trying to find out the essential things that linked them together while effacing the differences, which they believed were mere accidents of time.

The Kinfolk's whole goal was consciousness raising, to stage various interventions into people's lives to help disrupt the false logic of contraries. Their primary model was the situationists, and Guy Debord was a kind of patron saint in many ways. Everyone had to read Debord's *Report on the Construction of Situations* before moving in, especially since that corresponded to the more artistic liberation model of his career, not so much the political, which Tod saw as one more ideological trap. The Kin wanted to disrupt the habituated patterns of modern capitalist existence and to challenge people's single-minded and binary belief systems by doing guerilla graffiti pieces in random and not-so-random places, like Blek le Rat; striking up conversations with random people in malls and bus stops, only to talk them slowly into some contradiction in their beliefs that they had not noticed before, like Socrates; staging dramatic scenes in public spaces where the spectators could not believe what they were seeing, but would always talk about it for the rest of their lives.

One of their most successful and almost mythical interventions was a "hubristic inversion," as they called it. There was a local guitarist from out in Macungie, Andy Lawrence, whom one of the Kin knew through her brother. Andy had been working on a set of original material in hopes of getting a small record deal or at least some funding for a demo tape. He had been practicing for months, and finally got a gig at the Stonewall Club on 10th Street, where his brother worked. The gay bar was showcasing a techno house music trio called ABBAcadabra for a few Philly A&R reps, and the guitarist was going to have a shot at some actual labels listening to him. When they found out, the Kinfolk decided to arrive on the night of the showcase and pack the dance floor, screaming and mouthing words as if they were longtime fans who knew all the words. Their Beatlemania performance at first confused Andy, who thought that maybe they were just responding to his catchy songs. The more he was convinced of this, the more he got into his own performance, squinting his eyes and belting his lyrics like Eddie Vedder at his most Vedder-esque. In the middle of one of Andy's songs, the entire group stopped acting like fans and merely stood, staring at him with blithe, impassive faces, like they had just awoken from a fugue state. Andy tried to ignore them, squinting against them or staring at the stage, until he finally, and very obviously, missed a G# minor chord, at which the entire clan turned and walked out of Stonewall, leaving a group of bemused A&R reps and one devastated folk singer.

Ed shuddered. "And what in the world was the point of that?"

"Hubris, Ed. The inversion of hubris. The Greeks knew. On the one hand, they were one of the proudest cultures ever to exist. You read *The Odyssey?* Odysseus would stop by random cities like Ismarus on his way home from the Trojan War just to sack them for fun. A little rape and pillage for the boys to keep them happy. Yet the Greeks also invented tragedy. Originally, tragedies were part of religious festivals honoring Dionysus—the god of wine, ritual madness, and the obliteration of individual consciousness. A chorus of about fifty people would chant about fate and our ultimate dissolution, almost joyfully embracing the end. Then they added an actor, who would arise from the horde and say his bit before being eventually subsumed into the lot. The proud, hubristic individual, driven by his desire to be above the multitude, could not stand. Even the proud Greeks, the inventors of the Olympics—which, let's face it, was essentially a contest to see who could throw a stick or a disc the farthest like a bunch of five-year-olds—even they knew the limits of the individual. And to disrupt an individual's hubristic desire is just one way to dissolve opposition."

"But the kid just wanted to make music."

"No, he wanted to be famous. He wanted a record deal, and his fantasies of fame and power would have been his undoing. We just helped him to see it."

"I don't know," Ed sighed. "Seems pretty cruel to me."

"Well," said Ester. "I happen to know that now he's doing occupational therapy over at KidsPeace."

"The psych hospital?" asked Ed.

"Yep," she said. "He brings his guitar and shows the kids how to express themselves by submitting themselves to the music. It's beautiful."

"How do you submit to music?"

"It's like what Tod was saying. All religions have something to teach us. That's what Islam means: *submission*. Andy's work was all ego. The whole idea of 'lyrics' is to write about the 'I.' It's all like opera." She sang like a warm-up scale, "Me-me-me-me-me-me-me. The best musicians know that it isn't about ego. It's about summoning the muse—submitting to the higher power. Like the Romantic poets' idea of *inspiration*, which literally means 'to breath into.' Open up, and let the divine breathe into you."

"Look, Ed," said Tod. "This is hard to explain, if you don't have the background, but here is the crux. There is not one soul within us, you know. Consciousness and identity don't come without a cost." Tod took a napkin and drew a graph line with something that looked like a sine wave. "Everything we become," he said, tapping the sine, "every belief we attach to, everything we like or hate, creates an equal and opposite unconscious version." He then drew an inverted version of the sine wave in dashes. "There is another level—not deeper, but equal—an identity within us that is not always unconscious, although it certainly becomes so for most people. It's a balanced function. We call this the co-consciousness. The psyche's equal and opposite reaction against every empirical identity-forming piece of sense data it takes in and colonizes like some Columbus seeking immortality. The more we believe in something—the farther away from this zero line—the more we unconsciously believe in the opposite. Of course, we can't handle this desire, so we attack it, but the thing we're attacking is always ourselves. Jung called this the shadow archetype, and that's the thing we have to come to understand if we are going to stop the end of the world."

Ed looked at the napkin for a few seconds. Did he have an equal and opposite Ed, some *not-Ed* within himself? It seemed unlikely, and yet it might explain some things. Tod was talking over his head on a lot of things, and it seemed to Ed like he was mashing up a lot of different traditions and ideas into this meta-philosophy. Yet he was so passionate and persuasive that it was hard not to get swept up into his words, if not his argument.

"Okay," said Ed. "So, how do you stop the apocalypse by affecting one or two people, here and there? Seems like more of a global thing."

"Ever hear of the 'butterfly effect'?" Tod asked. "You'd be surprised by the rippling results of changing 'one or two people, here and there.' But you are right, that we might as well increase our odds by unleashing more butterflies. This is what is behind the next phase."

"This is so exciting," said Ester. "And this is something you might really be interested in."

"Ester tells me that you are an artist."

"I haven't painted anything in three years," said Ed.

Ester looked shocked. "Really? But you used to draw and paint and everything all the time."

"Aye, *non sum qualis eram*," Ed sighed. "The artist-priest is dead. Long live the unaffiliated custodian."

Tod looked confused at this last, but he ignored it. "Well," he said, "you might be inspired. In a couple of months, the Kinfolk are going to stage a happening, open to the entire community."

"You mean, like the sixties 'happenings'?"

"Exactly!" said Ester. "It is going to be amazing."

Tod explained. In two or three months, the Kin were going to plan a series of happenings—a kind of group art process that was staged, but also chaotic. The events would synthesize different kinds of art media and experiential events to bring the audience into participation with the art itself, collapsing the distinction between art and life, the spectator and the event, self and other. The whole idea would function as a kind of replacement religion, he explained.

"Religion?" asked Ed.

"Think about the Catholic mass."

"I always do."

"What's the point of the mass?"

"To receive communion."

"Right, but what is happening?"

"Homily. Reading. Chanting a bunch of hymns."

"No, no. Man, you Catholics," he laughed. "The final communion is to reenact the Last Supper. Think about that. To reenact the horrific moment when Jesus offers his body and blood to his apostles to eat and drink, right before his actual crucifixion. They must have thought he was bonkers. Yet this is what Catholics do every week all over the world. And for Catholics, this is no Protestant metaphor. The host *is* Jesus's body, and you'd better not drop it on the ground."

Ed raised his eyebrows in affirmation.

"Ultimately," Tod continued, "a mass is theater. By staging this moment from two thousand years ago and saying the same words, time collapses, and the people are united—they are in communion with one another and with Jesus. And as you know, when you are in it, it works. You remember that feeling, don't you?"

Ed nodded.

"We need a new religion, one that bypasses the cannibalistic snuff film qualities of the Christ myth, which only focuses on the tragedy—on the brutal takedown of an innocent man. We need a positive myth, and we need new ceremonies to transcend the false binaries that keep us apart. And once we hit the right form of ceremony, transcending dualistic thinking won't just be a metaphor anymore. It will *be* transcendent."

To that end, the Kin were working on various art projects and performance pieces that would break down barriers. Nothing overtly didactic, he explained. You don't want to turn people off with a bunch of preachy ideas that they're not even ready for. You have to create a completely unique space that combines imagery and multimodal sounds and lights, all targeted at disrupting our normal modes of perception. Unlike the mass, it would have to be something that could not be replicated the same way twice, since that would just set up a new dualism. We'll provide the space and form, and everyone will provide the content—an integration of structure and chaos—so that the participants will talk about it for the rest of their lives. Tod explained that they had to recruit people from all walks of life—the old and the young, the hip and the square. And the biggest challenge: they would have to make it a point to recruit people who normally would disagree with them. This was of paramount importance.

"You don't just want to get caught in an echo chamber," Tod laughed. "There's enough of that around."

"Just consider it," said Ester. "Why don't you come by the house tomorrow and get a sense of the vibe? If you feel inspired, maybe you'll contribute something."

"I don't know, guys. I'm not much of a joiner these days. I did enough of that in my adolescence, and it didn't work out too well. I doubt I'll be getting any tattoos anytime soon."

Tod smiled. "No pressure."

Tod looked around the room and saw Philos in the corner, reading quietly and taking notes. Tod turned his full attention to him.

"Hey, man. What are you working on?"

Philos looked up, pen in hand, and leaned back in his chair. Ed could not tell if he had been listening to them or not.

"Travel writing."

"What's that? Like Fodor's?"

He smiled. "Kind of. They're travel books that are partly informative, but they have the form of essay writing. Basically, I go from place to place and try to write about it from an outsider's perspective, to defamiliarize it for people. Make the reader see things that were right in front of them, but they were too close to see it."

"You do this a lot?"

"I have a few out."

"They sell?"

"Enough to keep me going."

"Going where?"

"Wherever I have to."

"And how long will that last?"

Philos sighed. "Until I get to the end."

Tod paused, smiling. "I like you, man. What's your name?"

Philos introduced himself, and the trio introduced themselves.

"'Philos' is unique," said Tod. "Is that Greek?"

"My father was. My mother was Jewish. Sephardic."

"This is fascinating," said Ester, almost clapping. "An actual author. The publishing world always seems so mysterious; you never think that you'd ever know someone who actually does it. So, what exactly do you do?"

Philos explained that he traveled from town to town, staying places anywhere from a few months to a year or two, depending on how many . . . people there were. He got to write his essays about the city—its spaces, its people, its history. He loved not just how people lived, but *why*. What motivated them, got them to get up in the morning besides habit and rote repetition. And often, this answer stretched far back into history, to times and places lost to the layers of history that the inhabitants had no idea about, places that often control who you are and what you do.

"How does a space control what you do?" Ed asked, thinking back to his architecture school days.

The spaces we inhabit are planned, Philos explained, or were planned. In America, the choices made in the eighteenth and nineteenth centuries set up the roads, institutions, government buildings, the factories, the schools, the bridges. Every one of those choices determines what is allowed today, what is even possible. Who owns what land, what jobs are available. You feel this every time you move to a new city. The locals usually don't even think that the way that they live is prescribed and proscribed by choices made for them a long time ago. It all feels inevitable, like the air and the rain.

"But there's always freedom of choice," said Ester.

Philos paused, eyeing his backpack.

"Maybe. Most of us just get born somewhere, spend a few years figuring out how the gravity works and where to pick up the best groceries; then we just . . . autopilot."

"Who can blame them?" asked Ed. "It would be exhausting to go outside every day and say, 'Golly, I never noticed that tree before.'"

Philos smiled a warm and sad smile.

"True. But there gets to be this point where we forget that almost everything that feels natural is a lie, or at least had an origin that we don't remember was chosen for us. And every time we are tempted to say 'natural,' or 'common sense,' or 'it is what it is,' that's exactly when we have to slow down and wonder how it got to be that way."

"Why bother?" asked Ester. "If it feels natural, maybe that's just our reality."

"It's only when you know the *why* that you can change the *what*," said Philos. "At least it is easier."

They were quiet a moment.

"Anyway," said Philos. "That's the way it seems from an outsider's perspective."

"And so you're going to write a book about Allentown," said

Ester.

"Pennsylvania, yes. You all are a chapter."

"How long do you plan to stay?"

"As long as it takes."

"It must get lonely," said Ester.

Tod and Ed both looked at her.

"It can," Philos said. "My girlfriend, Ruth, usually joins up with me on the road for a while. We talk almost every day."

"How long has that been going on?" Ester asked.

"About ten years."

Ed whistled. "That is one patient girlfriend."

Philos smiled, less sadly. "She is that," he said.

Tod told Philos about the happening and tried to gauge his response. Philos listened patiently to the pitch, nodding occasionally.

"I see what you're doing. And, honestly, I overheard part of your conversation from before. I understand your logic, but I'm not sure about your basic premises."

"What basic premises?"

"Doesn't matter," he said. "Look, I'm not really equipped to save the world. I don't know if I can even save myself."

"So, you're just going to worry about your own private ego? You worry about spaces, but you don't care if they are all blown off the face of the earth. You don't care about the coming apocalypse?"

"I'm not sure that that is an empirically verified truth, as of yet. The world does seem to keep on grinding on. Right now, I have enough to do in my life of creation and decreation."

Ed wondered what Philos meant by this last word.

"Well," said Tod, "then you're opposed to everything true."

"Well, then," Philos smiled, "I suppose that I'm part of the true, then."

Tod smirked. "Clever."

"Look, I wish you luck. I just have to deal with what I have to deal with."

"Your lone self."

Philos packed his things into his Eastpak, looking inside.

"Myself, and the sins of my father," he said, as though to himself. "To the third and the fourth generations." He stood and met their gazes. "Nice to meet you all. I'm sure that I'll see you around. Let me know when you get your event together. I can't say that I'm not intrigued."

CHAPTER THREE

Ester's parents, Richie and Ginny Donner, lived across the Lehigh River on the East Side of Allentown at the dead end of Howe Street. Their ramshackle farmhouse in the center of a half-acre lot incongruously nestled its bucolic oasis in the midst of the ferocious surrounding community. A dense wall of trees encircled the house, separating it from the desolate and crumbling row homes on the busy Hanover Avenue to the south, and Hanover Acres to the north. The Acres started life back in 1939 during the Depression as the fifth residential housing project ever built as a result of the 1937 National Housing Act. Three hundred and twenty-two brick-veneer units offered spaces for the prewar economic struggles that overtook the area. Eleanor Roosevelt even visited the development in 1942, meeting local housewives and giving her cotton-stockinged approval to the Housing Authority for a job well done, before she gave a speech to Muhlenberg College students about how men fight wars, but women carried on "the determination and courage of the nation." Richie's grandparents held out against the project, and the house sat as one of the only remaining single homes next to the development. Over the years, the Acres descended into a crime-ridden training ground for the future incarcerated. Just recently, two police officers were assaulted while trying to break up a twenty-person brawl. When you were on the Donner compound, however, you did not feel this tension right beyond the tree line; you were allowed to forget this imminent unrest, at least for a while.

Growing up, Ed spent many hours at the Donners' house. The families were very close, even though they were not technically related. Ester's mother, Ginny, was married to Ed's Uncle Glen, Teddy's brother. On the night of January 25, 1971, the same day that Charles Manson and three of his harem were convicted of the Tate-LaBianca murders, Teddy and Glen both got so drunk that for some reason they went up to Whitehall and sped down Water Street in Dark Town, missing the guardrail at the end of the road, sliding down the embankment into the Lehigh River below. Both drowned within a minute. Teddy left behind his wife who was six months pregnant, while Ginny sought solace in vodka tonics and Glen's best friend, Richie. Richie was a cotton spinner who was out on disability after contracting byssinosis, which they all called "brown lung," even though the lungs do not actually get brown. When people asked him what he did for a living, Richie liked to drawl, "That's my byssinosis, bub, not yours." The union had negotiated a small disability package, and Richie was able to live in semi-retirement in the family farmhouse that always looked like it was about to slide into the earth.

Ed's mother never really liked Richie, and she especially feared his temper. But she had no local family of her own, and was so close to Ginny that she and Ed just treated the Donners like blood. Lorel Leh gave birth to Ed on April 15, 1971 at Sacred Heart Hospital, and Ester was born two months premature that October in the same room, although she was already six pounds, three ounces, so it seemed like she was just ready to jump out. The doctors thought Ginny's smoking might have been the cause, and everyone was just relieved that Ester didn't have fetal alcohol syndrome. After Ginny lost some of her pregnancy fat, she married Richie two months later at Allentown City Hall, with only Lorel Leh and baby Ed in attendance. Ginny finally quit drinking when she started to breastfeed Ester, and she remained a teetotaler even in the midst of Richie's epic benders.

Their entire childhoods, Ed and Ester played together, dreamt of the future together, slept in each other's beds during sleepovers after playing round after round of *Asteroids* and *Missile Command* on their Atari 2600s. They even went to Moser Elementary together after Ed tested into the gifted program and was bussed every day over to the East Side. He still remembered the commute past the reeking air around the Arbogast & Bastian pork processing plant, which slaughtered over four thousand hogs a day. There were times when Ester even felt closer to Ed than her own younger sister, Angela, because of their proximity in age and experience. They had grown apart a little during the last four years after Ed left for college and dropped out. He seemed always to have some excuse for not coming back during the holidays, and Ester was busy herself, working for the Crisis Pregnancy Center while taking classes at Kutztown University, where she commuted the twenty miles back and forth every day. She was studying English, although Ed never knew her to finish a whole book after the *Little House on the Prairie* series, so he wasn't sure what kind of literature she was reading.

It was after dark when Ed and Ester drove down the long stretch of road that led to the house. As the car lights illuminated the compound that Ed knew so well, he remembered why he had decided to stay with Eva's family out in Quakertown for the last week. Everything had Richie's thumbprint on it: the chipped porcelain clawfoot bathtub with two missing feet, which served as an herb and tomato planter during the summer; the rusted-out '67 Chevy without wheels that Richie was going to refurbish back in the early years of the Reagan administration; the homemade chicken coop attached to the back of the west side of the house; the eight-foot Santa Claus that bent over from deflation so that he gently waved his entire body in the breeze to any passersby who dared come onto the compound; the large pile of scrap wood in various states of decay that Richie used to patch the numerous wood structures strewn across the property; the dun-colored sofa with the exposed springs that barely huddled under the back porch's overhang, next to a pile of crushed Miller High Life cans and an old washing machine that served as a makeshift prep table and storage bin. The entire first floor blazed in the dark, the curtains wide open and every light on so that Ed could see the entire layout of everything within. For a second, he felt like he was looking at the inside of someone's skull, with nowhere to hide the secrets.

"Well, looks like somebody's home," he said, stepping out of Ester's olive-drab 1972 Chevy Malibu that she had inherited from her father and into the fetid stench of Kline's Island, the sewage treatment plant that was only a mile away. It was still called an island, even though it was attached to the rest of the land, since City Hall decided it would be a good idea to use the western channel of the former island as a landfill dump. They walked past the sofa and opened the unlocked door to the familiar sight of an American flag hanging like wallpaper next to a Confederate flag in the tight entryway. Ed never understood that choice, since Richie's family had immigrated from Austria in 1914 and had lived in Pennsylvania for generations. The house hung heavy with the smell of turkey cooking and Richie's Pall Malls.

Ed locked the kitchen door behind him and as they entered the living room, he felt something was wrong. From inside the house, the windows backed by night reflected the room from eight large rectangles, and it was apparent just how on display they were from the outside. In the middle of the floor, Ester's ten-year-old sister, LeAnne, sat looking at a book with a lot of pictures of angels in it. Ed immediately started to close the drapes of the nearest windows, asking where her parents were.

"Oh, they're not back from the funeral yet."

"But that's been over for two hours," said Ester.

"They left you alone this whole time?" Ed almost shouted.

"Don't scare her, Ed," said Ester.

"Scare her? She could've been abducted or killed."

"Oh, no," said LeAnne, "Jesus watches over me. And God watches us all!"

"That's right, sweetie," said Ester. "You were fine. You are always safe."

Ed mumbled something under his breath as he closed the rest

of the curtains. During the day, the room shone bright and contrasted with the chaotic cluster of objects that flooded Ed's senses. Ed thought of Philos's claim about how spaces define us and wondered what part of their personalities this space was responsible for. The three-gallon tin can of Keystone Dutch Pretzels sitting permanently on the floor by the slipcovered sofa, stained and covered with cat hair; the pairs of shoes placed on the first five steps leading upstairs; the mysterious boxes piled against the west wall that had been there as long as Ed could remember, but never opened; the two empty Miller beer cases that Richie used to store his collection of Lynyrd Skynyrd, Charlie Daniels, and Marshall Tucker Band records. Along the north wall sat Richie's two tanks—one a twenty-gallon tank housing Richie's cramped five-foot ball python, curled up and sleeping from a full mouse dinner; the second, a seventy-five-gallon saltwater tank housing a spectacular eleven-inch maroon-and-white striped *Pterois volitans*, or red lionfish, whose dorsal and pectoral fins made it look like a floating explosion. Pete, the python, was Richie's joy until he got the lionfish, which he cared for with a tenderness that made everyone else in the house resentful. He preferred the lionfish because it was actually venomous, whereas the python could only constrict. He called it Lucy, even though he had no idea what its gender was.

Richie took great pride in being the opposite of everything he saw on *Lifestyles of the Rich and Famous*. He seemed deliberately to collect hobbies and affectations that had the least cultural capital as a way to reject the system that rejected him. He spoke with a slight Southern drawl, as though he had learned how to speak by watching *Hee Haw* on the Superstation, a trait that Ed had noticed in other Pennsylvanians outside the urban archipelago, but one he did not remember Richie having when Ed was growing up. It was as if the blacker and more Hispanic his neighborhood became, the more White-with-a-capital-W Richie wanted to be.

The kitchen door banged, as if the owner did not expect it to be locked. A fumbling with the keys, and Richie entered, followed by Ginny.

"Well, well, well," sneered Richie. "If it isn't Hippie Longstocking and the Grim Creeper, honoring us with their presence." Ginny pushed him slightly on the shoulder, as if this were all in good reciprocal fun. "Ball busting," Richie liked to call it, but Ed always sensed a real malevolence under all his jokes, as though that were not just a metaphor. They were still in their funeral clothes, which for Ginny meant a simple black dress with her most expensive costume jewelry, and for Richie meant a rayon polo shirt tucked into his best Levis. This he now untucked.

Ginny smiled meekly behind tearing eyes and hugged Ed.

"I'm so sorry, again, Ed," said Ginny. "I miss your mom so much already. But she was in so much pain there at the end, it was a mercy, really. She's with Jesus now."

Ed loosened himself from her hug.

"Yeah, tough shakes, Ed," said Richie. "She was a hell of a woman, your mom. It's not going to be the same around here without her stopping by all the time."

"You make it sound like she was mooching," Ester hissed. "She was barely here the last couple of years."

"She had a lot of personality," said Richie. "Maybe it just seemed like more." He headed off to the bathroom. "I'm gonna hit the shitter. Let's eat."

Ester glared at her mother, eyes widening. Ginny made her *You know how he gets* face. Ed sat down in a La-Z-Boy recliner, next to LeAnne. Ester and her mother headed into the kitchen.

"So, what's with the turkey?" asked Ester.

Her mother explained in a low voice that Richie was upset that Ed never made it back for Thanksgiving, saying Ed must have had some kind of anti-American bullshit problem about Indians, and claiming that it was partly what broke his mother's heart. Ginny did not think this was true, she reassured. But Richie was offended. So, he decided that since Ed was going to live under his roof, he was going to live under his rules, so they were going to have a proper goddamn Thanksgiving.

"Even though it is New Year's," said Ester.

"You know your father."

Ester rolled her eyes and started to set the table.

"Where'd Angela go off to?" asked Ester.

"She went to check in at the clinic. New Years is tough for a lot of people."

Ester's sister Angela worked for an off-brand weight loss center, counseling mostly middle-aged women on their diets and their attitudes. Angela herself had struggled all her life with her weight, and she had a particular weakness for the salty grease haven offered by a McDonald's quarter pounder with cheese, which she would often eat two of at one sitting. She thought of her job as supremely important, because she did not see her role as one that would shame women about their weight, as was often the case. There was enough of that in our world, and she suffered merciless taunting throughout her school years because of it. In fact, she counseled the women to accept who they were, no matter how heavy they were. She had a repertoire of slogans like "Say 'Yes' to the plus-sized dress!" and "There is no waste in a waist!" which she would tell the women to make them feel better about themselves. Angela did this behind the owner's back, mostly because when she was successful, the women dropped out of the program, happier with their bodies, if not exactly healthier. In Angela's ideal world, everyone would accept themselves for who they were, and she would be out of a job.

In the living room, Ed watched LeAnne copying one of the angels in fine-tipped felt pen into her scrapbook. She was a pretty good artist for a ten-year-old, Ed thought, and she was focusing on some crosshatch shading that Ed had shown her how to do a few years back.

"So, what are you working on?" asked Ed.

"Drawing, silly."

"I can see that. What are you drawing?"

"Angels."

"And which angel is that?"

"Leila."

"I'm not up on my angelology. Who is Leila? The patroness of My Pretty Pony dolls?"

She looked at Ed with a mock grimace.

"Ha, ha, smarty," she said. "This is Leila, the Angel of Conception."

"The who?" said Ed.

"The Angel of Conception. Isn't she beautiful? When a man and woman decide to have a baby, Leila is the one who picks the soul from the Garden of Eden and shows the soul how to enter the man's seed. The soul, of course, doesn't want to leave the Garden, much less *enter a man's seed*," she made a "gross" face, "but Leila makes it go. God looks at the soul and figures out what kind of life it will have. Will it be rich? Will it be pretty? Will it marry the man of its dreams? Then Leila puts the seed into the woman's belly and lights a candle for her to see, telling her all about the Garden of Eden and the Bible and showing her heaven and hell."

"There's a candle in her belly?"

"M-hm."

"She does this for everyone?" asked Ed.

"Of course! At least the Christian babies."

"Then why don't I remember the Garden or going to heaven?"

"Because, that would take the mystery out of life. As soon as we're born, Leila hits us on our lips, making this mark." She pointed to her philtrum. "When she does that, we cry, and we also forget all about heaven. But that's why when we learn about it, it sounds so right."

"Hm," said Ed. "I don't remember that in the Bible I read. So, why do Hindus and Muslims have that little dent, too?"

LeAnne thought for a second, and then turned back to her crosshatching. With her complete immersion in her projects, he thought how uncannily similar she was to Ester at that age, except Ester had dark brown hair, like Ed.

"I dunno. Must be a mystery. Isn't it fun to have mysteries?"

Ed looked down at her shoulder-length blond hair, her face intensely focused on her task, and thought about a line from Sartre: "I distrust the incommunicable; it is the source of all violence." Was that true? Ed certainly distrusted the mysterious and people who relied on blurry definitions to get by. But Aquinas believed in angels, after all, and there's no one more rational than the Angelic Doctor himself, the Dumb Ox.

"If I name my baby 'Leila,'" LeAnne asked, "do you think that will confuse the real Leila?"

"I'm guessing that an angel can figure out a doubling," said Ed. "Why do you like this angel so much?"

"Well, she wasn't there for Ester when she had her baby, so she must've done something wrong. Or maybe Leila left Eternity in hell. We're gonna make sure that that doesn't happen next time, me and Ester."

Ed stared. He put his head in his hands for a minute, thinking. LeAnne drew.

"So, how do you know this story is true?" Ed asked.

"Because she has faith," Richie's voice boomed from behind Ed. "You remember what that is, right? You wouldn't want to bring some of your Philadelphia atheism over to my house, would you?"

"Of course, Uncle Richie," said Ed. "I wasn't implying anything. I was just curious."

"Good. Then maybe you'll come to church with us on Sunday."

Richie loved being seen at church. He usually took the whole family to the 9:00 am mass, which was when all of his buddies went. Afterwards, he would drop the family off at the Donner compound and head down to "the Club," which was a members-only converted row home down on 4th Street that catered exclusively to Austro-Hungarians and their near relatives. They bypassed every civil rights law established in the 1960s by stating that it was not a bar, but a Veterans' Society, which just so happened also to serve beer. Richie met most of his friends there after mass at 10:00 to begin their true Sunday libations.

"Maybe, Uncle Richie. I'm still getting settled."

"Ready," singsonged Ginny, and the whole family gathered around their dinner table in a room decorated in country farmhouse style with furniture scavenged over the years from various places. The original family furniture had long since decayed, and Richie had slowly replaced it with this mismatched bric-a-brac. The walls were Ginny's province, and she coated most of the heavy yellowing wallpaper with religious icons and Precious Moments figurines. One of these had a central placement, so Ed assumed that it must have been important to Ginny, but he could not decode it. It was called "Trust in the Lord to Finish," and it depicted a boy with some kind of helmet and riding goggles from the 1940s, who held a trophy that said "WINNER" and a black-and-white checkered flag with a bird perched upon it. What exactly was finished? What race was run? A motorcycle race? Why does the Lord favor those who believe in Him? What happens when you have two people in the same race who trusted in the Lord? Was there a logic at all, or did the whole thing depend on an implied theology that he could not fathom? Ed wondered what part of the genome made some people go boneless at the sight of these icons and made people like Ed either want to laugh, cry, or smash the thing against the wall.

Richie folded his hands in prayer and waited until everyone else at the table did, too.

"We give thanks for all your benefits, almighty God, who lives and reigns forever. May the souls of the faithful departed, through the mercy of God, rest in peace. Amen."

"Amen," Ed said, with the others.

"Before we start this wonderful thanksgiving meal," said Richie, "I'd like us all to do a reading from a real American pilgrim." Richie tapped a dusty copy of William Bradford's *Of Plymouth Plantation*. "It seems that some of us are forgetting what this country was founded on, and its principles."

"Do we have to do this?" whispered Ginny.

"They don't even make kids read the Constitution anymore,"

his voice raised, "just a bunch of multicultural hymns to the great and noble Indian and the poor and always oppressed black man. I know. Just ask LeAnne."

LeAnne looked at everyone at the table and shrugged her shoulders.

"So, today, we'll each read a passage. Do we all remember William Bradford? Born a little rich kid on a big ass farm, his parents died even younger than Ed's here. Got shuffled around to a bunch of uncles until he started to read his Bible. Looked around him and saw that the world was filled with a bunch of hypocrites who didn't practice their Bible right. Then he got right with Jesus, and decided he needed to go somewhere where he could be a real Christian. So, he sailed on the Mayflower and came to help found our great nation at Plymouth Colony. Over half of the hundred settlers were dead by the end of the first winter. And they offered up their lives for us."

Richie opened the book to a passage he had marked and intoned, "May not and ought not the children of these fathers rightly say: 'Our fathers were Englishmen which came over this great ocean, and were ready to perish in this wilderness but they cried unto the Lord, and He heard their voice, and looked on their adversity, &c. Let them therefore praise the Lord, because He is good, and His mercies endure forever.'"

"And this is something we should all be keeping in mind when we think about the difficulties our Founding Fathers faced, which we can't even imagine in our cushy lives. What have we done to give back to this country?"

Richie passed the book to Ester, who flipped through to find a passage. He sat back in his chair and lit a Pall Mall. It just occurred to Ed that Richie had been out on disability for his lungs for the last twenty years, even though he was a chain smoker.

"Here's one," Ester said. "'Thus out of small beginnings greater things have been produced by His hand that made all things of nothing, and gives being to all things that are; and, as one small candle may light a thousand, so the light here kindled hath shone unto many, yea in some sort to our whole nation.'"

"Beautiful. And a good lesson for us all to remember. Ed?"

Ed took the book and his heart sighed. He turned to a random page and began to read: "'Being upon it examined and committed, in the end he not only confessed the fact with that beast at that time, but sundry times before and at several times with all the rest of the forenamed in his indictment.' Um." Ed skipped ahead. "'And whereas some of the sheep could not so well be known by his description of them, others with them were brought before him and he declared which were they and which were not. And accordingly he was cast by the jury and condemned, and after . . . executed about the 8th of September, 1642. A very sad spectacle it was. For first the mare and then the cow and the rest of the lesser cattle were killed before his face, according to the law, Leviticus xx. 15 and then he himself was executed. The cattle were all cast into a great and large pit that was digged of purpose for them, and no use made of any part of them.'"

"I don't get it," said LeAnne. "Why did they kill the animals?"

"Someone else read," said Ginny.

"I don't understand," said LeAnne.

"What the fuck was that?" said Richie.

Ed scanned up the page to the heading.

"'A Horrible Case of Bestiality.'"

The table was silent.

"What's bestiality?" asked LeAnne.

Ester snorted and tried to suppress her laugh.

"What?" implored LeAnne. "What is it?"

Ed tried not to smile, but raised his eyebrows at Ester.

"Don't you dare," said Richie.

"Yep," said Ed, scanning the part he missed. "Apparently some poor farm boy, Thomas Granger, was caught with a mare, a cow, two goats, five sheep, two calves, and a turkey."

Ester stared at the gravy boat.

"A *turkey*?" laughed Ginny.

The table erupted in laughter. Even LeAnne laughed along, as if she understood.

"That's what it says," said Ed, gesturing to the bird before him. "Just like this one here."

Richie reddened and clenched his hands.

"I have to say, dad, you were right," said Ester. "The old ways are the best ways. I think we have a new tradition."

"Now," said Ed, "who wants first dibs on the bird?"

Richie slammed his fist on the table and pointed a blunt finger at Ed's head.

"You shut your goddamn mouth," he hissed, breathing heavily.

"Dad!" said Ester. "Come on. No one was going to say anything to LeAnne."

"Richie, don't," said Ginny. "Please."

"No, fuck that. Big man! Big fucking brain. Can't even finish college like your cousin's going to. Your mom sold your goddamn house for you and lived in that shitty little apartment out in Whitehall. No, screw that, Gin. I don't have to put up with his bullshit now that Lorel's dead. I've listened to your art-faggotty nonsense for years. No more. You can stay the night, but you start looking for somewhere else to stay in the morning."

Ginny stared at the table. LeAnne cried softly to herself, and Richie stared Ed down.

"Now, you get the fuck away from my table."

Upstairs, Ed sat on the bed in Ester's room, while she lit lilac-scented tea candles, which she had placed on most free surfaces. They added a gentle glow to the fairy lights she had strung above her bed. The air hung heavy with the scent of patchouli that mixed with the synthetic lilac in a way that irritated Ed's senses. Batik tapestries that Ester and Angela had made covered the walls, giving the room a gently flowing ambiance. Ed thought of how he could read the exact moment that Ester started to change her persona by looking at the New Kids on the Block and Menudo posters that the tapestries covered. On her dresser, on top of a pashmina decorated with purple and gold paisleys, sat a hodgepodge of trinkets that Ester had picked up in various thrift stores and second-hand shops: hand-blown glass vases, strings of beads, a three-inch statue of Shiva dancing in a wheel of flames. On the wall above her bed, she had a large print of the Venus of Willendorf that she had learned silk-screening just to make.

"Don't worry," she said, blowing out the match. "I don't think he meant it."

"Oh, I think he meant it."

"He'll settle down. I'll talk to him tomorrow when he's sober. You know how he gets."

Oh, I know, Ed thought, wondering if it was too late to get his job back at the hospice. Ed looked around the room. In the corner by the only window was a five-foot ficus tree, which Ester had had for as long as Ed could remember. He marveled that she was able to keep it healthy for so many years. He could not keep the cactus that Eva had given him alive for more than a month.

"Hey," he said. "Do you remember that time that you put labels on everything in your room?"

"Oh, god. Don't remind me."

"That was the weirdest goddamned thing," he laughed, "coming in here and seeing every little object with a printout from that labeling gun you found. *CUP. BOOKS. BED.* You even had one for the ficus tree."

Ester grinned, a sadness in her eyes.

"What was that all about?"

She picked up a cloth of some kind and was silent a moment.

"It was a bad time," she said. "It was just after I lost Eternity. You can't imagine what that felt like, Ed. And, because you're a man, you'll never have to find out. I was in a really bad place, and I felt like I was losing my grip on reality. I couldn't eat. I couldn't sleep. I didn't want to talk to anyone or do anything, even things I liked doing. Everything seemed so far away from me, like it was behind a veil I couldn't pull from my eyes. I was trying out the label gun by typing 'DESK,' which is where I was sitting, and I held the word up to the thing, and I just couldn't make them match in my mind. Where did the word 'desk' come from? What possible relationship did the word have with this hard thing that was sitting in front of me?" She knocked the desk lightly. "Where did any of the words come from? *Desk. Love. God.* It's like when you say a word or a name over and over until it doesn't make sense anymore: *Gilligan . . . Gilligan . . . Gilligan.*"

Ed smiled.

"So, I stuck the word to the desk, and it seemed to have a little more solidity. And after that, I couldn't stop. I had to try to fix things right, to get them solid in my mind. I even put one on this."

Ester handed Ed the small flannel cloth she was holding. It had a hood that had flowers embroidered across the surface.

"What's this?"

"Eternity's wee wrap. They use it to put stillborn babies into so we could meet her. She was just so small, and delicate, and . . . lavender. We even got a picture of the three of us, but I'm guessing you might not want to see that."

Ed felt nauseous, and wanted to drop the wrap quickly, but held it gently a few more seconds before handing it back. Ester placed it gently on her dresser.

"So, it was a girl?"

"Ah, yes," she said. "Caught in my own words. I didn't think I'd be able to keep her gender a secret forever. Tod's idea. Yes, she was my little girl. I lost my little girl, and there's not a moment that goes by that I don't imagine what she would look like today."

She leaned against Ed's shoulder, and he held her gently as she wept.

Ester walked Ed up to the attic, where he was supposed to sleep. The attic was Richie's studio space, where he did his projects. Ed was never allowed to go up before, so he was intrigued by what exactly he would find. As they opened the door, Ed jumped back a little when he saw a woman standing in the middle of the room, naked from the waist up. Ester laughed as she turned on the light.

"Ed, Agatha. Agatha, Ed."

"What the hell?"

Ed stared at Agatha, Richie's full-height store mannequin of a blonde woman that he used as a model. To bring in extra money, Richie designed and made doll clothes and sold them to a local upscale children's store that specialized in high-end wooden toys from Germany, like Ostheimer animals and Fagus trucks, handmade by the handicapped. Richie lacked the imagination to dream up his own designs, so he used Ginny and their daughters' clothes and dressed Agatha, as he called her, to model as he crafted a miniature version. For some reason, one of the breasts was cracked like a priestess of Cybele, and the whole thing gave Ed goose bumps. Agatha stood in the center of the room, and Richie's work bench—covered with fabric, an old Singer sewing machine, and a large pile of threads and bobbins—faced the model. The mannequin had no face, and this unnerved Ed even more. Apparently, Richie found the individuality of a woman's face distracting from his work. This way, Agatha could be any of his family members.

In the back corner, behind Agatha, sat a twin bed where Richie would sometimes crash after working late. This was supposed to be Ed's new home. Ed put his suitcase over by the bed, although he thought it best not to unpack yet.

"So, tell me," Ed said. "Why don't you move in with Tod and the Kinsmen?"

"Kinfolk," she corrected. "Are you kidding? My dad would kill me. It was bad enough when we got pregnant without being married. After Tod broke it off, I thought my dad was going to go after him with his Remington 870. Let's just say that that relationship was over, whether we wanted it to be or not."

Ed noted the "we got pregnant" and wondered if that phrasing really made women feel better or more upset. *We* weren't hauling around a bowling ball in our bellies and throwing up twice a day, were we?

"Maybe. But you're twenty-one now. He can't control you."

"I don't know. Partly it is his cosigning my student loans."

"Which you're going to have to pay back yourself."

"But part of it is that I can't leave LeAnne just yet. Angela's getting married in June. LeAnne's only ten, and I just can't leave her alone here."

Ed sighed. "Your mom can protect her."

Ester raised an eyebrow.

"Yeah," said Ed, "I get it."

Ester pulled herself up, straightening her dress.

"You'd better get some sleep," she said. "We should probably head out early before dad sleeps it off. Tomorrow has to be a better day."

Ed gave her a hug.

"Goodnight, cousin," she said.

"By marriage," said Ed, and she smiled at their old exchange. She kissed his cheek and left. Ed watched her go down the stairs and closed the door behind her.

Ed got into the bed and stared at the walls, smelling, or imagining he smelled, the faint scent of patchouli and Pall Malls coming up through the cracks in the floorboards, listening to the old farmhouse creak like an antique whaling ship, groaning under the weight of its load. The attic's exposed rafters added to the effect that he was trapped within the hull of a boat, and he felt a nauseous sense of vertigo even though he was lying still. He wondered what this space would do to him if he stayed. As the digital clock's glowing red numbers informed him of time's transformation into January 1, 1993, Ed lay naked in the attic twin, looking at the back of a half-naked Amazon, and for the first time in as long as he could remember, he drowned in a sea of nostalgia for a home that never was, and a home that never again would be.

CHAPTER FOUR

"Nothing is so immoral as developing old rolls of film," Felicia Berger said, as she darted around the room. "Spring cleaning, Saturday afternoon. Five rolls of film packed for the move or from lack of funds. Crammed in the bottom of an old U-Haul box. Excitement brews: What did I photograph? What images had I considered important? And now to the Fotomat: $10 a roll for the classy Tri-X pan 400 Black and White Film. One hundred and nineteen exposures; one drops off into a void. They say that primitive cultures dread the photograph as an enslavement of the soul. Balzac feared the daguerreotype. We all do. This is a just fear. A photograph is just a slice of time, a still moment of a being, an essence removed from the flow of the temporal. The photograph is death, a Platonic Idea that exists nowhere but in the mind. That which *was*, by definition *is not*. The photograph offers immortality—by annihilating our existence. We should feel the cringe in the face of a photographer; we should resent those who present an image of what we were. We should despise the lens-up-to-nature, since it is a perversion of the natural. Beware the person who loves having her picture taken."

"Will you please shut up," said Lavinia.

As she said her speech, Felicia took pictures of Lavinia, who perched naked on the edge of a wooden stool, her legs splayed wide. Felicia's camera was a Nikon F90 SLR, and it was her primary love object. She disassembled and cleaned it every morning like a marine field stripping his rifle.

"Look, I'm not saying that I like it," Felicia said, continuing her photographs, "considering it is my métier and my muse. I'm just saying that I don't blame people for hating it when I take their picture. I am in control. I am the master of this moment. I will make you into what I want you to be. My camera's gaze is worse than a person's gaze, because you really can do nothing about it."

Lavinia looked at Felicia with an ironic submissiveness. Lavinia yawned slightly.

"Modeling has a different kind of power," said Lavinia. "I remember doing this in college for the first time, and I was terrified. I wasn't one of those beautiful, cut models with the runner's body who was doing it primarily as a glorified version of exhibitionism. I was a chubby Jew with bitch bangs, and my girlfriend at the time asked me if I would fill in for a last-minute cancellation in her painting class."

"Oooh, clever."

"Oh, yes," Lavinia said. "Because *obviously* she had never seen my body before."

Felicia smiled.

"So, there I am, standing before this group of abstract painters, each rendering an image resembling anything but my body, as far as I could tell, and each claiming to have captured my pure essence—purer than what was revealed on the surface, apparently."

"You civilians seem to forget that abstract art means abstracting the fundamental deep structure of reality; it isn't just some random pile of colors and lines."

"Yes, well, Janelle—the young woman I was dating—would actually read to me from Mondrian's art theory book."

"Mm, hot," said Felicia.

"Right? There's that one line that got me: 'I want to come as close as possible to the truth and abstract everything from that, until I reach the foundation of things.'"

"Come, indeed."

"So, he makes a bunch of horizontal and vertical lines. And

some color fields. Can't say I ever got the relation between the two, really, but Janelle made it sound pretty sexy at the time. And so there I am, naked under my towel before disrobing, shivering at the studio temperature in the school's old crumbling building, goose bumps and nips sticking out like they could cut glass. Almost immediately, I wanted to hide, just crushed by the desire to run to my pile of clothes in the corner and cover myself. But then I had an epiphany and realized what all models have to: that to allow these insane creators to warp me out of recognition for their own purposes, pleasures, and ends, was right. It was just. And to allow this misinterpretation of my true self—or at least the self that I thought of myself to be—I had to remain naked, so that they could find what they needed."

"In the service of art," said Felicia.

"We all do it to one another, anyway. We just usually don't know it's happening."

"Was this about when you started stripping?"

"That was a little later. It took a while for me to fully get comfortable with my body. Stripping was just a little experiment with myself in my twenties. It was like an art piece of my own. I treated my body like a block of marble that I chipped away at. I developed a lovely bulimia and got down to a size two and wanted to see if I could pull it off. I did it for about six months and got out right before my teeth started to rot away from the stomach acid. Obviously," she said, stroking her hand along her size fourteen frame, "that is no longer a problem for me."

The doorbell rang, and Felicia capped her Nikon and placed it in her workstation like a priest handling the chalice. She headed to the door.

"Well, my little lamb, I certainly found what I needed."

"Oh, good," said Lavinia, lighting a clove cigarette. "I aim to please."

Felicia opened the door with arms gloved up to her elbows. It was her peculiar affectation, and she never took them off from what anyone could see.

"Well, if it isn't our other little lamb," said Felicia. "And she's brought along a specter from a Tim Burton film. Where's Winona, my good sir?"

"Hey, Fel," said Ester. "This is my cousin, Ed. Tod wanted him to stop by."

"Come on in," said Felicia. "Lavinia was just regaling me with her tales of her Explorations in Paraphilia in the Service of Art."

Lavinia stuck her tongue out at Felicia. "I suppose you want me to put on my clothes again," she said.

"Suit yourself. We have a stranger here. Maybe he can paint you looking like a skyscraper."

Felicia and Lavinia liked each other. They saw their careers as two halves of a similar project. Felicia was tall and blonde with a Midwestern athletic build, and she had grown up in an all-white section of Emmaus, Pennsylvania, in the suburbs of Allentown out by the Lehigh Country Club. Her parents were both epidemiologist MD/PhDs who focused more on the research side of their degrees. They each had a private consulting practice and worked at the Allentown Health Bureau, and each shared a worldview that from the moment of birth, the human body was in a slow but steady state of decay. Each individual was a collection of infections, microbes, and latent diseases, her DNA just waiting for the opportunity to flip a genetic switch, and everyone could be categorized by how far away from a perfect human specimen they were. Felicia had attended the very private Swain School for her elementary years, and her mother pulled her out for homeschooling after eighth grade. Since both parents worked so much, however, her mother hired a full-time governess out of a Henry James novel, through whom Felicia began to see the limitations of her parents' worldview. By that time, however, her personality was formed, and while she ideologically opposed how her parents treated reality and rarely talked with her parents unless she had to, she already shared their repulsion at everything that was fleshy, decayed, and human. She contributed to the Kin and learned from them as much as she could, and she especially liked Tod's emphasis on transcending the limits of binary thinking. Her long-term project was a book of photographs, *Re-Visions*, which embraced everything that she found revolting in the world in order to turn it into a pure aesthetic that she could finally objectify. The more she found it disgusting, the more she needed to capture it in her Nikon. Besides the fleshy protuberances of Lavinia, who neither cared if Felicia was repulsed by her nor would have been terribly surprised, considering her upbringing, Felicia catalogued skin lesions, close-ups of decaying teeth, cleft palates, and crossed eyes. She took a series of fifty photographs of a dead squirrel she found in the front yard, its innards bloated and skin peeling away to reveal a kind of cottony white froth while one half of its body, which had been ripped away and semi-masticated, was slowly decomposing and dissolving into the lawn that surrounded it, so that you could not tell where the squirrel ended and the landscaping began. Felicia had one of these blown up in a frame above her bed.

"Hey Lavinia," said Ester, "Your big ol' crack face is starting to peel. I hope we don't lose it forever."

"Ah, the end of an era," said Lavinia, as she put on her corduroys and red and blue checkered flannel shirt.

Ester referred to the giant billboard out on MacArthur Road, right by the Rt. 22 exit by the Lehigh Valley Mall. When she was in college and needed to make some extra money, Lavinia spent an afternoon modeling for a company that provided public domain images for a small fee. Twelve years later, she was surprised to find that she had become the face of the Allentown chapter of DARE's anti-crack campaign. In a fourteen-foot-tall close-up of her face, heavily airbrushed with dilated pupils and the self-lacerated skin look of an extra from *New Jack City*, Lavinia stared over the entrance to Allentown like the glasses above the ash pit in *The Great Gatsby*. She thought this was hilarious, as did the artists who hired her to model, and it made her a minor celebrity in the Allentown underground scene.

"So," said Lavinia, "what brings you to our neck of humanity, Mr. Donner?"

"Pullman," said Ed. "We're not actually related."

"Wait," said Felicia, remembering. "Eddie Pullman? Your mom isn't Lorel Leh, is it?"

"Was, yes."

"Was? Oh, shit, I'm sorry."

"Oh, it's okay. The funeral was just yesterday."

Felicia thought.

"Huh, weird. I'm sorry to hear that. A few years ago, when things were really tight around the holidays, I picked up some hours at the Whitehall Mall Portrait Studio, god help me. Your mom and I worked together. I mostly did darkroom. She was great with the filthy little urchins up front, making them coo and smile on cue. I just made them cry. She was a lovely woman. She'd talk about her Eddie, who seemed to be taking a lot of painting lessons."

Ed smiled at this behind-the-scenes glimpse. He had never visited his mom at her weekend work, although she had taught him to handle a camera.

"Where is everyone?" asked Ester.

"Finishing up the sandwich run," said Lavinia. "They should be back soon."

The Kinfolk believed in living off of as much of the waste of capitalism as possible. On trash nights, they would make dumpster runs to the Allentown Farmer's Market, especially after the weekend, to bakeries, which had to scrap the day's unbought bread, and to upscale restaurants like the Bay Leaf, which had the largest amount of waste, especially from the female patrons who liked to order food, but not so much to eat it. After rinsing the food off and adding enough condiments, they generally could sustain themselves for a large chunk of the week. The first dumpster run was usually a good exercise in humility, Tod laughed, and they allowed themselves scented soaps for their post-run showers.

Ester showed Ed around the house, which was not quite what Ed had expected. The upper floor and the basement of the Victorian had been converted so that most of the bedrooms and other spaces had flimsy drywall partitions to accommodate the six to ten people who squatted there at various times, all on mattresses lying on the floor. Ed never quite understood that squat feature, as though a bed frame would be capitulating to the Man. He assumed that it was so people too high or drunk would not fall out of bed in the middle of the night. Tod had the master to himself, and they all congregated in the large annex rec room addition off to the east side of the main house's living room. Ed thought back to Agatha and the upcoming nights ahead.

By the time they came back to the annex, Ed saw that Tod had returned with Serge Cieco and Tim the Enchanter, both of whom looked both worse and better than when Ed had seen them last. No longer bobbing with that acid head-cum-meth shuffle, Serge seemed to have cleaned up a bit and gained some weight back, but he looked much older than his twenty-one-year-old self. Tim's slow face looked about the same, although he too was graying a bit. They looked up at Ed and Ester's approaching footfalls.

"Dude," Serge said from somewhere far away, wrapping his arms around Ed's torso. "Good to see you, man. We heard you were coming back to do some revisions to the poem."

"What poem?" said Ed.

"Life, man," he said. "Life."

Ed played with his lighter.

"Hey," said Tim. Ed nodded.

"So," said Tod, "thanks for stopping by, Ed. Your cousin tells me you might be looking for a place to stay."

Ed looked at Ester. She shrugged. "I talked with mom this morning. She thought it might be good to keep your options open."

"It's no problem, man," said Tod. "Lexi and Augie are out on the Philadelphia mission for a while, so there's plenty of room. Just get unpacked in one of the upstairs rooms and get your bearings. Come on back by the prayer meeting tonight by five. You can get a sense of what we do."

Ed and Ester spent New Year's Day getting Ed's things out of storage and buying some basics he would need out at the Lehigh Valley Mall. He forgot just how much he missed her, and he felt more comfortable around her than almost anyone else he had known. They reminisced about their childhoods, comparing memories and perceptions of different events. Ester got very excited whenever they remembered things differently, which seemed to happen with almost every major flashbulb memory they shared. No, that could not have happened then, because I was only in second grade and Reagan wasn't even president then. Uh-uh, Joey was the one who used to pee himself every day in fourth grade, not his brother Rabin, so it must have been in Ms. Harmony's class.

"Our memories are so useless!" Ester squealed in delight. "We were talking in my psych class about this one study done on people right after the Space Shuttle Challenger exploded. I still remember that day vividly, even though I was only fourteen at the time."

"Oh, yeah," said Ed. "That was ninth grade. We were talking about *Wuthering Heights* in English when the announcement came on the loudspeaker to tell us."

"Yeah, but *were* you? This one guy, Ulric Neisser, followed up three years after with his freshmen and found that most of them made huge mistakes in their memories. One of the students thought she heard about it from the TV, when she actually overheard some students in her religion class; one woman remembered a girl running through the dorm, screaming, 'The space shuttle blew up!' when she actually heard about it over lunch. That one really struck me. It's like she projected the way she felt on the inside into a tangible reality. Twenty-five percent of the participants were completely wrong about everything, yet they were all completely sure that they were right. Can you believe it? Something so vivid was just absolutely wrong. A complete misremembering. Amazing, isn't it?"

"Amazingly disturbing," said Ed.

"It gets even weirder," Ester said. "My psych professor was talking about this one researcher, Elizabeth Loftus, who had people watch a tape of a car accident and asked them how fast the cars were going. The only difference between the two groups was how they were prompted, using the word 'hit' verses 'smashed.' When people heard 'How fast were they going when they smashed into one another,' they were much more likely to remember seeing shattered glass, even though there was none."

"What the hell?" said Ed.

"I *know*, right? Think about how much of our lives might be shaped just by the ways we talk about them. All those memories of our childhood could be completely wrong."

Ed paused, thinking. He could not see why Ester took such great pleasure in these moments. He lived so much in his head with his memories that he had started to feel that the only thing he could be sure about was his own story. But if so many of our memories are mistaken, confabulations, or just plain lies to ourselves, and if we could be so easily manipulated just by the use of language, then who the hell are we? He also was disturbed about something else. If our own testimony that we are so absolutely sure about can be so completely misguided today, even when we are the very witnesses to our lives, how can we trust anything that came before? History was written by the winners, yes, but it was also written by people misremembering the past. And then it struck him: Neither Socrates, Jesus, the Buddha, or Muhammad ever actually wrote anything down themselves. Muhammad was illiterate, for heaven's sake. The only thing we know about them was from the memories of others. Ed was uncomfortable about how far he wanted to take this line of thinking. For Ester, this indeterminacy was liberation. If the old rules and traditions and histories were just narratives of error or narratives of control, then we could dismiss them all for the pure liberation of the self.

"And think about what our relationship would be like if we hadn't just always called each other 'cousin,'" she said, smiling into his green-brown eyes.

Ed broke the gaze.

"Judging by the way your dad treated me, we never would have seen each other, ever."

"Ugh, leave him out of this. There are some people in this world you just have to tolerate and negotiate. There is no solving them." Ed wondered if it was that simple, even if it sounded wise.

That night, they returned to the Kin, who were already congregating in the annex. Felicia was showing her latest blow-up photo of Lavinia's clitoral hood, which they all learned was pierced with a small J-bar.

"My god, Fel," said Serge. "Why do you hate the female body so much?"

"What are you talking about?" she said. "This is a celebration of the female body."

"It looks like a Georgia O'Keeffe flower, lifting weights."

"I think it is striking. This is what she looks like. Maybe you are the one with the problem with reality."

"Maybe, but you framed it. You could have picked anything, but this is the detail and angle you chose."

"Hey," said Lavinia, yawning. "Clit is, what clit is." She turned to Ester and Ed, approaching. "What do you think, Captain Apollo?"

Ed looked closely, squinting, then looked at Lavinia.

"I'm not sure we were formally introduced. Hi. I'm Ed."

Lavinia snorted laughter.

"So, what did you guys end up doing today?" Ester asked.

"Fel and I went to see *Husbands and Wives* up at the dollar theater," said Lavinia.

"How was it?" asked Serge.

"Good. Really good. I thought I wouldn't be able to see past the headlines, but I forgot about it pretty quick."

"No surprise. You like everything Woody Allen does," said Tim. "Even the shitty ones."

Serge started laughing. "You liked *September*!"

"I enjoy his work," said Lavinia.

"Blech," said Ester. "He left his wife for his adopted daughter."

"Not officially either."

"Still, how could you still like him after that?"

"I said that I enjoy his work," said Lavinia. "Never confuse an artist with the art. You'll end up not appreciating anything. Dickens. Baudelaire. Pollack. Assholes, all. Joyce was a huge prick, from what I recall—wanted his wife to have an affair when he had writer's block. Party game: Name an artist who wasn't a giant cock, and I don't exclude my gender. Nature of the beast."

"In my experience," said Serge, "most artists are pretty fucked up at some level. Otherwise, why create?"

"Well, here's hoping not," said Tod, coming into the annex. "Otherwise, we might be in trouble."

"Where were you last night, anyway?" asked Ester. "We thought we'd see you at Origen's."

"Hooked up with Clare," said Lavinia. "I know most of you are a bunch of breeders, but if you ever get the chance, I highly recommend making love to k.d. lang's 'Constant Craving.' Whoosh."

They all looked at Ed.

"Are you kidding? If I get the chance to have sex again, I'll be playing John Philip Sousa."

They all laughed. Tod gestured to Ed and Ester.

"Come on in, guys," said Tod. "We were just getting started."

Tod put on a mix tape, which started halfway through The Doors' "The End." They sat in a circle like a prayer group or AA meeting, sprawled out on couches or in a couple of tattered armchairs. Tim got out a bowl and packed it, taking a drag and passing it over Felicia to Ed, who took a drag and passed it to Ester, who sat close to him on the forest green sofa. Tod picked up the *Dhammapada* and opened to the first chapter.

"So let's begin," Tod said. "In the words of the Buddha, fifth century, B.C."

What we are today comes from our thoughts of yesterday, and our present thoughts build our life of tomorrow: our life is the creation of our mind. If a man speaks or acts with a pure mind, joy follows him as his own shadow. "He insulted me, he hurt me, he defeated me, he robbed me." Those who think such thoughts will not be free from hate. For hate is not conquered by hate: hate is conquered by love. This is a law eternal. Many do not know that we are here in this world to live in harmony. Those who know this do not fight against each other.

For the next half hour, Tod wove an intricate argument around these basic themes, mixing an apparently random amalgam of religious, intellectual, philosophical traditions. Ed tried to keep up with them all, but some he had simply never heard of. Taoist versus Zoroastrian views of the world; Gnostic versus Manichean thinking; Kantian antinomies versus Hegelian dialectics; eschatological narratives versus the Great Wheel. As the smoke from the weed and from the incense nuzzled around their faces like a drowsy cat, Ed started to lose focus, and he was beginning to see the logic of illogic, the pleasures to be found in the fuzzy boundaries between self and other. Lavinia got up to flip the mix tape, this time beginning with Pink Floyd's "Careful with that Axe, Eugene," and sat back next to Ester, who squeezed in closer to Ed, who felt the warm press of her body and thighs next to his. Roger Waters's hypnotic D minor repetition between root and octave made Ed realize after a few minutes that his entire body was tense, and he had not even noticed that he was clenching his muscles, as though ready to be hit. He tried to unflex. He looked around the room at the artworks draped across most surfaces, at the stacks and shelves of books, at the intensely focused and unfocused faces, listening to the cadences of Tod's speech weave a world that Ed had never known, and for the first time in as long as he could remember, through this group of almost random strangers, Ed began to feel himself. If this is what the Kin were about, he thought, he might have to be a joiner after all.

On Monday, Ed began his new job at Greif Industries. From the outside, the factory looked like every other building in a large modern industrial complex. His job was largely a rotation of cleaning the management offices and the workers' locker room, lunchroom, and other areas, and the constant movement between the two worlds disturbed him. The swing shift was responsible for cleaning the floor, where most of the work was actually done, so Ed spent most of his day away from both the other workers and the management, who never made eye contact anyway. He liked the long swaths of quiet time. It amounted to a less glamorous version of the job he did at the hospice, although he felt more at ease not being constantly surrounded by the dead and dying.

He had thought that he would enjoy the physicality of the labor, to get outside his mind for once. He had not anticipated just how much inertia had atrophied his muscles, and by the end of the first day, he was exhausted and felt aches in muscles that had disappeared from memory. It was as if his own body had been on loan to him, and without that pride of ownership, he had been treating it very badly. He remembered reading about how Tolstoy would look forward to taking breaks from writing and go out and work with the serfs for a while to reattach himself with the land and bond with the common people. Of course, like Thomas Jefferson, Tolstoy also fathered a child by one of those serfs he owned, and Ed was starting to understand a little bit about power and desire. He was quickly learning that there was no romance to the working man or woman, except by the people who claimed to be speaking for them or denouncing them. Labor was something that demanded respect, not fetishization. Labor was labor, and it hurt like hell. He started to wonder what the serfs thought about the help they received from the great writer. Did he actually do anything, or was he like a four-year-old boy helping his father shovel snow, knocking more drifts into the path that he could possibly clear? Who could tell the story of those who had no voice of their own?

He fell asleep quickly after prayer meeting on a twin mattress in a basement partition. The area was small, but cozy, and he was able to relax, knowing that there was not some hillbilly raging down below him and about to blow his head off. He did not understand why the Kin insisted on calling them "prayer meetings," since what they talked about did not feel like a religion, exactly. Tod discussed religions as though they were all false and yet had deeper truths that those who claimed to believe in them did not see. Ed presumed that it had to do with Tod's idea about creating new myths. It was as though by using the words they had all grown up with—*soul, god, prayer, sacred*—he tapped some very deep spring of faith they had all lost, but desperately, desperately longed to believe. But it unnerved Ed, because he never knew exactly when Tod was speaking metaphorically and when he was being literal. Did he really think that the apocalypse was imminent, or was that a metaphor for some spiritual transformation? And if he really did think it was coming, what were they all doing there?

CHAPTER FIVE

Every building is a palimpsest, a layered history of all the aspirations of those who plan, those who create, and those who live. The most rundown shotgun shack in Appalachia to the highest cathedral spires of Ulm are products of human creation, and therefore can be read like a text—a text of intentional form, both conscious and unconscious. Anything created by people is like a text in that way. Perhaps nature, too, since nature is always defined for us, framed for us, by the unnatural, by the human.

Whenever Ed's teacher, Professor Kunstkeller used to go off like this, which was usually every class, Ed always thought of his favorite buildings—the Alhambra, which he hoped to see in person one day; Frank Lloyd Wright's Fallingwater, a masterpiece of organic integration of the natural world and the necessary habitats of humanity. Even though he was long out of architecture school, he still loved looking at buildings, walking through the spaces, and thinking about the intent of the architects. What was the space communicating with its form?

Ed also thought of Kunstkeller's other favorite comparison, which often took on tones as though he did not see it as merely a metaphor. Every building isn't just where people live; it is a person itself, a host for often innumerable beings that have lived within it, depended upon it, fed upon it. Sometimes these relationships are symbiotic, the inhabitants giving back, keeping it up, renovating, making it at times better than it was before, allowing the building to exist at all. Take Beijing's Forbidden City: "You may know it as the backdrop of Mao's giant portrait next to Tiananmen Square, where the Chinese showed who was really in charge of the illusions of freedom they gave." The Forbidden City was like this, Kunstkeller explained, and laborers ran an endless cycle of upkeep that lasted ten years before it had to start all over again. Sometimes these relations are parasitic drains on a once healthy specimen, and the host dies an inglorious death, wasting away like a cancer patient, skin draping down over the voids where the fat used to be. Some buildings are planned, lovingly desired and prepared for, prenatal vitamins and dreams for the future; some seem like the product of too much booze and a broken condom—the structural equivalent of one of those 1950s films on *Mystery Science Theater 3000* that you can't believe a hundred people got together to shit upon the silver screen. But most of all, a building, like a person, is defined by its traumas, by the history of shocks and upheavals that added to the slow entropic erosion of its foundations, until its inevitable passing into the next world . . . Usually as the site of a future Walmart.

The students usually laughed dutifully, though they were still too young to understand the implications of what Kunstkeller was saying. Like the other students, Ed was usually amused, sometimes shocked, but often inspired by these apparently off-the-cuff speeches and metaphors, and they always led him to other thoughts and associations. This was education, he thought, and people outside this random day's rant would never hear what I heard.

On the Saturday after Ed started at Greif, Ed thought about Kunstkeller's words as he drove into the parking lot of the old Phoenix Clothes building, Adelaide Mills at 333 Court Street, down by the Jordan Creek.

Ed met Stan and his daughter, Joanie, who was just in for the holidays. Joanie was twenty-five, and she was getting her master's degree from Penn State out in University Park, writing her thesis on Lehigh Valley labor history. Stan wanted her along to give the context in a way Ed might appreciate. She dressed simply in jeans and a maroon jacket; she pulled her hair back into a ponytail and wore no visible makeup as far Ed could see. Ed could not tell if this was her usual uniform when she was at school, or if she was performing this identity for her father's benefit.

"I know that you're not very excited about joining the union," said Stan, "so I thought that you should see some of your history. It's part of my job as the shop steward, but I love talking about the union. We obviously didn't start out in that giant industrial park in Hanover Township. That's only been there the last ten years or so. This is the original Adelaide Mills. Your mom and dad met in this very building back in the mid-sixties. When they got your old house up on 5th Street for ten thousand bucks, they'd drive together over here every morning. It was only, like, two miles."

"I don't get the Adelaide Mills sign," said Ed. "Wasn't it always called Phoenix Clothes?"

Joanie explained. Built in 1881, the Adelaide Silk Mills operation in Allentown, Pennsylvania was one of the largest of its kind in the world. After the 235,000-square-foot site was constructed, it revitalized the area after iron making, the key industry in the region, started to decline following the implosion of the railroad boom. The Mills were built by a silk-making firm that relocated from Patterson, New Jersey, called Phoenix Manufacturing, run by a young man named Albert Tilt. Tilt thought of himself as a great industrialist after he had inherited the company and control of his father's firm. The family had been in silk making, which was a fairly new industry in his father's time, since the 1830s. Albert's father, Benjamin B. Tilt, came to the States from Coventry, England in 1835, and his arrival in America was preceded by a fortuitous antecedent. In 1830, the Chinese Mulberry (*morus multicaulis*) arrived on America's shores. While perhaps a mundane occurrence in other times or with other trees, the silkworms that fed on the Mulberry produced superior silk, it was said, so Congress promoted its culture, leading to wild speculation and bidding, referred to in the media as "the morus multicaulis craze." This craze helped to establish Tilt's rise from silk apprentice to the founder and president of the Phoenix Manufacturing Company. Eventually the value of the tree soared beyond the value of the actual silk, leading to the inevitable crash around 1840. Somehow, no one saw this coming, yet Benjamin weathered this slump. Albert was born from the ashes of that slump the next year.

In 1862, when he turned twenty-one years old—the "attainment of his majority" as the law referred to it at the time—Albert was added as a partner in Benjamin's new business, B.B. Tilt & Son. At first, he did not mind only being "& Son." His father was a great man, after all, and embodied everything a booster could possibly say about what American industry promised. The entrepreneur's poster boy: talented, shrewd, and fortunate. He saw the state of the world and exploited a desire that the world did not know it had. Father and son had many productive schemes, such as representing to the 1876 Centennial Exposition the many benefits and possibilities of silk by handing out a lot of free souvenirs—an event they repeated at the Paris Exposition two years later. After his death in 1879, Benjamin willed the Phoenix to his son, who immediately became president and general manager.

Of course, the heir is not the creator. It is one thing to build something from nothing. It is another thing altogether just to inherit it. The year after his father's death, the thirty-eight-year-old tycoon wanted to move the company, looking for easy waterpower and even cheaper labor, not particularly caring that he would be putting all of the current employees out of work. Albert also expected the new community to pay for the privilege, while his wife, Adelaide, would have her name christen the new plant.

"Now, is that romance, or what?" quipped Stan.

Allentown's desperate town leaders champed, and Albert had his back scratched so hard that he was almost flayed alive. The Silk Factory Fund Association, with a little greasing from a Philadelphia bank, got the locals to pony up the money to construct their own factory for their own future owner. The robber baron required the funds of the people, and they, for some reason, required someone to own them. The locals funded the factory. The locals provided the materials for construction. The locals built the damn thing. Phoenix provided the machinery to the tune of $150,000 of the latest silk weaving equipment to start the new venture, a good chunk of it moved from the old mill in Patterson.

The factory's grand opening on November 17, 1881 was catered by a chef brought in from New York's Metropolitan Hotel. Fanfare, faith, and fairgrounds. Adelaide had her own two-step named after her by the Allentown Band, whose name continued that city's ongoing tendency to name things after itself. Imagine a stereotype of late nineteenth-century pomp and circumstance, and that is what Allentown looked like until the wee hours of the morning.

The mill was a massive success, depending on how you define that word. With the hard and cheap labor provided by the company's employees, the Phoenix soared, creating wealth for both the workers and their owner—mostly the latter. Of course, this was not an idyllic world, and there were the inevitable tragedies. Kids started working in the Adelaide as young as ten or twelve years old; widowed women would often pull kids out of school to "help out" in the mills. Work went from six in the morning to six at night, with only a half-hour lunch. In the late nineteenth century, the occasional horror story was par for the course. There was no OSHA back then, and management felt little pressure to make workers' safety a real priority. In 1888, a seventy-horse boiler exploded at seven o'clock in the morning, killing three men and wounding many others. One of them, Hiram Sell, was pinned alive, his right leg broken, and his left leg crushed by a heavy iron lever. No one could move the machinery, and he screamed in mortal anguish. Foreman to the end, he instructed his coworkers to amputate his leg, the only way to move him. He died three hours later in what the papers described as "excruciating agony." Both of the other men were horrifically disfigured. One of them, Henry Bohrans, was only twenty-seven years old, and his wife gave birth to their second son that same night.

"I've always thought of that story about Hiram Sell," said Stan, "as a perfect metaphor for the history of labor in this country."

Joanie smiled somewhat primly at her father. Before she went off to college, he wasn't exactly one to find metaphors in anything.

"And imagine poor Mrs. Bohrans," Joanie said. "What kind of life was she to look forward to with two kids and a newborn in tow, a newborn not even old enough to work in the mill? This is long before government cheese and Medicaid."

By Albert Tilt's death in 1900 at age fifty-nine, the Adelaide Silk Mills employed 1,900 people, a strange symmetry not marked by any of the local papers. In that entire time, Albert and Adelaide never lived in Allentown itself. They still resided in Paterson, New Jersey until 1888, after which they moved to New York, where they became citizens.

"Tilt was an interesting case," Joanie said, "because he serves as a sign of the changes that have happened in the history of American labor. The libertarian fantasy of the genius industrialist who through a little gumption and can-do spirit rose above the lowly crowd is asinine when you look at the history of these movements. Albert's father was the closest to this archetype, but his son merely inherited the wealth and learned how to consolidate power by exploiting the desperation of the poor."

"Remember this, Ed," said Stan. "Power accretes. Just like money."

"And still," said Joanie, "as the sole owner of the firm, Albert felt an obligation to make his workers happy. Upon his death, the leftist *American Economist*, which had as its subheading, 'Devoted to the Protection of American Labor and Industries,' offered an almost hagiographic obituary."

Joanie pulled out of her jacket pocket a printout from a microfiche copy of the *American Economist*:

In the death of Mr. Albert Tilt the silk industry of the United States loses one of its great captains. At the time of his passing away, May 2, 1900, Mr. Tilt was president and treasurer of the Phoenix Silk Manufacturing Company and president of the Silk Association of America. As a member of THE AMERICAN PROTECTIVE TARIFF LEAGUE Mr. Tilt was an active supporter of the cause of Protection, and he lived long enough to witness the splendid triumph of sound economic principles in the phenomenal development of silk manufacturing, one of Protection's most stalwart children.

"Protection" meant protecting American markets by raising taxes on imports to keep American goods competitive. Back then, the Republicans were the Lefties, and people like Lincoln made their careers in backing tariffs. "I am in favor of a national bank," Lincoln said in an early 1832 speech. "I am in favor of the internal improvement system, and of a high protective tariff." Of course, an industrialist like Albert Tilt loved tariffs because it protected his silk mills, but the workers loved it, too, because it secured them a livelihood.

The Silk Association of America made a resolution the day after Albert's death, pointing to the fact that he was "always closely related to every progressive movement both in the industry and in the association.":

> *Resolved*: That we unfeignedly mourn the loss which has come to us; that we take pride in his conspicuous relation to the development and upbuilding of the silk industry in this country; that we recall with pleasure his record of fairness and justice to the many employees in his mills, and that his highly esteemed personality will ever be a delightful memory to his surviving friends.

Of course, not all tariffs worked to the benefit of the common people, but it sustained the employment of entire industries. Tariffs were never going to provide a blanket protection of any job that ever existed. The McKinley tariff of 1890 actually hurt several industries, but Phoenix did fine.

After Tilt's death, Phoenix Clothes seemed to take on a life of its own, and it continued to provide the blood to the veins of an entire community in a way almost unimaginable today. By 1929, one-quarter of Allentownians were employed by silk makers like Phoenix Clothes; Allentown alone had over twenty silk mills, and the Lehigh Valley was recognized as America's silk-making center. The Great Depression, not caused by a single laborer in the country, decimated the silk-making industry. Manufacturing slumped. Luxury products like silk fabric were decidedly out of fashion. In four years, half of the workers lost their jobs. Wages were slashed seventy-five percent to maintain high profits. Think about that for a while. The belt that tightened around the workers' waists began to tighten around the industrialists' necks. Labor unrest made the great industrialists nervous, so in the 1930s, ten silk plants migrated south for cheaper labor and more easily controlled desperation.

"This is what I'm talking about, Ed," said Stan. "When a company is owned by one or two people or a family, people are accountable. If you want your company to survive, you can take a hit in an economic downturn. It's like getting laid off from a job. Just because, you dip into your savings or put some things on credit cards for a bit. You don't liquidate your family. And when you live in the community and come to work and see where your workers live and how they live, then you can't be that surprised when they want to negotiate higher wages and better working conditions. At least guys like Tilt seemed to be that way. Don't get me wrong. Plenty of the robber barons couldn't give two shits about their workers, which is why we needed unions in the first place. But that all goes out the window when the company incorporates. Once it is owned by faceless investors, profit is king. Fuck community. Fuck the local schools. Fuck whether your employees have health insurance without a $2000 deductible."

"It's true," said Joanie. "Phoenix was bought out and merged with Greif Brothers of Baltimore back in 1982 during the last recession, because Phoenix was struggling and couldn't compete against cheap, non-tariffed Korean imports. Greif was, and is, a subsidiary that was gobbled up by a giant corporation out of Nashville, Genesco, fifty years before. Genesco was started by a couple of men, James Jarman and William Wemyss, back in 1924 as the General Shoe Company. They went public in 1939 and have been buying up everything in textiles throughout the eastern seaboard. Genesco needed to keep growing, because that's what corporations do. After Greif bought Phoenix, there were 'redundancies,' as they chillingly refer to human beings after a corporate takeover, so they consolidated the two divisions to become the company you're now working for today."

"And don't kid yourself, Ed," said Stan. "If they could ship everything off to be made in Indonesia tomorrow, they would. Thank god it is still too expensive to do so; what do you think would happen to this city if industry just left? To this country? If a corporation could get away with paying you ten cents an hour, why wouldn't it? And yet in less than two weeks this Slick Willie Clinton is going to get sworn in, and his first priority is to push through NAFTA, a Republican wet dream."

Ed looked confused.

"The North American Free Trade Agreement," said Joanie.

"Never heard of it," said Ed.

"Most people wouldn't have if it weren't for Ross Perot. Do you remember the debates?"

"Was he the little *Lord of the Rings* character? I was a little preoccupied this election. I didn't vote."

Stan rolled his eyes. "It could just mean the end of America as we know it."

"Without being too alarmist," said Joanie, "it would decimate American manufacturing. NAFTA will get rid of all tariffs in Canada, the United States, and Mexico. Ross Perot was the only one in the debates who warned of the 'giant sucking sound' of manufacturing plants relocating to Mexico, since they only pay a dollar an hour—about one-seventh or so of what we pay, sadly enough, but enough to make industry excited. They have no health benefits, and no pollution controls, so no one from the EPA, which we fought so hard for in this country, is going to go and tell you that you can't dump industrial waste into the groundwater. This is the free trade fantasy: getting rid of all borders and acting like countries are equal. Of course, that's just the beginning. Neoliberals like Clinton share the Republican worldview that only absolute free trade is the way to prosperity for all. And of course, corporations are funding most of these campaigns."

"Why wouldn't they?" said Stan. "The only function of a corporation is to make profits and to keep growing to make more profits. The corporation just *has* to do it, like a fungus or a rabid dog. The CEO is a figurehead: if he doesn't do it, the board of directors will just fire him and get someone who will. It's nothing personal. As the Don says in *The Godfather*: 'It's just business.' The union doesn't take it personally. But we're not going to kid ourselves, either. They're not our friends."

"You can't be friends with a headless hydra," said Joanie.

Stan sipped his coffee, thinking.

"Usually when we want things to grow," he said, "there is a

reason for it. A corporation has either to pay out the profits every year to shareholders or they have to spend its profits on expansion projects, which is why they keep buying up other businesses. Their only capital is in their holdings. So rather than save, they have to keep growing."

Joanie smiled, sadly, as though watching some slow ship head towards its fated iceberg partner. "Growth as an end in itself is the logic of cancer." Ed looked up into the darkened windows, thinking of his mother.

Stan sat up, erect, stretching his back a little. "The last two hundred years have been a long, proud tradition of the struggle of the common worker, Ed. While you might be slumming it with us and don't think it is important, the union helps keep people employed and helps them to put food on their tables. The only reason we make a decent living at all and have some self-respect is because we got together and demanded it."

"It's true," said Joanie. "Until unions, labor was treated like a commodity, but a commodity that couldn't set its own price. You wanted to start a silk mill, you had to put up the capital for the silk threads, and the silk thread providers set the price based on the cost of their insanely expensive trees. You had to pay for bricks at a price set by the brickworks. Yet labor was the only commodity where the employer could say, 'This is what I'll give you.' Once people came together and unionized, they could say, 'This is what we cost.' It was one of the greatest developments in labor history."

"Look, Ed," said Stan. "You may have dropped out of college because you were bored or unfulfilled, or whatever, but the only reason you went in the first place and weren't dead of black lung or rickets from being entombed in some godforsaken coal mine during the only twelve hours a day when the sun was out is because of unions. And don't ever forget it."

Ed promised he would think about it, said goodbye, and headed back to his car. He looked up at the long-abandoned and decaying building, thinking of Hiram Sell and wondering at the palimpsest histories of all the traumas within.

CHAPTER SIX

A raid on the heavily armed compound of a religious cult here erupted into a bloody gun battle on Sunday, leaving at least four Federal agents and two cult members dead and at least 15 agents injured.

The cult's 33-year-old leader, who has told followers that he is the Messiah, told a local radio station that a 2-year-old inside the walled compound had been killed in the shootout and that several other people were hurt.

- *New York Times*, March 1, 1993

The Kinfolk all gathered around the television, watching the CNN coverage of the raid on a religious cult's compound in Waco, Texas. There was an exquisite banner, and every time they came back from commercial, they followed a station identification from the guy who did the voice of Darth Vader with a lovely video graphics package bearing an intern's sly reference to R.E.M.: "It's the End of the World as We Know It." The Bureau of Alcohol, Tobacco, and Firearms were medevac-ing the corpses of the four ATF officers out of the area, and each of the Kin separately could not help but think about how this looked like a scene from a movie. Was it just the television frame? Was it something about all the professional camera angles the ATF established because they thought this was going to be a big public relations coup? CNN also kept replaying the same scene of an officer getting shot through the wall next to an open second-story window, and it had the uncanny effect of a Super Bowl instant replay. It probably did not help that the botched operation was called "Showtime."

"That David Koresh has kind of a Jesus-y vibe," said Lavinia, who was working on a movable mural for the happening.

"If Jesus had a mullet," said Felicia.

"Nah, that's more of a Jewfro," said Lavinia, who was allowed to, wearing her ethnicity mostly for the humor these days.

"What, you don't think Jesus had a tight coif of black Middle Eastern curls? Nice Jewish boy from a little town called Bethlehem had those golden Leonardo locks?"

"Seems an unlikely Messiah," said Serge, pointing at Koresh.

"He convinced over a hundred people in this day and age that he was the second coming of Jesus," said Felicia. "There has to be some serious charisma there somewhere. I personally can't see it through the Don Johnson facial stubble, myself. But it must be there, somewhere."

Tod was animated, and he took another hit of sativa. "This is what we've been talking about," he said. "This is not some random accident. This is the mark of what's coming. These aren't accidents. Gog and Magog, man. Two days ago, the World Trade Center almost came down. 'And the mountains shall be thrown down,' says Ezekiel, and I'm sure that's what the Twin Towers must've looked like in his vision. And why? Why were those car bombers trying to hurt America?"

"They hate us for our freedom?" snarked Tim.

"Ridiculous. Oppositional thinking. Us versus them. We're still fighting the Crusades against people who we are convinced aren't like us, and they're still fighting back to establish the Caliphate. We're both Abrahamic cultures, for fuck's sake.

"And this Waco disaster is just the result of a bunch of gun nuts on both sides trying to show whose is bigger. Stockpiling weapons like the federal government is the seven-headed beast. Like you can fight off an apocalypse with conventional weapons. But the State's not our enemy. We're our own worst enemy. We have to find the commonality. We have to show the world that we are just like them and they are just like us. We are just coming out of a Cold War, where we had permanent opposition for fifty years. And the Moscow Soviets were *Europeans*. Can you imagine if these Muslims were successful in taking down the World Trade Center? What kind of horror would that begin? Permanent war. And fighting jihadists would be like Mickey Mouse fighting the brooms in *Fantasia*; every time he smashes one, they split into two. Like trying to nail Jell-O to a tree. How could we ever find that common ground?"

"I'm not sure it was just ignorance of commonality," said Ed. "Targeting the World Trade Center seems to be a pretty clear message about money and America's global influence, don't you think?"

"But the root is misunderstanding," said Ester. "If we could just get together in the same space, we'd find that commonality."

Ed hoped they were right, though he still couldn't tell how seriously Tod took this prophecy stuff. He seemed to be talking more and more about it the closer they got to the happening, as though he really thought that this performance art thing would change Biblical prophecy. Still, Ed agreed that talking was better than not talking, and he certainly shared his generation's belief in talking it out rather than taciturnly staring off into the middle distance. But could you come to an understanding when one side still had its boot on the neck of the other?

"And, thanks to Ed, we're one step closer to getting there." Tod patted Ed on the back and smiled.

After his meeting with Stan, Ed had had the idea to rent out part of the Adelaide Mills as a performance space for the happening. Tod was still working on the agreement with the owners, but everyone agreed, including the city, that it would be wonderful to re-envision the area with something productive, and that repurposing the abandoned factory could be a key symbol in that revitalization. They set the date for April 19, which was the earliest they could get clearance and liability coverage. A 102-year-old factory was bound to have some safety issues, and the city wanted to make sure that part of it was usable. Tod and Ed had toured the interior and found one room large enough for a performance space without being in the main factory floor, which would have been far too large for their plan. Maybe one day, said Tod, but not yet. The room had a separate entrance next to a loading dock on Court Street at the south side of the building, so they could bypass most of the safety concerns.

"Let's watch some MTV," said Lavinia. "I need to focus on something positive and not these poor shmucks." Ester turned the channel to a blond Thom Yorke, playing this new Radiohead video that was in constant rotation.

You float like a feather
In a beautiful world
I wish I was special
You're so fucking special

But I'm a creep
I'm a weirdo
What the hell am I doing here?
I don't belong here.

The simple video of the band onstage mesmerized Ed, and the words of alienation sounded to his ears like an augury for his own fate, a fate which he both wanted and resisted. He had longed for so many years to stay unattached, and now it seemed that everyone wanted to pull him from that. He just did not want to hurt anyone or be hurt by anyone anymore, but how was that possible, when the world seemed constructed so that hurting was inevitable? As soon as you set up your lovely tea party, some asshole was going to come along and piss in the pot. Or worse.

"Ooh, that guitarist is pretty," said Lavinia. "Almost makes me want to switch sides."

During the next few weeks, Ed continued to work at Greif, and his evenings were spent planning the happening. He still was not feeling particularly creative, but he enjoyed helping Ester in her projects. Even though she was an English major, her true passion was in making little crafts for herself and friends. She owned her own glue gun, which never ceased to amaze Ed. When they were growing up, Ed would watch as she spent two weeks making an elaborate poster collage for her friend Janie's birthday, ignoring her schoolwork and everything else just to make Janie smile for one moment. Ed always admired her selflessness, if that's what it was, especially the more and more self-conscious he became. He wanted some of that ability to bleed into another. He wanted the lines between them to blur, and he wondered if she felt the same.

On a Saturday in March, Ed took the afternoon to go up to the dollar theater at the Whitehall Mall to catch a film that everyone had been talking about, *Reservoir Dogs*. Mr. Blonde's sadistic severing of Nash's ear was like a harbinger of a new era. There was no motivation, it seemed. Just pure torture for the fun of it, for the sheer aesthetic pleasure of destruction. To Ed, the film seemed to match this general aggressive unease he was finding in all the apocalyptic arts around him. It seemed like punk rage was morphing into punk despair, and Nirvana's "Smells Like Teen Spirit" was matched by the rising female belligerence in the riot grrrl bands like Bikini Kill and L7. *Reservoir Dogs'* almost entirely male world of naked aggression disturbed Ed, and he was reminded of all the years of his childhood when he had had to negotiate the rough boys and jocks who tormented him and his "art fag" friends, as everyone called Ed and his crew. Yet while the film disturbed him, he wondered: How different was that from the whole history of representation? St. John of Patmos kind of seemed to get off on the horrific imagery of the apocalypse in Revelation. Dante's *Inferno* was a vade mecum of sadistic chicanery, putting people from his hometown up to their eyeballs in excrement, and it was far more memorable than *Purgatorio*, which Ed's life was feeling like these days. And what was the cultural legacy of two thousand years of crucifixion paintings? Ed remembered going to Sacred Heart Church at four years old, staring up at the giant bleeding statue that hung below a duplicate, triumphant, and radiant Jesus, both strikingly lit with gold and white linens surrounding the dais, a dual messianic vision that confused and frightened Ed. The magnificence of destruction. And that was one thing that Ed truly loved about *Reservoir Dogs*—that even with the nonlinear chronology, the nihilistic sense of doom, and the hyper-stylized violence, the overall feeling he left with was pleasure as the parts all came together in their inevitable finale, as though fate had marked them all before they even began. Ed found this aesthetically satisfying, and he wondered why.

He left the theater and decided to walk over to the portrait studio where his mother used to work. Ed was struck at how much more depressed the mall had become in just the few years since he was in high school, although it was always a little sad. The mall opened in 1966 as the first enclosed mall in the Lehigh Valley, and it led to a boom in retail shopping outside of Allentown proper, helping to decimate Allentown's downtown shopping and tax base. Ed still remembered how when he was five, the pomp and circumstance over the opening of the newer, larger Lehigh Valley Mall across the road perpetually relegated the Whitehall Mall to a second-class status. Ed's mother had talked to him for months about it as a very exciting development, and they went together in October on the opening day. He still remembered walking through the JCPenney, which he thought was pretty average, and crossing into the main interior space of the mall, decorated already for the Christmas season. The indoor fountains, Santa's talking reindeer, the soft pretzels at Mr. Dunderbak's all seduced Ed with the pure shopping pleasure of an anesthetized, climate-controlled simulacrum of the filthy world outside. For the rest of his teenage years, he always had a sentimentality about malls and the spaces that they provided, even when John Hughes films taught him how problematic they were. His friends would meet there at the giant circular wheelchair ramp on a Friday night, and they would walk up and down the length of the mall, stopping at Spencer Gifts to look at the black-light Led Zeppelin posters, whoopee cushions, and racist joke books; playing the latest video game at the Space Port arcade; browsing records and audio cassettes at the Listening Booth, usually too poor to buy much, but loving to hear Pink Floyd's "Another Brick in the Wall, Part 2" blaring from the in-house sound system, which was second to none.

The Whitehall Mall always felt a little sad and tawdry in comparison, with its mid-sixties décor and sunken seating areas. Unless you were going to a specific store, it mostly consisted of elderly people looking for a clean, well-lit place for some slow-motion exercising. Ed walked over to the portrait studio, and he watched his mother's friend, Cheryl, who worked at the front counter. Ed stayed back, looking into the store, since he had not seen Cheryl since the funeral, and he did not want to face anyone else's pitying stares. He turned from the area and was surprised to see Joanie standing near the Orange Julius. He called to her.

"Oh, hey Ed. How've you been?"

"Been worse. What are you doing in town?"

"Spring break. I needed to come in to check the *Morning Call* microfiche at the library. Of course, I have to come on the eve of Snowpocalypse. They're saying it could be two feet of pileup. I'm thinking I might be here a while."

"Well, if you are around tonight, come by Origen's around seven. A friend of mine from Philly is coming up to play a show, and she's really good."

"Folk music, I'm guessing?"

"Folky rock, I'd say. It has some balls to it," he caught himself saying, too late. "She's hilarious."

"Maybe. I'm more of a jazz fan."

"I thought working-class hero types had to love themselves some Woody Guthrie."

"Ha, ha," she deadpanned. "You have to get past your stereotypes, Ed. You shouldn't condescend, especially since you are one of them."

He bristled a little, although he was lately beginning to wonder how long you could play at an identity before it became who you were. "I know. I just had a lot of bad experiences in my neighbor-hood growing up. You might not believe this, but dyed black hair and leather pants don't go over so well on the North Side. One of my earliest memories of the bus out to the gifted and special needs school was getting my ass kicked by a nine-year-old thug who didn't take kindly to my implication that professional wrestling was fake. I had so many fantasies of escape when I was a kid. People like my Uncle Richie just terrified me when I was little. Well, he still terrifies me."

"What's that got to do with it?"

"I just wanted a gentler life. I had this fantasy that going to England would be the one way out of this American cesspool. I used to watch *Masterpiece Theatre* and Monty Python reruns on PBS late at night, and I would just marvel at how smart and witty everyone in England seemed."

"First of all, I appreciate what you are saying, but from what my dad says, your uncle has been pulling a con for the last twenty years that he scammed from the company. That's not union, Ed. That's someone exploiting the union. For every system, there are bound to be some moochers giving it a bad name, like Ronald Reagan's whole Linda Taylor 'welfare queen' nonsense. Second of all, you really should get more involved with the union. My dad says you don't even attend the meetings. There is a lot going down this year, and they need everyone together to be effective."

"I have a real problem with crowd mentality. Getting in groups of people and shouting just feels too much like Nazi groupthink to me. Isn't that why the Soviets finally lost?"

"The USSR fell apart for a lot of reasons, but that is not really the point. The Soviet Union was never Marxist or pro-union, if that is what you are implying. It was a totalitarian state. Same with the Chinese. There's never been a Marxist socialist country in the world, Ed, or a purely capitalist state, either. But there have been social democracies like Denmark and the Netherlands, and democratic socialist countries, which blend capitalism with the checks and balances that things like unions and the EPA provide. I know, all we hear is 'capitalism' and 'communism,' even though neither side was that at all. We tend to dissect with a very blunt blade in this country. And either way, Marxism was never about collective thought. If you actually read Marx, you'll see that it is all about liberating the individual by breaking out of the ideologies and mindsets that have been controlling you. Engels called it 'false consciousness,' and it is as relevant today as it was a hundred years ago."

"Controlling me? Who's being condescending now?"

"Look, Ed. You need to improve your analysis. You are never alone in this world, making choices that are free. You are a function of history and economics, and the only way to get freer is to see the lines of force and chains of causality. Otherwise, you are just a pawn of power."

Ed thought about this. Was it true? It seemed in line with what Tod had been saying about not seeing the world correctly, but Joanie seemed so clinical and cocksure about everything. And her focus on accurately defining things and seeing some things as fundamentally opposed was exactly what Tod was warning against.

"Please think about the union. Tough times are coming."

"Why, what's the problem?"

Joanie explained. Up until 1989, the company had been regularly pulling in profits of four to five million dollars per quarter. When the recession hit, sales dropped off, and they were now making six or seven million dollars per year.

"So, again, what's the problem? Six million dollars is not nothing."

"Of course not. And just five years ago, the company only could have dreamt of those kinds of profits. The recession was preceded by three years of soaring profits—seven million in '87; thirteen million in '88; sixteen million in '89. After the first year of the worldwide recession in 1991, they made it sound like end times, but Greif still made the same four million in profit they made in '87. But corporate memories are only as long as the last quarter. Like I said, if this were a family-owned business, they would have hundreds of millions to lean back on to weather the recession, even if they had a negative year. But as a corporation, they can't just have money; they have to have *all* the money, and it has to keep growing, or it is seen as a failure by the investors. The word is that the company is going to ask for massive cuts in salary and benefits from the workers while they go bidding on After Six tuxedos, which just went bankrupt, and while they go after another old company, LaMar Manufacturing in Georgia, to get a cheaper suit line covered."

"You can't expand while you are claiming to be contracting."

"Watch, Ed. Doublespeak is the name of this game."

They talked more about her thesis, which she was finishing that semester, and her upcoming plans. She was hoping to come back to help work for the Amalgamated Clothing and Textile Workers Union to do public relations. God knows, Ed had never heard someone talk so eloquently and passionately about the topic, and he wondered what the state of unions would be if they had better figureheads than that union organizer, Aaron Blumenfeld. He certainly had the rhetorical gifts, but he also had the uncanny ability to alienate even those sympathetic to the cause. Blumenfeld also had the tendency to sound like the anarcho-syndicalist peasant in *Monty Python and the Holy Grail*, whose language was a little too rehearsed and often made people roll their eyes: "Come and see the violence inherent in the system! HELP! HELP! I'm being repressed!" Joanie also talked about her father, whom Ed genuinely had affection for, even though he did not always agree with him. Stan reminded him of pictures and stories of his own father, with their Eastern European stockiness and broad shoulders, and the hotheaded tendency to anger quickly at injustices—arguments playing out in their heads all the time. Joanie told Ed about her father's anxieties and loneliness, especially since her mom passed the year before. Also, cancer. Ed couldn't help but wonder if the cancer rates outside of his industrial side of Pennsylvania were as high. It seemed that everyone he knew had watched someone close to them die of it. Maybe something in the groundwater.

The more Joanie talked, the more Ed liked her, too, and he found her passion and intellect to be very attractive, even though she seemed to do everything she could to deflate everyone's desires. She had an entire life of the mind that he felt he was only seeing the iceberg tip of, and he wished he could get to know her better. Her world seemed so foreign to his, as though both of his parents were not factory workers and as though he were not working at the exact same plant. Yet he knew that if the fates had lined things up just a little differently—if his mother had been in any way neglectful or hostile, or if she had not shared her interest in the arts with Ed at a very early age; if he hadn't scored well on that IQ test, which led to him being bussed out of his community to a program that local educators set up to meet the special needs of kids like Ed, and so on and so on—he would be a very different person today. Set out this way, Joanie seemed right that his entire self was a function of socioeconomic and historical forces that predated every choice he made, but inside, it did not feel that way. Inside, he felt that he was in control, making rational choices in response to the world he was given, even if he chose not to choose. Which was it? Or was that a Tod Griffonian false binary?

That evening, Ed met Eva and Kevin at the Kinfolk's house, and he was delighted to show them around. Tod talked with them for a long while about their plans, and Eva asked a lot of questions, while Kevin seemed nonplussed. They all drove over to Origen's together and sat in the back room, at their usual corner table, until Eva's set. They saw Philos had returned with a short, black-haired woman in her thirties, who had the eyebrows and the striking gaze of Helena Bonham Carter in *A Room with a View*, which disarmed everyone who looked at her. She looked like she would have been a good therapist if the gaze were not so unnerving, like she was seeing a sin you had forgotten was there—a "bullshit detector," but people felt it whether they had something to hide or not. Of course, everyone had something to hide.

They all greeted each other, and Philos introduced them to Ruth Barbello, his "partner" he called her, as though they were a gay couple or in business together. Ed noticed a large maroon book on the table in front of Philos, with the word *Conversions* on the cover, and he was overwhelmed with a strange sense of déjà vu.

"How's the book coming along?" Ed asked, pointing.

"Oh, it's getting there," said Philos, putting the book in his backpack. "This is a different project."

"That's getting there, too," said Ruth. She had Lauren Bacall's velvety voice, although she did not seem to be a smoker. She smiled wanly at Philos, who looked at the Kin. Ed squirmed. Without Tod or Lavinia around, he always felt a little uncomfortable talking with people older than him.

"So," said Ed, "what do you do that you put up with this guy traveling around so much?"

"Oh, I have my own life," she said.

Serge and Tim showed up with the photocopied invitations to the happening, and Serge handed these out to everyone they knew. Philos and Ruth took their invitation, asking if there was anything they should bring. Some art or a donation or anything?

"Oh, no," said Serge. "We'll provide the event, but you may have to donate your bodies."

Ruth frowned. "I'm not sure I like the sound of that."

Serge smiled gnomically and went back out front to distribute the rest of his invitations.

Tod arrived with an intense flash around the room, and he moved to the Kinfolk present. "So, get this nonsense. I have to go to Philly in a couple of weeks. I got a call today, and apparently I'm named in some relative's will."

"Oooh, exciting," cooed Eva. "It's like we're in a Victorian novel. Are you rich? Inheriting some crazy Jamaican in the attic?"

"No clue," said Tod. "As far as I know, the family has been poor white trash for over a hundred years. Maybe I'm inheriting Great Uncle Billy Bob's collection of NASCAR model cars."

"Special edition Jerry Springer bobbleheads?" said Serge.

"A large python in a fish tank?" said Ester. Ed grimaced.

"You know," said Ed, "except for Felicia and Lavinia, we're all more or less from this background. Maybe we should be a little more generous."

Tod looked at Ed, somewhat surprised. "Ed's right," he said. "Sorry, man. Just a remnant of my class shame. Hard to shake. But there's nothing that says that one culture is better than the other."

Eva played her set, and within seconds she owned the room with her blend of sass and vulnerability. After her normal setup of self-referentially ironic songs, she moved into Ed's favorite of her originals, "In the Country of Last Things," a slow-burning song based on a small scene from the Paul Auster novel. Ed sat transfixed, watching Eva disappear into the arpeggiated minor chord progression leading up to the intense "slaughterhouse bridge," as she called it, which moved between an E minor and a C diminished 7 chord, giving an uncanny feeling of ethereal intensity. He forgot how much he missed hearing her practice, and he could almost feel her fingers pressing upon his spine instead of her guitar, as he often fantasized.

By the time the show was over, the Great Blizzard of 1993 had begun, and they all went back to the Kinfolk's house, where Kevin and Eva would crash for the next three days. Their cars were all buried under eighteen inches of snow, which they could not shovel out until the plows finally made it to their street. By morning, twenty-nine people were dead from the blizzard across the East Coast. Allentown had an otherworldly glow about it as everything ground to a halt—industry, traffic, shopping. It was even difficult to walk down the street without hip boots, which none of them had. Snow draped over every surface, even the power lines, bizarrely enough, and it dampened the sound so much that the complete lack of reverberation made it sound like you were talking in your own coffin after being buried alive. The snow stripped the air of all smells, a blank slate in the senses. Without traffic or any movement, the world looked as it would look after Armageddon, Ed assumed. Stillness. Quiet. He could see the draw of seeing the world without humanity, without even the sound of a bird in the distance. And yet there was something deeply unnerving about this quiet. If Tod was right, and our desires and fears canceled out in our unconscious into a flatline of non-existence, then this scene seemed to exemplify that annihilation. One must have a mind of winter, Ed remembered from a Wallace Stevens poem, and he shivered against the emptiness, returning back inside.

The house was full now that Lexi and Augie had returned from Philadelphia and Ester was stuck, so she shared the bed with Ed, as they had when they were children. They slept with their backs to each other, acting like this was the same thing as when they were eight-year-olds. They tried not to touch each other's bodies, yet allowed their backs to come so close that there seemed to be a warm pillow of energy rubbing against them. In the morning, Ed would wake before Ester and quickly jump out of bed before his morning erection gave him away.

During the day, the entire Kinfolk gathered in the annex and worked on their projects. Kevin borrowed some of Tim's paints and canvases, and he started an abstract form that Ed could not quite place. He had given up painting in excrement, for the less than aesthetically pure, but highly pragmatic, reason that his landlord would evict him if he continued. Besides, for some reason, he never sold a single work, which made his fantasy of living off his art a dream farther and farther away. Kevin lived with the ignominy of watching Megan Dee's star rise extraordinarily fast in the Philadelphia art scene, while he was merely hoping to get in a show somewhere. Knowing that Megan's success was largely attributable to her father's connections did not help, as Kevin was starting to realize that most success in the art world seemed to be a matter of connections, and Kevin's acerbic wit was not helping him. He was terrible at networking, and even though he reveled in postmodern subversiveness, he still took his play very seriously; he also, he was finding, maintained a romantic attachment to the image of the loner genius artist whom time would reward. He was broke. To pay the rent, he worked at a Lowe's Home Improvement Warehouse, whose advertising tagline, "Never Stop Improving," made Kevin wretched every time he saw it branded throughout the store.

In the evenings, Tod still ran prayer meetings, and Kevin and Eva attended these, too, although they mostly remained very quiet and listened attentively. Tod was smoking more pot than ever, and his disquisitions were increasingly as laced with paranoid fever dreams as his joints seemed to be laced with something stronger. The ongoing events at Waco had started to affect his sense of mission, and he swung from identifying with the Branch Davidians, whom he saw as under attack for beliefs outside of the mainstream, to blaming them for a divisive and misguided version of religion that was going to doom everyone. The Kin all thought that the stress of the happening was getting to him, so they ignored these eccentric flights. Ed hoped that the happening would be a success so that Tod could go back to his endless optimism, which, he had to admit, was very contagious.

After the third day, the roads had cleared enough for Kevin and Eva to dig her car out and return to Philadelphia. They both had work, and they would have to move slowly. Forty-nine people had died in the storm in Pennsylvania alone, and the roads were still treacherous. Before they left, Eva pulled Ed aside to one of the downstairs rooms. She looked at him in the eyes as though she were trying to decode a particularly difficult modernist novel. Ed felt self-conscious.

"So, what are you doing, Ed?"

"What do you mean?"

She looked at him as if he were being willfully obtuse.

"This group. This 'Kin' thing. What are you doing?"

"I'm just staying here for a bit. Things didn't work out with Ester's parents."

"No surprise with good ol' Richie the Peachy. But you seem pretty involved with the . . . goals of the group. And with Tod."

"Well, yeah. I mean, Tod's a pretty visionary thinker. I think this happening has a lot of potential to bring people together and do some real good."

"Sweetie, you do realize what this looks like to an outsider, don't you?"

Ed thought for a minute and shrugged.

"Don't you think this whole place has a bit of a . . . culty vibe?"

Ed blanched and his eyes looked like they were trying to read a space four inches in front of his face.

"What?" he said. "Like those Waco wackos? No, no. No, no, no. This is totally different."

"Really?"

"Do you see any glassy-eyed stares from me or Serge?"

She looked at him.

"Well, okay, bad example. But he's had that for years now from all the acid. No, Eva. This is nothing like that."

"I don't know, Ed. The tattoos; the communal living; the limitless pot reserves; the dumpster diving; the bizarre-o religious sermons. Tod might be a low-rent David Koresh, but there is something not sitting right for me here. I just have to be honest."

"They lied about the whole it being the 'best policy' thing."

She smiled her smile. "Maybe so. But I'm just worried about you. You're all pretty much completely dependent on him for your living arrangements, and it seems like for a bunch of people talking about breaking down hierarchies, you all are doing a lot of listening to his talking."

"Well, he's been around longer than most of us. You heard him. He's read a library's worth of some really interesting ideas. He has some good points."

"Ever since I've known you, you've been this little puppy, running back to the master who kicked him, wondering what he did wrong. Ever since your mom's diagnosis, you've been one big shoe waiting to drop. I knew that I shouldn't have let you move out right after the funeral. You're just too vulnerable. I can see why all this Kin stuff might sound like the Answer, or something." Ed looked at her like she had just started talking in fluent Mandarin. "Just stay critical, okay?"

Ed tried to reassure Eva, whose opinion he valued above everyone else's. All of this sounded like it was coming out of nowhere, and he could not see any connection to what was happening on the television and what they were trying to accomplish. Was it possible that Eva was jealous of his growing closeness with Ester? That seemed unlikely, as she had never seemed interested in Ed in that way. But perhaps there was such a thing as emotional infidelity that was harder to quantify and track. Perhaps.

The last big project that Ed had to accomplish was to invite someone whose point of view opposed his own. This was not easy. Not only had Ed been gone for so long from the area, but his entire social group at this point largely consisted of people just like him in the Kin. Inviting his Uncle Richie would just get him more scorn, and Stan was unlikely to hang out with a bunch of artistes on a mission, even if the whole idea of unity might appeal to his union goals. On the Wednesday before the happening, he sat in the annex, still trying to think of someone, while Lavinia and Felicia finalized their contributions.

On the television, MTV News announced a revelation in the history of the Pulitzer Prize: the best drama award went to the first part of Tony Kushner's *Angels in America: A Gay Fantasia on National Themes*—a title alone which would freak out the Christian Coalition and the other arbiters of America's national morality. Ed noted the strange synchronicity of the title of the first play: *Millennium Approaches.*

"Yeah!" screamed Lavinia. "Suck it, Clinton!" Lavinia was still angry that one of Clinton's immediate acts in the first ten days he was in the White House was to agree to compromise on the ban on gays in the military. Her sister was in the Air Force, and while she wasn't expecting the Clinton White House to be a *Cosby Show* for queers, she said, she was hoping for *something*.

Felicia smiled. "I'm not sure that it would have been better for you all if Bush would've won reelection."

"Bah!" said Lavinia. "I don't care that he probably has a few gay friends. This is the fucker I'm stuck with. A politician is only as good as his policies. Liberals just aren't what they used to be. I still can't figure out why your cousin works at that goddamn antiabortion clinic, if she's such a hippie chick."

Ed shrugged. "She says she wants to protect all life."

"Feh."

"That's the real difference between Republicans and Democrats," said Felicia. "They never break ranks, whereas we can't seem to resist destroying our messiahs."

"My messiah doesn't have such a greasy smile," Lavinia sneered. "Ball-less cracker motherfucker."

Ed wondered about their banter. Here they all were, so committed to overcoming oppositions and false binaries, but when it came close to home, it seemed virtually impossible to resist taking sides. He tried to imagine what it would really be like to reach the no-wind of nirvana—to really be beyond all desires and fears. Would that be peace, or was that just a metaphor for death? And what would it be like to be married to a hardcore Theravāda Buddhist, for whom the Buddha's Fire Sermon was no metaphor, and to know that they were actively trying to squash all desire for you? Find *that* Hallmark card.

Ed decided to try Joanie, even though she wasn't exactly opposed to his thinking. She just took all the union stuff a lot farther than he ever did. He was worried about the happening being on a Monday and her being almost three hours away, but it turned out that she only had morning classes on Mondays, so she could make it over afterwards. Besides, how could she turn down an opportunity to get a look into the old Phoenix plant? Ed offered her a place to stay after the event, but she demurred, saying that she'd have to drive back to get some sleep before her afternoon classes the next day. Ed still prepared the house in case she would have to crash there.

His final mission accomplished, Ed set about helping the others with their projects and enjoying the process of getting lost in the collective. There were only five days left, and there was still so much to do.

The happening approached.

CHAPTER SEVEN

A monstrous fluorescent vagina waved gently in the breeze. At over twelve feet in height, it swayed its labia minora like the wings of Ishtar, the Babylonian goddess, offering protection and threatening destruction. The flesh swooped in ridges like the folds of an ear, always listening. At the top, the clitoral prepuce perched atop the glans, bathed in blue light like a beneficent mother, encircled with a nimbus. At the opposite side of the room, a twelve-foot flaccid penis drooped its purplish length downward, pointing to the main performance space with a small drop of ambiguous moisture at its tip. Between these, and ten feet higher, perched a golden griffin with a lion's back and an eagle's front, surrounded by a block-shaped capital "G," guarding the priceless treasures below.

The stylized griffin logo was Greif's attempt at rebranding the 125-year-old emblem back in 1988 to reflect "the new company image and attitude," as reported in the *Morning Call*. What was this logo capable of? What futures would it bring? The old logo used two traditional griffins that projected a staid confidence in the solid and stolid ways of tradition. This new solitary griffin had a futurist hardness to it, as though Marinetti designed it to strip all organic matter and softness out of the world. And what did it mean that a phoenix had been replaced by a griffin? When Ed first saw it, it reminded him of the German coat of arms in the highly formal sweep of its wings. The logo must have been installed after the plant closed, as a joke, or perhaps it was in place before the later public unveiling of the logo. The griffin hovered high above them in the old loading dock at Adelaide Mills, where the Kin had finished setting up their installations that afternoon. Felicia projected her Brobdingnagian genitalia onto two large cloths on either side of the room with a slide projector, and small circular fans sat behind them, giving the tapestries their slightly sinuous motion. At that size and with the various filters she used, you really could not tell what they were unless you stood at the farthest point of the room. At close range, they merely offered a surreally pleasant wave of color and texture.

Looking up at the tapestries, knowing what they were, but not able to discern much from his angle, Ed thought again about Philos's comments about spaces. He remembered how back in his architecture class they had discussed that naval barracks out in Coronado, California. The building complex was built in the 1960s, and they were so obviously laid out like a swastika that he could not believe that the developers did not know. One glance at the blueprints would have given that away, yet the American military still built it. Kunstkeller drew no conclusions from this example, and the significance of the buildings remained ambiguous to Ed. He wondered how many other spaces would reveal different messages when viewed from the right angle.

The audience was beginning to come in as the Kin hovered around their own pieces, getting them ready for the performance. At the entrance, Tod greeted the guests while overseeing the refreshment table. Over one hundred small Dixie cups were set up in the shape of a mandala, based on a design Tod devised after a lucid dreaming experiment, and each one was filled with a small amount of liquid that looked like sangria. "Drink the Kool Aid," a banner behind the table quipped, and most of the guests sipped their cups while milling about the room that was about sixty feet long by fifty feet wide. The main performance area was flooded with a pulsating light wave pattern that made it seem like they were all underwater, and the room was large enough and the lights dim enough that you could not see the edges or corners, making the space seem to stretch into eternity.

Ed looked around the room at the people he recognized. Ester was over near the entrance, talking with her sisters, Angela and LeAnne. He had not seen Angela since he came back, and he had no idea that she had gained so much weight; she wore a smock, just like Ester, but she ballooned in every direction like Violet from *Willy Wonka & the Chocolate Factory*. LeAnne ran around the performance space, fascinated by this motley blend of people and art, and jumped in front of Philos and Ruth who were talking together, not drinking anything; LeAnne introduced herself, and the three talked with animated smiles. Carol, the epicene barista from Origen's, regarded one of Kevin's paintings, which he had donated as a thank you to the Kinfolk for putting him up during the storm. The painting was an ironic version of Hans Holbein's *The Ambassadors*, updated for a postmodern era. Kevin's version had all the worldly accoutrements of two renaissance men, but this time in 1993: a Sony Discman, a laptop with a "Pentium Processor" sticker across the front, a large Motorola DynaTAC phone that looked like a small brick. One of the men wore aviator sunglasses and an acid-washed denim jacket with matching jeans; the other wore an unbuttoned flannel shirt over a gray T-shirt. Serge's younger brother, a white kid with dreadlocks and a Bob Marley T-shirt, had a hazy mien that suggested he was following in his sibling's footsteps. Freak Ferguson looked far less freaky these days, wearing Chuck Taylors and a simple untucked Oxford over some stonewashed jeans, his hair sweeping off his face in a curtained hair pattern like Keanu Reeves in *Point Break*. He talked in muted tones with Joanie, who planned to walk through the mill with Ed after the event.

Ester left her sisters and came up to Ed, a look of expectant exultation across her face. She gave Ed some of the sangria.

"Here we go," said Ester. "To Dionysus."

Ed laughed as they clicked Dixie cups and drank. "The die is cast," he said.

"Looks like we're going to have a full house," Ester said, her voice ethereal, gazing out at the crowd. Ed watched her watching the world.

From two loudspeakers in their rented PA system, a voice started to whisper in tones too low to hear above the din of the crowd. Tim the Enchanter was beginning his musical piece, which fused over fifty different tape loops playing in forward and reverse, like a modern version of The Beatles' "Revolution 9." The left speaker had a mumbling speech from *The Omen* and the right speaker began a few seconds later with the same speech played in reverse. Other layers of sound started to add to the cacophony, which alternated between moments of chaos and moments of extreme clarity. Ed remembered hearing some of the clips back at the house while Tim worked on the piece, mixing jazz, classical, and hip-hop music with political speeches; teary testimonials of people confessing their crimes in front of Oprah Winfrey; sports cheers and Mussolini chants; wisps of Carl Orff's *Carmina Burana* and Dvorak's *New World Symphony*. There was no official beginning. In the confines of the old factory space, the piece slowly increased in volume, echoing its alternatingly discordant and consonant tones, so that the audience only gradually could tell that the performance had already begun.

The area had bleachers installed along the perimeter, but some atavistic impulse brought the audience down to the performance space itself, some people lying on the floor, some sitting cross-legged, and some moving their bodies to the strange sounds that Tim wove from a mixing console beyond their sight, as though it were the chant of an old Greek chorus and the speakers intoned in call and response, strophe, antistrophe. The lights dimmed even further, and the central space pulsated with the seawater lights in time to a kind of heartbeat, like the beginning of Pink Floyd's *Dark Side of the Moon*.

Ester started to rub Ed's neck, and his body wound and unwound at the same time. Lavinia walked to the center of the performance space and spun once, the people moving back to make room for her mock Stevie Nicks pirouette, and everyone noticed for the first time a plastic tarp underneath them. She began to strip down completely, revealing a body painted head to toe with what looked like tattoos, but was actually dried latex paint, incorporating familiar images such as a yogic Aum sign and a Soviet hammer and sickle, but also Maori tribal symbols that no one could read except for Lexi, who had copied the images onto Lavinia's body the night before from a book of Polynesian symbols. Lavinia sat cross-legged and pulled out a large bowl of a clear fluid, which she proceeded to rub on top of her paint. Most sitting nearby sat hypnotized as Lavinia rubbed each symbol into shiny relief, and the lighting shifted to make her briefly the center of this scene. Those nearby seemed to feel an invitation, and they dipped their hands into the fluid, rubbing parts of her body that were nearby and blending the paint with their hands, which in the dim light seemed to blend with her body and each other. Lavinia's head dropped down and flung back in bacchante-like ecstasy as the twenty different hands covered her flesh.

Something began to change. The audience moved from individual response to a kind of communal movement, a mass vibration playing across their faces and bodies. They were outside of their selves and yet their mass consciousness felt still, pure. Ecstatic. Their limbs collectively began to droop and sway, as though something had unplugged them from their daily concerns and let them float passively under the breath of a divine presence. They were no longer in control of their actions, and they embraced their detachment from self as they began to embrace one another.

Ed watched this display, his breath seeming to come in time to the seething horde and the music that measured them. He looked into the pit of bodies, which started pressing their limbs against one another, the soft and hard press of flesh on flesh moving in rhythm to the pulsing sounds. Ester took his side again, seizing his hand in hers and rhythmically stroking the fleshy palm and scarred wrist. Ed did not recoil, and he felt both out of his self and also deeply embodied at the same time. They looked at each other as though for the first time, and then a silent clairvoyance passed between them as they both decided to leave at the same time. Ed led her to the back of the space, and they passed through a door under the griffin, which led down a long corridor to the factory floor. Ester looped her arm into Ed's as they made their way to the main room, where both of their fathers and Ed's mother once had worked. The exposed brick looked both steady and delicate, and Ed marveled that the masons had put so much detail work into such a functional space. The heavy oak floors were coated with a thick layer of dust, onto which their bodies collapsed near some machinery that they had no idea how to name. Within seconds, Ester pulled her smock over her head and gazed at her cousin, baring herself freely, her body pulsing with expectant desire. For the first time in four years, Ed wished he was not wearing his ten-hole Doc Martens as he struggled to get them off in the dark.

As Ed and Ester had passed through the back doors, the main entrance in the performance space had opened. The harsh outer light of the loading dock fluorescents briefly disrupted the throbbing horde in the main space. Philos and Ruth looked back at the sight of a crew of six black-clad skinheads under the front exit sign. Tod saw them and walked back to greet them, giving a firm handshake to the tallest one, who had a maniacal grin and a scar running from his left temple to his chin, "Sieg Heil" tattooed across his forehead. The others hailed Tod as well, three of whom, Ruth realized, were women. Skinbyrds, they were called, although she did not see them as women at first because of their uniform hair and clothes. Two of the men had "Berserker" tattooed on the sides of their heads, from what Philos could read at this distance. They all wore Doc Martens with either red or white laces. From their air of amused aggression, the protection of numbers and the interchangeability of their personas made them feel secure. The tallest one had the number eight tattooed on each cheek in Gothic script like upended eternity signs. The shorter male had a National Front symbol tattooed on his neck. For a second, one girl looked like she had hair, but Ruth realized that her head was just covered in tattoos, including a black sun surrounded by a wheel of flames across the entire tip of her head, like a skullcap. They moved away from the sangria table without taking any and started to spread around the perimeter of the space, laughing and pointing at the spectacle in front of them.

Ruth scanned the chamber, looking for LeAnne, and saw her on the edge of the pit. She flashed her gaze across the room, seeing Angela kissing the young man to her left and not seeing Ester anywhere in the area. She moved towards LeAnne while Philos went to the back of the room.

"What's your game, Tod?" said Philos.

Tod looked at the sight, the sounds, the unity, and he smiled at Philos. "What do you mean?" he asked.

"Is this what the Kinfolk are? Some kind of neo-Nazi group?"

"No, no, man. We just invited them tonight. The Compton brothers are harmless."

"You know that Ruth and I are Jewish, right?"

Tod squinted his eyes, like he was grooving to some inner song.

"Which is awesome. Everyone's welcome here."

Philos looked out at the growing storm. The figures dispersed through the darkness. "There are limits, Tod," he said.

"No way, man. Only the illusion of limits. It's like Kesey and the Hell's Angels. We *need* the angels of hell."

"What the fuck for?"

"The balance, man. The balance."

Philos looked through the throng for Ruth, who was talking with LeAnne in the distance.

"You're too tense, Philos. Have you had some of the sangria?"

"What? Your Electric Kool-Aid Acid? I don't think so. I thought your sign might've been literal, and this would end up like Jonestown. What's in it?"

"Ecstasy," he said, rubbing his chest. "Isn't it beautiful? You can just see it, can't you? They all want it. They all need it. They're all in it together. This isn't LSD, like Kesey's trip. This is something better, something new, something *purer*." As he said the word, something clicked in his DNA, and he was gone, smiling down within.

Philos met with Ruth. "We've got to go," he said. "Now."

"I know," said Ruth, turning to LeAnne. "Sweetie, where's Ester? Did you see where she went?"

"She hasn't been around for a while," said LeAnne. "She and Ed went into the factory to explore." This last word she said almost mystically, Ruth thought, and she started to get panicked the more LeAnne would not.

They moved over to Angela and tried to pull her away, but Angela just curled further into the man she was kissing. Philos and Ruth gave up and started to pull LeAnne toward the EXIT sign. "We'll just wait for your sisters outside, okay?" LeAnne began to move with Philos and Ruth, the room's energy force shifting palpably behind them.

From the back of the room, over the pulsing beat of the electronic music, there was a primal scream that sounded like it came from the depths of some atavistic rage. They looked over in time to see Tim's mixing console crash to the floor, spools and tapes splaying across the oak flooring. The tallest skinhead jumped on top of the table, shouting, "Anarchie!" At that moment, the giant vagina burst into flames as the shortest skinhead set fire to the tapestry with a Zippo lighter, emblazoned with Skrewdriver's *Hail the New Dawn*. The skullcapped Skinbyrd let out a Valkyrian shriek and booted a young Hispanic woman across the face, shattering her nose in a spray of blood and cartilage. The rest of the crew jumped into the pile of bodies with their steel-tipped boots and started curb stomping as fast as they could. As the tapestry swept in flames to the ceiling, the fan that animated it shot across the room, hitting the opposite fan, and the two forces created a vortex, sending the other tapestry spinning round and round in a giant column that tumescently pointed upward to the griffin logo. Screams raged from the pit of bodies as everyone scrambled individually to get to the exit sign, stepping over one another as violently as the skinheads themselves. Ruth and LeAnne made it to the exit first with Philos right behind, protecting them with his body to prevent them from being trampled. A wave of people started to surge behind them, pushing one another aside like a zombie horde, and Philos just caught sight of Tod and Joanie getting trampled by part of the crowd. The three burst out onto Court Street and leapt off the loading dock just in time as the sea of people crashed from the factory onto the street outside—dispersing individually into the night, running to their cars or fleeing up Race Street toward Hamilton, not looking back at the holocaust blazing behind them.

Back inside, under a reeled silk throwing machine long since abandoned and rusted into place, Ester and Ed came together in sweat and heaving chests, and Ed collapsed next to her with a smile she had not seen in a long time. Ester spooled her body around him, purring soft pleasure as the music continued to beat in the room down the hall. She thought about the last few months. She thought about the last few years. She thought about how triumphant Tod had been in the end, and she thought how happy she was that she could be a part of something so positive. She thought about revisions and redemption, and she knew in her heart that in the end, she would be forgiven.

Ester exulted.

PART III
ALLENTOWN
APRIL 20, 1993

CHAPTER ONE

The Messiah has a hole in the center of his chest. A shorn loaf, the Eucharist of sorts, tries to fill the space, but his torso tabernacle provides no support. The Christ child looks not at the viewer, but down at his own negation, his right hand resting on a ball with which he does not play, his left hand resting on a closed book, as if swearing an oath we cannot hear. Both ball and book hover, unsupported, corpuscular. He floats, bodies untouching, over the Madonna's lap, inches ahead of her chest, which also has been gored and cauterized, exposing the featureless horizon line behind. Their bodies are framed by a dilapidated archway, the smoothly painted surfaces eroding at the farthest radial points. The keystone is missing, and in its place dangles an ostrich egg on a line from an empty shell, as though the two feminine symbols cancel each other out: incipient and complete versus exhausted and empty. Even the mountain ranges hover, cast shadows, as though the laws of nature could not apply to the items in this scene. At the Madonna's feet, an altar of atomized elements: an empty sack, an unplanted white rose, an unfilled earthen vessel, a breathless fish. Everything floats, disconnected, foundationless, unknowing.

In the middle of the night, Ed sat in bed, looking at the cover of the collection of Dalí postcards he had brought from his mother's apartment after the funeral. The painting on the collection's cover first caught his attention: *The Madonna of Port Lligat*, in which Dalí used his wife as a model for the Virgin Mary. The last time he had held this collection, the one with the torn Borders Books price tag and the error-wracked little reproductions, he had been with Dana four years ago. It was during the somnambular summer after graduation, and he had bought this collection during one of their monthly visits to Philadelphia, which had had the only decent bookstore in eastern Pennsylvania. Ed was preparing for college, working graveyard shift in a motel to give himself time to philosophize in a vacuum and keep himself in oil paints and used Penguin Classics, and this was the best he could afford in lieu of one of those coffee-table books that were so massively cumbersome that they couldn't be opened. Dalí, Bacon, Giacometti—the twentieth century's whole psychically stable Top 40—he had them all in four-by-six-inch collections of thirty, and some, like the beloved Dalí, had a twin: one for sending, one for keeping.

"Oh, you like Dalí?" Dana had asked flatly, smoothing the line of her Brylcreemed Betty Boop hair. She was crisply clad in black, careful not to get Ed's mom's cat's hair on her. Ed said nothing.

When he was an early adolescent, just beginning to become deeply interested in Dalí, Ed had found this painting from Dalí's Christian period to be quite comforting. Transubstantiation, consubstantiation, and all the other Catholic mysteries he still believed seemed harmonized and centralized in a way he had not found in other works. The serene face of the Madonna and the mysterious morphing cuttlefish female angels worked well with his surreal and decadent aesthetic preferences while still supporting his substantial Catholic beliefs. Yet when he began to lose his beliefs in a very hard way, this Dalí, like so many other icons and images that had once buttressed his young faith, began to shift and expose the latent anxieties within the painting. To this day, he found it difficult to look at the credulous descriptions Dalí made of the image, and Ed found it almost bewildering that Dalí sent a copy to Pope Pius XII for approval. In another century, with a different Inquisition, he never would have lived to 1951.

Ed had somehow left these postcard collections behind in his mother's new apartment after he went to architecture school. He later found them buried at the bottom of one of the boxes of dusty sketch pads, nude figure drawings, and dried-out Rapidograph pens—the only things he was willing to rescue from his mother's apartment after her death. The rest went into storage purgatory.

Ed put the collection down on his milk crate nightstand and looked in the box, pulling out several novels, including a dog-eared copy of James Joyce's *A Portrait of the Artist as a Young Man*, which he had read in his senior AP English class. The exposure had had the same effect on him as on so many generations before him. Ed identified intensely with Stephen Dedalus's deep sense of cultural and familial apostasy, even though he was, at the time, still a believer in his childhood Catholicism. Nice Mrs. Brightfoy, with her chemo wig and "Have a drug problem? Talk to me!" posters, proffered her novels as an escape, a life raft to her class of poor white coal miner and steel plant descendants. She thought this would come through even while assigning Joseph Conrad's *Heart of Darkness*, in which mad Kurtz's lofty Enlightenment ideals were reduced to a single line scribbled in his papers: "Exterminate all the brutes!" When Mrs. Brightfoy spoke of Stephen's quest to escape the nets of religion, family, and nation, her voice oscillated between the thrilled staccato of the newly-converted Born Again and the hushed pitch of the inclusively conspiratorial mutineer. When she spoke of Stephen's flight from Ireland to France at the end of the novel, she taught the plot as it was taught the first fifty years after its publication, focusing on the penultimate sentence of Stephen's journal: "Welcome, O life! I go to encounter for the millionth time the reality of experience and to forge in the smithy of my soul the uncreated conscience of my race. Old father, old artificer, stand me now and ever in good stead." This was the seduction of large forms, eternal truths beyond the local, the minor, and the contingent. This was the seduction of Culture. A flight to Paris has no Friday night cow tippings after the Game. No *Benny Hill* reruns on the Superstation. No gnarled or disputed family trees. And Stephen had used a working-class smithy metaphor, no less.

During his time working at the hospice, Ed picked up a copy of *Ulysses*, wanting to tackle something big. He had already cycled through *Crime and Punishment*, *Moby Dick*, and *Middlemarch*, and he liked the feeling of landing the big whales of literature. At first, he was delighted to find that *Ulysses* continued with Stephen, but he could not figure out why he was back in Ireland. By the third chapter, Stephen walked along Dublin's Sandymount Strand, thinking of his previous self, back in the time of *A Portrait*: "Reading two pages apiece of seven books every night, eh? I was young. You bowed to yourself in the mirror, stepping forward to applause earnestly, striking face. Hurray for the Goddamned idiot! Hray!" Something was wrong. What had happened to the romanticized artist? What had happened to the Stephen with whom he identified for so long? When he looked back at *A Portrait*, he was able to read for the first time the final sentence of the novel. With Stephen's invocation, "Old father, old artificer," he finally realized that Stephen Dedalus was not Daedalus, the mythic creator of the labyrinth and the wings that killed his son, prideful Icarus, who flew too close to the sun. Stephen was Icarus himself. Not the creator, but the function of the creator. For the first time Ed found that there were texts that could only be read in retrospect, and worse, that an entire perception could be undermined by a simple structural irony, that most serpentine aspect of language. At the end of the chapter, Stephen laid a chunk of snot on a rock ledge "carefully." In Joyce, Ed had hoped for yet another way out of his upbringing, through something that might be discussed in the *New Yorker* or NPR. But he was slowly realizing that if Joyce were alive today, he wouldn't be able to stand Ed's mirthless presence.

"I gave up on art a long time ago," he said aloud in his empty room.

The Mrs. Brightfoys wanted the best for us, Ed thought, but they never quite thought through what *the best* meant, or why the best art so often started as the most subversive. The Mrs. Brightfoys had promised a world in which class would be annihilated by the torn borders of a cultural meritocracy. She was nice, nice. Very nice. But in a recurring nightmare that Ed had again after the previous night's conflagration, when he woke up panting at 4:20 in the morning, Mrs. Brightfoy—Janice Brightfoy—wrote a single line in her day planner, next to his name: "Exterminate all the brutes!"

Ed set Joyce back in the box and looked again at the Dalí cover, thinking of last night. Thinking of the past, wishing that history would fade like those space shuttle memories Ester was so excited about. He lay back down on the twin mattress, alone, and as he closed his eyes again, his mind saw nothing but the horizon line through a transparent Messiah.

CHAPTER TWO

Just after two o'clock in the afternoon, Ester walked into the annex's desolation of abandoned art materials, pizza boxes, and a smashed reproduction of *Winged Victory of Samothrace*. She found Ed sitting on a sofa, staring at a blank space on the wall where one of Felicia's photos used to hang, its rectangular form defined by the layers of pot and cigarette smoke that clung to the drywall. He started at her footfalls, looking somehow ashamed.

"Where is everyone?" she asked.

Ed made a sweeping gesture. "Gone, mostly. Lavinia's still in ICU. Everyone else went to their family's houses. Serge is in that wheelchair. I don't know how he's going to get up to his mom's third-floor walkup. Lexi was gone without a word. But what else is new?"

"Where's Tod?"

"Gone."

"He had a shattered rib!"

"Oh, I know. He had those compression wraps around his chest, and he sat around the annex all morning, wheezing. You could tell he was in a lot of pain, even with the medication. He was obsessing over the Waco coverage."

"Why, what happened?"

"The FBI and ATF came through and leveled their compound."

"What? Why?"

"Who knows? Janet Reno says they were abusing children, but

who can say? I think they died of boredom. There were over seventy of them in there. Nineteen of them were kids under six."

"Christ."

"He has nothing to do with this."

Ester looked down and started sobbing silently. Ed let her.

CHAPTER THREE

No one had died in the previous night's carnage, but only about a quarter got out unscathed. There were almost one hundred people crammed into the performance space at Adelaide Mills, and the Compton crew were effective, but they were not gods. Many who filled the ER alongside the Kinfolk were there from the effects of being trampled by the other guests or from smoke inhalation. Tod had fractured a rib under the weight of the panicking horde; Joanie was still in the hospital with a collapsed lung, currently undergoing a procedure to remove the excess air around the trauma site; Serge had a shattered kneecap, which would need massive reconstructive surgery. Felicia was far back from the crowd, taking pictures near the main entrance, so she had been protected by distance and time. Ed and Ester had been trapped by the fire, but the steel doors and the massively long factory floor had protected them until the firefighters could put out the blaze. They knew that if they had to, they could have smashed out one of the windows at the far end, but they stayed huddled together against the north wall, waiting for a sign. Afterwards, they stayed in the ER with the Kin until around two in the morning, when it seemed that everyone was more or less stabilized. Neither of them could get in to see Lavinia, as access was restricted to family members, and she had few family members recognized by the state. They knew that Lavinia had been curb stomped almost by accident, her mouth falling open on the edge of the stage floor when the skullcap's leg jumped on her head from behind, shattering almost every tooth in her mouth and breaking her jaw; she would be in oral surgery for hours. They last saw her in severe shock, being led on a gurney into surgery, the symbolic images across her body smeared beyond any recognition by the Vaseline lubricant she had used on stage. The fire was finally put out by 12:30, and the old factory maintained its structural integrity. Most of the fire came from the oak flooring and the other wooden objects left scattered around the room. The fire never even spread to the hall leading to the main shop floor, although the smoke certainly made it as far as Ed and Ester.

The Compton crew was on the run, and the police had out an APB as they tried to lock down the city. But Allentown was too porous and its police too few, and most people thought that they were probably already heading toward a safe house somewhere out in the Midwest, where the Comptons had family connections. No motive had been established, but none really needed to be. A universal force met a universal desire. The police were mostly wondering why such events were on the rise throughout the Valley and the rest of Pennsylvania, and was there anything they could do to curb its growth. For the cops, especially the ones on the night shift, civilization was a thin veneer stretched across nature's chaos, constantly being buffeted by volcanic eruptions from below and meteors from without. This state was constant. There was nothing to be done but to try to minimize the impact so that reconstruction could begin soon enough again after destruction.

Ester went home amid the cursing threats of Richie and the cloying wings of Ginny's ministrations to sleep fitfully until noon, while Ed merged with his mattress, haunted by the specters of the night, finally getting up at eight to a silent house, the antithesis of the energy that had driven the space for the last six weeks. Tod returned to the annex after being stabilized and collapsed on the sofa, where he remained until twenty minutes before Ester arrived. His breathing came erratically through the wraps. The doctors had been very worried that he might have a flail chest—the condition where multiple ribs were shattered, losing the structural integrity of the body—but the other ribs were only bruised. He sat around all morning, Ed explained, smoking hash and coughing spasmodically from it, watching replays of the destruction of the Branch Davidian compound. He kept saying that something had to be done, but Ed could not tell if he meant about the disastrous night, the Compton crew, the Waco siege—or some mixture of them all together in his hash-addled brain. He finally got off the couch, saying that he had to get to a meeting in Philadelphia in the next week. Ed could stay there as long as he wanted, he said. He did not know when he would return.

Ester joined Ed on the couch, and both of them stared at the empty space on the wall, feeling guilty that they were not among the ones trampled, yet hoping that their union was one good thing to arise out of this darkness. Ed remembered the short-lived feeling of ecstasy under the heavy machinery, and he wondered absently how long it would be before they could try to return to that moment. But even to think about such a thing, even vaguely, while their friends were suffering, seemed a kind of sacrilege.

Ester wanted to visit Philos and Ruth to thank them for saving LeAnne. None of them were aware that Tod's final solution was to spike the drinks, and she never would have left her younger sister alone with Angela, who had had two of the Dixie cups and was beyond all caretaking ability. Ester went over to Origen's to see if Carol had come into work, as she was the one person who seemed to know the couple very well. Carol was haggard, but okay, and had not had the sangria either because of her shift this morning. She gave Ester their address, which was a furnished apartment just a few doors down from the coffee shop.

Ester rang the bell, and she was buzzed in without announcement. She went up the dark creaking staircase with peeling heavy brown wallpaper out of some movie about New York tenements in the 1930s, and the heavy oak door, laden with at least ten layers of shiny black paint, opened at her arrival. Ruth let her in, and Ester gave her an immediate hug, which she held for longer than was required. Ruth gestured for Ester to sit on a couch in the main living area.

"Carol called to say you were coming," said Ruth. "I'm glad you did."

"Is Philos around?"

"He's out working on his project."

"Which one?"

"The long one."

Ester felt Ruth's calm and steady gaze, and her body decompressed a little.

"I really have to thank you two for last night. My baby girl—my sister—I don't know what I would have done."

"She's a perfectly sweet girl."

"She's our pride and joy, and we never would have brought her if we knew how it was going to go. She's just so innocent. I think that there are some people who are just so naturally pure and innocent, that the world owes it to them to keep them that way, don't you think?"

Ruth considered this.

"There are some theologians who think that the Garden of Eden story is a story about growing up," Ruth said. "When we're born, we listen to our parents, we follow the rules during what you are calling our innocence. Eventually we hit adolescence and develop the ability for abstract thought, and we realize that the world isn't quite what we thought it was. In fact, we start to look around at history and our parents and our society, and we realize too late that we've already bitten from the Tree of Knowledge of Good and Evil. Think about the first time you learned about slavery. Or the Holocaust. From then on, none of us are innocent. We're all out of the Garden."

Ester looked down at the pattern in the carpet that she hadn't noticed before. "But I didn't choose that," she said.

"None of us chooses the life we discover we're leading. That's our tragedy and our challenge."

"Challenge for what?"

Ruth smiled. "Would you like some tea?"

Ester sighed, "God, yes." Ruth got up and went to the kitchen. Ester looked around the room. The main living area was large but cozy, if spartanly furnished, with two sofas, a reading chair, and two separate desk areas, each obviously the respective territory of Ruth and Philos, and each facing different directions. On Philos's teacher's desk were a number of reference books about Allentown, the Lehigh Valley, and Pennsylvania. There were several notebooks open with writings throughout. In the middle of the desk was the Lehigh Valley AT&T phone book, next to the large maroon book with *Conversions* on the cover. On the other desk were stacked a number of books Ester had never heard of before, all apparently linked to something called apophatic theology. She gazed across the titles, marveling, as she always did when looking at someone else's shelves, at how there were entire worlds of knowledge that you could never know—that no one would ever have time to read in their entirety. Emmanuel Levinas's *Otherwise Than Being*; Maimonides's *The Guide for the Perplexed*; Raimundo Panikkar's *The Silence of God*. Ester had never even heard these names, and they could have been either divine writ or the ravings of a cult leader in Waco, Texas. How could you know? How could you discern? Ester picked up one of these by someone named John Scotus Erigena, and she opened it to a page that Ruth had bookmarked, reading: *We do not know what God is. God Himself does not know what He is because He is not anything. Literally God is not, because He transcends being.* This had a chilling effect on Ester and she put the book back, less out of the fear that Ruth would see her and more out of the fear that the texts would ask more of her than she was prepared to answer.

"Kettle's on," Ruth said, returning to the room.

Ester prepared her face. "So, if you don't mind my asking, what exactly do you do, Ruth?"

Ruth smiled at her apprehension. "I teach religious studies up in Toronto. I'm on sabbatical this year."

"Theology?"

"Mm . . . Religious studies. But theology is part of it."

"You're Jewish, right?" Ester asked.

"Ethnically, yes."

"What's the difference?"

"The word 'Jewish' is both an ethnicity and a religion. If your mother is ethnically Jewish, you are Jewish, like being Irish or German. The other is a religion. In America, there are a lot of variations. It causes no end of difficulties for people's understanding. I sometimes wonder if we shouldn't call the religion something else. Jebbism or something."

"So, you are not Jewish, by faith?"

"No. Not in the sense most people mean."

"You are an atheist, then?"

"I'm not a believer, in the traditional sense of the word."

"Yet you made it your life?"

"Oh, you'd be surprised how many people who teach religious studies are non-believers and even outright atheists."

"So why teach religious studies, then?"

Ruth paused. "I believe in the Bible as a historical fact, not that what is in it are historical facts. I believe that most of the world has faith that guides the foundations of everything they do. And I think that it is of fundamental importance to understand why people do what they do. Didn't they say something like that to you in college?"

"I don't know," said Ester. "We don't have to take religion classes at my school. We have core classes, where you get to take a bunch of courses from the humanities or the social sciences; that kind of thing. But honestly, you can get through a lot of classes without really thinking about why you are studying them."

Ruth nodded, somewhat sadly.

"I'm supposedly an English major, but I can't say that I embraced that for all it was worth. The professors offered so much, I think. But I graduate this semester, and I wish I could do it again with more discipline. I guess I just am more interested in relationships than books."

"You might be surprised at how the books can help the relationships," Ruth said.

The kettle began to sing, and Ruth got up to get it. Ester walked over to Philos's desk and ran her finger down the spine of the large maroon book. Glancing over her shoulder, she opened it and saw page after page of signatures, all categorized under different states and different cities. The order of the states seemed geographical rather than alphabetical, as though by going through the book, you were going across America, so Ester easily wound her way across America through Pennsylvania to Allentown, which had, it seemed, over fifty names signed. About one-third of them had lines through them with some kind of code afterward in a different color of ink. Her eye was immediately drawn to the name Pullman, and Ester was stunned to see that Ed's mother, Lorel Leh Pullman, was crossed off, and below her name read:

Eddie Pullman

Behind Ed's name was a question mark, a few random dots, and the address of the Kinfolk's house. Ester was just as surprised to see her aunt Martha's name written below Ed's, with her address added later too.

She closed the book and turned just in time to take a cup from Ruth.

"I hope you like chai. It's what we have in the house."

"Oh, that's great," she said. "Thank you." They sat back on the sofa.

"So, what exactly is Philos's project all about?"

"The Pennsylvania book? Pennsylvania, of course."

"No, the other one."

Ruth smiled. "Oh, you'd have to ask him that yourself. It is not my place." They sipped their chai. "Can I ask you a question?"

"Sure," Ester said.

"What exactly were you all thinking?"

Ester paused, almost tearing up again, but containing herself.

"We were just trying to do something beautiful, you know? There's just so much hate, so much hostility. So much pain in the world. Just look at the news on cable. Just 24/7 tension, all the time. Like Israel and Palestine, right?"

Ruth looked at her. Ester looked away.

"We just wanted to remind people that there is no real difference between people, once you get past the things that divide us."

Ruth got up and walked to the window of the apartment, looking down onto the 19th Street Theater. "Maybe it is not my place to say, but you seem awfully influenced by Tod's thinking—the Kinfolk, I mean."

"Well, Tod's a great man," Ester said, almost surprising herself by using the phrase. "He—he thinks about the world and what's coming. Why things are the way they are, but also how to change where we're heading. To improve humanity. How many people can you say do that on a regular basis?"

Ruth looked down at the street.

"I don't know," said Ester. "There are so many people with ideas, but who is trying to change the world for the better, and who is trying to revise the world for the worse? I just want to align myself with life."

Ruth did not look back at Ester, and the street did not look back at Ruth.

CHAPTER FOUR

When you shoot a game of pool, how do you describe *why* the ball fell into the pocket? Gravity? Did the ball cause its own fall? Was it the last wall of the table it ricocheted from? The last ball it careened into before sending it on its final trajectory? The cue ball? The cue itself? The pool player's arms? Her intent? Her psychology? Her unconscious desire to use a big stick to smack into a ball? The moment of her coming into being? How to draw the chains of responsibility, the lines of cause and effect? Where do you begin the narrative of something that happens? Which event is the first cause? And if each of the smaller paths is contingent on what came before, and if you can trace causality all the way back to the Big Bang, then who is responsible for anything that happens?

Ed had thought of this question often in the last few weeks as he found himself visiting Joanie daily at Sacred Heart Hospital. Ed and Ester were keeping their distance from each other out of a kind of respect for the damaged, and he found Tod's house to be haunted by the living. Joanie's diagnosis was pneumothorax, or collapsed lung, and hers was not a simple collapse. She would take weeks to heal, even though she avoided the complications of hemorrhaging and hypotension. During that time, Ed kept her company during the evenings after work and on the weekends, bringing her books and other things she needed to finish her thesis. Penn State found a replacement teaching assistant for her classes during the last two weeks of the semester, and she was able to continue her work from Allentown, getting her master's degree announcement while lying in her old twin bed back in her room at Stan's house.

Joanie did not seem to draw the lines of causality directly to Ed, although she was incredulous at his credulous belief in the Kin's plan. She looked at her injury as a historical reality the prognosis of which was predictable, so she turned to those prognoses that were not. After she finished her thesis, she began thinking about the union full-time, and it seemed to Ed that the deflation of her lung paradoxically gave her inspiration and an even more voluminous voice. For Joanie, being within the old factory itself was like descending into the belly of the whale, and after she was spat out onto a shore where history and theory met practice, her future was clear.

A battle was brewing, she said, and the company was planning even more draconian measures for their upcoming contract battle at the end of September. Rumors fell down like acid rain from the workers, but Joanie heard more direct confirmation from Aaron Blumenfeld, the international representative at ACTWU, the Amalgamated Clothing and Textile Workers Union, which had given Ed a $500 scholarship for his first year of college. The company wanted steep cuts in wages and benefits "to remain competitive," they said, and they were using the looming threat of NAFTA as leverage to scare the workers into submission. The union had to be ready for a fight.

Stan never overtly held Ed responsible for Joanie's injury, but a silent contract passed between the two men. Ed knew that a debt had to be repaid. He started to attend the union meetings, and as he entered a world he had resisted for so long, he began to see these people not as a horde of hostile, uncultured takers, the way his mother started to talk about them at the end of her life, but rather as a group of individuals united in a common cause—a desire to protect a better life for themselves and the families they were raising. Ed actually was surprised when he first came to Stan and Joanie's house, a thousand-square-foot brick bungalow at 5th and

Florida Streets in Whitehall, just a half-mile away from the house where Ed grew up. When he was a kid, Ed had passed this house and others like it every time he went this way up to the Lehigh Valley Mall and felt envious of the clean and happy lives that must have been within. At that age, Ed had thought that anyone who lived in a detached single home must be rich. Stan's house could not have been worth more than $60,000. Whatever else it was, the union was not exactly a factory for making Stan a Rockefeller.

Being in Joanie's childhood room was like looking at her previous self, embalmed like a fly caught in amber. Her mother never wanted to change anything after Joanie left for college, even though it was only a two-bedroom bungalow and the extra space would have made a difference. Stan was motivated more by inertia and a desire to simplify everything in his life now that Sheila was gone. Joanie's bookshelves were lined with two full shelves of Victorian novels—Dickens, the Brontës, and Thomas Hardy—and also childhood copies of *Little House on the Prairie* and Judy Blume. But what to make of the *Calvin and Hobbes* and *Bloom County* collections? The wallpaper was goldenrod with light red accents, and the walls were decorated with framed pictures of Monet's *Water Lilies* from the Met and several Impressionist artists that Ed loathed for what he thought of as their sentimentality. The largest reproduction was of Gustav Klimt's *The Kiss*, which Dana used to love as well.

"Did you know the original of this is about my height?" he asked her one day in June. "There's a whole Klimt museum in Vienna I hope to see one day. Some of them are enormous."

"I wouldn't mind seeing the Wiener Staatsoper," Joanie said.

Ed looked at her, perplexed. Joanie smiled. "The Vienna Opera House. Sorry. I had six years of German, and I never get to practice it, so I try it on everyone I know. Most schools in America don't even offer German. All these Pennsylvania Dutchies around here, eating their fastnachts and 'throwing the horse out the window some hay.'"

"I took French. Much more practical." They laughed.

"I have this longstanding fantasy to see all four nights of Wagner's *Der Ring des Nibelungen* at the Staatsoper. Ah, Ed," she hummed. "Wagner does it for me. All that 'Liebestod' in *Tristan und Isolde* is hot, hot, hot." She sang:

> *ertrinken,*
> *versinken,—*
> *unbewusst,—*
> *höchste Lust!*

She translated melodramatically, "'To drown, to be engulfed—unconscious—the highest bliss!' Yum," she laughed.

"I don't know, Joanie. You're ruining it for me. I'm trying to synthesize these different versions of you. I get the Victorian social realist. That's allowed. But mythic German romanticism, half in love with easeful death? I hate it when a good stereotype fails me."

Joanie laughed. "Yes, nothing but Clifford Odets for me. 'Sacred War' on infinite loop on my CD player."

"Only the best to get the imprimatur of Chairman Mao."

She sighed. "Oh, Ed. You laugh, but this is what the last decade has done to us. People get all misty about the good old days of the fifties. Well, in the 1950s, over a third of the country was union, the top marginal tax rate was ninety percent, and we had the largest middle class in history. We're down to about twenty percent union today, only eleven in the private sector, and the income inequality is growing exponentially. Where is it going to end up? People have no sense of history. The Triangle Shirtwaist Factory. Matewan. Your old namesake, the Pullman Strike. There are powers working so hard to revise what we've worked so long for. And they're winning. You have working-class people scoffing at unions and voting against their economic interests. Its maddening that we're losing the rhetoric war. You can see why I want to do public relations."

"It's like all the women running around now, scared to call themselves feminists because they 'don't hate men.'"

"Gah! I hate that! My dad even gets caught up in that rhetoric."

She looked at a picture of her mom that hung near the bed. "Progress does not always develop at the same pace, sadly. Dad's still got some of that Old World Polish in him. He was always good to mom, but they were never what you and I would call equal. Happily, he's never used the word 'feminazi.' Too closely associated with Rush Limbaugh, I think."

Stan watched this growing closeness between Ed and Joanie with cautious approval. He was caught on the dilemma of his own commitments. On the one hand, he loved his coworkers and the labor they did—well, most of his coworkers; best not to sentimentalize, he thought. He despised the fat cats and the cultural elites who condescended to them; he was sad that people stopped using "fat cats." On the other hand, Joanie was his pride and joy—proof that the honest labor he did could improve the life of the next generation. Yet when she went to college and then even graduate school, he found himself having fantasies of her entering a "different class" of people, as he put it, though he was not quite sure what that meant. And here was Ed, a nice enough kid, he supposed, if a little arrogant. But he had absolutely no ambition, it seemed, and Stan wanted someone who tried a little harder for his daughter. Happily, Joanie implied that Ed had some other girlfriend or something, so maybe they were just going to be friends. Stan had a little trouble with that one, since no one in his generation had friends of the opposite sex that weren't already in couples—and certainly not people outside of work who were as intimate as they were becoming. He vowed to himself to keep an eye on them, while appreciating Ed's increasing involvement with the union. They were going to need all the help they could get.

In the weeks after the happening, the world did not seem to get any further away from longing for the apocalypse. The twenty-four-hour news cycle went through a seemingly endless stream of End Time signs. An IRA truck bomb decimated Bishopsgate in London's financial district, killing one person; the former Prime Minister of France committed suicide while the Sri Lanka president, Ranasinghe Premadasa, was himself killed by a suicide bomber; UN troops were killed in Somalia; and a 7.5 earthquake hit Japan, wiping out more than three hundred and fifty people. If those were not images out of Revelation, what was? All they needed was a plague of frogs.

One evening in June, Ed returned from Joanie's house to the sound of movement within Tod's Victorian. Ed came in expecting to see Tod's half-shaven head, but instead opened the door to find Kevin Maro sitting in the annex, watching news coverage about a woman named Lorena Bobbitt who had cut off her husband's penis and thrown it out the window of her car into a field in the middle of the night.

"Holy hell," said Ed. "What are you doing here?"

"The Plan, Phase Two, apparently," said Kevin.

"Oh, god, no more planning, I hope. It didn't go so well the last time, in case you didn't hear."

Kevin explained. Tod had shown up to his apartment in Philly last week and made him an offer he couldn't refuse. To be honest, any offer would've been an offer he couldn't refuse, considering his last roommate had moved out and he wasn't going to be able to make rent with his salary as low as it was at Lowe's. How the hell are you supposed to live, Kevin wanted to know, on $4.25 an hour? He couldn't afford to buy canvases, which were absurdly expensive, even if you stretched your own. And he only got a few sales of some of his work that was hanging in a nearby coffee shop. When Tod showed up, he told Kevin of the failure at Adelaide Mills, and the conclusion he had come to after two months of meditation alone was that he hadn't dreamt big enough. He was recruiting Kevin for a new project that would synthesize all of Tod's philosophical ideas with his marketing background, and he would finally deal with the larger issues in the culture—the issues that had caused such a thing like their tragedy to happen. What exactly that entailed, Tod would not say yet, but Kevin thought he could go along with just about anything for a while, especially if it paid decently. Tod hired him to do the graphics, public relations and advertising work; in exchange, he'd have free housing and the room to do his work, even on the larger canvases that Kevin liked to use. Before Tod returned, Kevin was to rip out the drywall partitions in the basement and use that for his studio, since most of the Kin were gone for good. "That took me about thirty minutes," Kevin said. "You weirdoes lived like serial killers."

Kevin had already begun to work on the new plan's logo, which he showed to Ed in one of the black sketchbooks—Ed had often filled the same kind, so many years ago. On the page in several different permutations was a slick futurist version of the symbol Ed knew so well: two parallel lines hovering across the eternity symbol. Below this was the legend in a bold Impact font:

Harmonic Energies

Ed wondered what rough beast was slouching back towards Allentown, and what role Tod was birthing for them all.

CHAPTER FIVE

As long as I can remember, I never asked anything from life except that it always be plentiful. Be growing. Be beautiful. Be kind. When I was a little girl, Nature provided everything I needed, everything I did not get from other parts of my life. When I thought of Nature, I always thought in the kinds of absolutes that people use to describe God: all-wonderful, all-nurturing, all-forgiving. The opposite of what people are. In the summers, I would play in our backyard behind my father's coops, watching the chickens cluck and pluck at the seed, as if they had no conscious intent behind what they did, and I knew that they were blessed, because they had no sense of self. No sense of pain. No sense of their eventual death. The one thing that truly separates us from the other animals: They have no idea that they're going to die. No chicken ever clucked, "to be, or not to be." No rabbit ever feared the wrath of an abusive father. No mother failed to protect its young. Most mothers in nature would destroy any animal that tried to hurt it with a vicious impersonal righteousness. And so I loved Mother Nature, long before I learned that to do so was a sin, and I pictured her like the Virgin Mary, radiant with a beaming halo.

I don't remember much of my childhood before twelve or so, except some vague impressions. A Raggedy Ann doll my mother actually made of rags, so soiled with love that it stank from rot. The painfully magnificent chill of an early spring dive into Jordan

Creek, baptizing away the haze of winter's idleness. Playing *Star Wars* with Ed in his tiny backyard, him getting so bent out of shape over the littlest things. The day they brought LeAnne back from Sacred Heart and let me hold her and nurse her with a bottle. I still remember looking down into her squinting eyes that couldn't focus on anything yet as she sucked so hungrily and innocently from me, as though nothing else could ever fulfill her, and I knew that this was what they meant by grace. And just like our *Star Wars* religion, as Ed used to joke, the force of life was everywhere if you knew how to feel it, radiating from every object as though giving the world its silent benediction. No, I don't remember much of my childhood, and I don't want to remember the parts I don't.

And so adolescence came, and when I started to bleed it was like they said, that the blood of Christ came to wash away the past and all my sins. I was in harmony with Nature, and she let me know every month that I was a part of the cycles of life. Things stopped, but I kept going. It was a matter of calendar time, now, that most male of ideas. In another century or another culture, I would've been paired with someone by twelve and could begin my family, the way nature intended. I remember in my senior developmental psychology class, Mr. Singh started to lecture us girls who were planning to go to college, saying that we were throwing away our prime fertility years, when we were most prepared to give birth. Everyone was incensed, even the boys, and Mr. Singh was reprimanded after everyone launched a complaint. But deep down, I knew he was right, that I had already wasted six of my best years that I could never get back.

And so, when I met him, I knew that he was probably too old for me. I was almost out of high school, and he was already thirty years old. But no boys my age that I had dated were ready for the kind of commitment I wanted, the kind of love I needed. We met at Origen's, where I was working at the time, and I had never heard anyone talk like he did. Even Ed, who really is so smart, never had the passion for life the way that Tod did. Everything he said was like the sun's warm caress, and he made me want to reach up to the heavens and cry mystic prayers to the sun, my god, my goddess . . .

Have you ever heard of ATP?

No, I don't think so.

I learned about it in my biology class. Adenosine triphosphate. It is a chemical that stores energy. The energy from the sun comes down and gets stored in plants as ATP, and this becomes the basis of all the energy in living organisms. When we eat plants, or heaven forbid, eat the animals that have eaten the plants, we get this ATP, which gives us life. We literally are animated because we consume the sun. When I heard that, I thought of how close that was to what we teach about how we eat the Son during Communion. And triphosphate literally means it has three phosphate molecules, so it is structured like the trinity. Don't you think that's a beautiful way of looking at it?

. . . Go on . . .

Well, Tod changed everything, but only in the way that he was helping me to become more me, if that makes sense. I resisted at first, because I knew that in that other culture in which I could give life at twelve, he could be my father, but I just felt drawn to him like a planet circling the sun. And that time when we lay in bed and he held me, soft, gentle, and mollifying. He stared into me with his emerald and earthy eyes, the whites always a little bloodshot, alternating between understanding clarity and the piercing glare of an omniscient being. His hand extended as he pulled away gently, the pinky and ring fingers curled back to himself like the statues of the saints in all of those interminable museums Ed used to drag me to. And his hand reached my face, eyes fixed on mine, fingers tracing the curve of my brow and cheek as he painted a silent nimbus about my head. And he looked to the side, as though he saw something important in me for the first time, and said, *Did you know that you have a tiny little birthmark right here on your cheek that disappears when you smile, as though it wants to hide?* And I knew that I loved him. And I gave myself to him that night though every part of my being screamed against it, knew that it was some kind of sacrilege, though of what kind I could not imagine.

And those seven months were another kind of grace. Through Mother Nature and a man who could be my father I was going to enter into the great cycle of being. You can never know what it feels like, to be a vessel so laden down with your own being, to feel the weight of my baby and me lying in bed, glorying in the sheer dimensions of my expanding self that was no longer myself. I stroked my belly endlessly, telling her of her future, telling her of all the beauty that I would be able to show her when she joined her father and me in this wild and wondrous world. My own father hated it, but the die was cast, as Ed would say, wherever he got that phrase, so he skulked around, giving Tod a hard time every time he came to visit. But it just didn't matter anymore. He didn't matter, and he knew it, and it drove him a little insane. It was almost worth it just for that.

When we lost Eternity, I was seven months along, just like I thought my mom was when I was born. That was the story I always heard, anyway, so as I went into labor, I thought she might be just like me, just dying to be born. But she wasn't dying; she was already dead, and had been for a while, they said, but I never knew exactly how long. I had been talking to a dead thing for weeks, it seemed, so she might not have heard all the joyous things I was promising. My poor little girl. Never even time to learn what she lost.

I was a little hysterical, they told me later, and they had to sedate me while they cleaned her little lavender face and body to let me hold her, to caress her just one time in her little wee wrap, so impossibly, impossibly soft. If I could have had Felicia's camera to freeze time forever there, rather than the regular camera they used, I would have gladly given my life to become one with art, and I remembered that passage from Yeats that we read in class:

> *Consume my heart away; sick with desire*
> *And fastened to a dying animal*
> *It knows not what it is; and gather me*

Into the artifice of eternity.

And then I knew what her name was, and I started to weep hysterically again. After we buried her the next day, I started to wonder why God had punished me. Why would he grant the one thing I dreamt of so intensely for so long, only to take it away? I remember learning in CCD classes that the reason we suffer is because God had to give us the gift of free will so that we could appreciate our salvation. But as I looked down into my beautiful girl's innocent face, I could not imagine a deity who would want to see his children suffer. I would gladly have taken away her free will to protect her from her fate. I would gladly have given up my own.

When Tod told me that we were called to be on different paths, I could not help but see the logic of his reasoning. Whatever God it was that killed my girl, beneficent or malign, had clearly marked us because of some transgression. And so I waited. And when Ed came back to me, I knew that I had a chance for redemption. We had always loved each other, even if he did not love life the way I did, even if, in fact, he seemed hell-bent on embracing death, and I thought that our different ways of thinking might come together to produce something wonderful. And so we did come together under the decay and old gaslight fittings of a factory burning down around us, a fire that we didn't even know about. And then he went away for a while, out of a sense of loyalty to the fallen, I suppose, but that was okay, because I knew immediately that I was pregnant again. I could just sense it. Eternity had come back, and this time, I would be whole.

And so Tod returned, eyes blazing like he had been to the mountaintop and had had a vision, with the other half of his head shaven so that he was completely bald. He said he liked the "streamlined look" that would help guide his vision into the future. It scared me a little, especially after we had just gone through all that horror with the people with no hair. Tod said that I was being silly and swore that he saw no connection between the two. He needed a radical baptism for his mistakes, he said, and there was not enough water to symbolize his rebirth. Perhaps he is right, but I can't help but feel that maybe God was protecting Eternity from some hidden force that even Tod did not understand.

And so the days went on, and Ed started to be part of my life again, even though he was starting to get fired up about all that union business with Joanie—you might have heard about some of the unrest in the papers. He even came around the house when my dad wasn't there, and we started to smile again in the spaces that our friends had left behind. And perhaps that simple kindness is why I have to do what I have to do. But maybe not. Maybe I would have found out another way.

Found out what, exactly?

The one thing I never should have known. As I entered my third month, I was starting to show, but my mother couldn't tell, because I always like to wear beautiful, loose dresses that allow me to move and feel my body swimming underneath, like I have a secret to hide from the world. Or maybe Momma was used to poor Angela, and she couldn't see my weight gain for what it was. Or maybe her conscious mind just didn't want to know, so she deliberately did not see it. And maybe that trait, too, is my birthright, which is why I am being punished for my sins.

Which sins, exactly?

The sin of—Father, is it a sin if you did not really know what you were doing?

That depends on your confession and hope for redemption.

Well, my mother noticed Ed and my closeness, and apparently, she got nervous. It was July 19th. I'll never forget, because the president was just announcing his "Don't Ask, Don't Tell" policy about gays in the military, and I couldn't help feeling later like God might be good or evil, but he sure loves a sense of irony. My mom took me outside, and we gently rocked on the swing on the back patio area. She needed to tell me something she was hoping she would never have to, because it was just easier not to know the truth for everyone involved.

Twenty-one years ago, my mother had had an affair. Her

husband, Glen, had been abusive, just like her father had been with her. She did not consciously set out to find these men, but there seemed to be some magnetic pull that drew them to her, she thought. She just assumed, as her mother assured her, that all men were that way, one way or another, so she had to put up with it. And it wasn't like she could get a divorce, anyway. She had run off to a friend's house three times, but still ended up right back with him, because, she said, no one understood him the way she did. After the third time, she knew she needed some kind of revenge, although she wouldn't use that word. "Revision," she preferred. She wanted to own some piece of herself that he could not get to, so she had an affair with his brother, Teddy, one night when he was too drunk to care. For my mom, it was a one-time affair, and she just wanted to hold onto that secret knowledge, to have that private transgression that he did not own. But when Teddy sobered up, he suddenly did care. The old guilt kicked in, and he felt that he had to confess to his brother. At least that's what Mom thinks happened, because the next night is when the two of them drove into the Lehigh River. Teddy was stone sober, but Glen's blood alcohol level was over .20. They were both dead within minutes, trapped by the weight that dragged them both down.

Was it an accident? She doesn't know. Did Teddy confess and did Glen want to destroy them both? No one knows. No one can ever know, although the possibility destroyed my mother. She spent the next two months in a haze of alcohol and what comforts she could find in her husband's friend, Richie. They were married less than two months later. What's the line from *Hamlet* about "funeral baked meats"? And so the miracle baby comes along at seven months, three days, and everyone is so delighted when I jump out like Athena, fully formed, that no one bothers to do the math.

What exactly are you confessing, my child?

. . .

I'm sorry, I'm sorry. I've been a little . . . teary . . . the last few days . . . Oh, Father Anteil, I know that I have not been a good

Catholic. I know that I've had premarital sex with two men; I know that I have not been keeping the sacraments. But I don't even know what to confess. How do you make orders of sin? How can you tell which is worse? . . .

Please go on.

My mother has no way of knowing, but what if I was not premature? What if my father . . . What if my father was actually Teddy? . . . Don't you see what that makes Ed? . . . .

But, no. You can't be absolutely sure.

No! And it isn't right not to know. If my dad really is my dad, then everything is fine. Then God has forgiven me for whatever I did to Eternity. But if my dad is not my dad, which would make other horrors slightly less so—but if my father is actually Ed's, then I cannot allow . . . I'm sorry, I'm sorry again. I'm running out of tissues. Hold on . . .

Do you wish to make an Act of Contrition for your fornications? For your premarital relations?

No, no. I need you to forgive me for what I have to do . . .

. . .

I'm sorry, my child. No. No, no. That is not possible.

Why not, Father? I can't know. No one can. Nothing is certain, except that I cannot allow an abomination to come into this world. I have sinned too much already. I must have. Look at what I've been through. Can't you see it in your heart to forgive me? Ed never knew, and he still does not know, even now that I am three months along. No one ever has to know.

You don't understand. Ester, please try to understand. Such forgiveness is not in my control. No one can be forgiven for a premeditated mortal sin. Canonic law clearly states that anyone who seeks a successful abortion receives an automatic excommunication. Latae sententiae. Do you understand? You would be forever outside the house of the Lord. This would apply to you and whomever you could convince to let you do it. It is nothing personal. It's the letter of the law.

But, Father, how can God judge me when I don't have all the

knowledge I need? There has to be some possibility of redemption, doesn't there? God can't want a child of incest born, can he?

. . .

Well, now, it is not exactly approved, but if you look closely, there is actually a lot of evidence in the Bible that consanguineous relation-ships were in fact very common in the ancient world, which actually preferred endogamy, or marriage within the family structure. First cousins were ideal, but there are other examples. Lot had relations with both of his daughters, right after God killed the true sinners in Sodom and Gomorrah. Moses's mother was his father's aunt. Even the great patriarch, Abraham, was half-brother to his sister, Sarah. There are lots of examples . . . No, really! I mean, think about it. If you go back far enough, we are all descended from Adam and Eve . . . There is no outside to our blood relations.

I . . . I . . .

I'm sorry, Ester, but you cannot undo what you and Ed have done without losing God forever. Do you understand? . . . Do you want to ask forgiveness for your other sins? . . . Do you? . . . Yes? . . . I will take that as a yes.

God the Father of mercies, through the death and resurrection of your son, you have reconciled the world to yourself and sent the Holy Spirit among us for the forgiveness of sins. Through the ministry of the church, may God grant you pardon and peace. And I absolve you of your sins, in the name of the Father, and of the Son and of the Holy Spirit. Amen.

At dawn, Ester walked into her bathroom and got ready for the day. She showered slowly, sitting cross-legged on the floor of the tub until the steam gave the entire room the air of floating in the midst of a cloud. She did not wipe the haze from the mirror, and she stared down the entire time. She brushed her teeth, fixed her hair, and put on just a dab of perfume scented like lavender. After she was ready, she locked the door and laid on the floor of the bathroom. She curled on her side, pulling her legs up close to her chest, cradling her stomach with gentle ministrations. The world continued to turn outside, indomitable and indifferent, while she started to whisper to her little bit of eternity, who would not be there by the end of the day, all the things that she would have to miss—all the beauty in Nature's world that Ester would never be able to share with her little girl. And why.

CHAPTER SIX

Battling Union, Greif Threatens To Close 2 Plants
August 17, 1993 | by MICHAEL HERNAN, *The Morning Call*

Apparel maker Greif Cos., setting the stage for a nasty union contract battle, has threatened to close manufacturing plants in Shippensburg, Cumberland County, and Virginia if workers don't agree to concessions.

The Hanover Township, Lehigh County maker of men's suits told workers earlier this month that the Shippensburg and Verona, Va., plants, which employ a total of 950 people, may close if workers don't agree to wage and benefits cuts as part of a new three-year contract.

The contract would also apply to the Hanover Township plant, which has about 700 workers. However, Greif has no plans to close that plant.

The Amalgamated Clothing and Textile Workers Union fired back yesterday, calling for a national boycott of shoes made by Greif's Nashville parent, Genesco Inc., and vowing to win what a union official said is shaping up to be a "tough fight."

The union's current three-year deal expires on Sept. 30. The two sides met for the first time last week.

Greif, which in the past has bargained with the union as part of a big industry group, this year decided to negotiate a separate contract.

"Neither one of us (the union or the company) would like to close any factories but we have to be competitive . . . and we need to come to terms that would allow us to do that," said Nathan Freeman, Greif's president.

"We're going to keep negotiating in good faith," he said. "At this point there isn't anything that is a *fait accompli*."

Freeman said competition from foreign apparel companies has cut profit margins and forced Greif to scale back production and trim its work force. Over the past two years, Greif has reduced employment by about 15 percent.

Though those moves have helped shore up Greif's finances, he said, the company still needs to find more ways to keep costs down.

"It's a step to make ourselves more competitive," Freeman said. "We're in a global business now and some of the domestic companies haven't done that well. We need a product that we can offer at the right price and to do that we need lower costs."

Michael Zucker, a spokesman for the Amalgamated Clothing and Textile Workers Union, said Greif has asked for "a minimum 20 percent cut in wages and benefits."

Freeman wouldn't disclose details of the company's offer.

CHAPTER SEVEN

"*Fait accompli,*" Stan spat. "Of course he's using Latin to fuck us in the ass. I'm surprised he didn't use Greek."

"Dad," said Joanie.

"I'm sorry, little girl. He makes me mad enough to kick babies."

"Oh, Jesus. Take it down a notch. Its rhetoric, and you know it."

Stan threw the paper to the side of the kitchen table and put his head in his hands. "It's just words to keep sixteen hundred people in a constant state of fear? And all their families? And the entire community that depends on them?"

"It's exactly words. And that's the battle we need to win."

"*Twenty percent?* That's Nate's 'good faith'? Why not just require us to go back to twelve-hour days for ten-year-olds? Sure would help the goddamn profit margin. Can't just have a shit ton of money, can they? It's got to be *all* the fucking money."

Joanie backed off. She knew her father knew how she felt, but she also knew how he liked to wage the war in his head with anyone who happened to be nearby, even people who agreed with him. She shared his passion, but she also wanted to pick her battles to be as effective as she could be when the time came. Although her father loved his job, he carried the responsibility for those seven hundred workers in his plant too fully on his back, as though a failure on his part would get them tossed out onto the streets.

"Oh, and just so you know," she said, "Ed's on for the boycott march if it comes to that."

"Really?" said Stan, derailed. "I never would've thought. I guess guilt sure goes a long way."

"Guilt? No, that's not it. At least not anymore, I don't think. He's not against the union. He's just a little scared of crowds."

"He fears the people?"

"I'm sure there's a word for it. Can you be 'demophobic'?"

Stan looked at her and started to laugh. "Oh, that's just great. 'Look for the union label, by yourself, over there, if you don't mind.'" He leaned back in his creaking kitchen chair. "A few more demophobes on our team, and we'll be in a right fucking mess."

In the coming weeks, contract negotiations intensified. The actual terms were not exactly twenty percent, which was leaked to the press largely to scare the workers and to make the offer look better. But it wasn't good. Greif wanted a cut in their two weeks' vacation time, a huge contribution to their health coverage, and a three-year wage freeze. This amounted to about a fifteen percent cut, but it sounded better spread out among the three benefits. Rhetoric, Joanie thought. If the workers did not agree, Greif threatened they'd close all three plants and ship the work to a non-union factory. Some of the workers were beginning to dissent. They were scared of unemployment and were willing to take scraps, if that meant that they could keep their houses on a shoestring budget. Aaron Blumenfeld, the union rep, thought that they were bluffing, and he organized a nationwide boycott of Greif's spring clothing line. He would show the bosses that they were not powerless. Of course, thought Joanie, if he's successful, they'll all be out of jobs anyway. Work slowdowns and strikes were fine, but she did not see the logic of decimating the demand for the product that your job depended upon, which seemed to her like a snake eating its own tail. But Joanie was just a public relations representative, and she had to listen to the union leadership.

Greif suits were largely higher-end brands like Perry Ellis, Ralph Lauren, and Kilgour, French & Stanbury. Most people had no idea that they were largely the same suits, made in the same factory, just under different covers and slightly different materials. Few of the workers could afford to buy any of their own suits, unless they bought an irregular from the outlet. The boycott targeted Macy's and Today's Man, which were their largest retailers.

On Saturday, September 11, the workers began the first round of the boycott. The morning paper galvanized them with a story about Jake Edgman, the Amalgamated Clothing and Textile Workers Union president, who proposed that the union hire consultants to help cut costs in other ways in the factory—an offer management roundly rejected. Edgman hardlined it, saying that the union expected "raises and improvements to our benefits, not cuts." The workers were very excited by the tough talk, although Ed pondered if always expecting more for the workers was much different from the logic of the corporate brass, and he wondered how much of that was rhetoric, too. Growth as an end in itself was the logic of cancer, Joanie had said. Did they really expect more all the time? What would happen if there were zero growth for a while—a kind of steady state economy that would reach an equilibrium that maximized the quality of life for everyone? Was that even possible?

The ACTWU coordinated protesters from all union membership at all twenty Today's Man stores in the five-state region. Ed, Joanie, and Stan met at the Whitehall Square Mall store with four other union members. They all wore royal blue T-shirts with the slogan, "We're fighting for our future" written across the front, a refrain that gave Ed a strange sense of déjà vu from his Spring Garden College days. "Let the Garden Grow" had been their chant when they demanded action from the president, and that had not turned out so great for anyone involved, although their protests could hardly be called organized. Ed felt uncomfortable being in someone else's uniform, and he thought his tendrils of black hair dangling over his eye looked a little ridiculous with the bright blue shirt. But he agreed out of loyalty to Stan and Joanie. Pamphleteering was not Ed's forte, and for the first half of the day he mostly watched alongside Joanie as she approached customers and he handed them fliers saying, "Boycott Greif at Today's Man." Ed had seen a documentary in high school about the Homestead Strike during the early days of the labor movement, and he half expected the Pinkerton Detective Agency to roll up at the behest of Greif and gun them all down. Most of the people he and Joanie talked to, however, were sympathetic to their cause and identified with the plight of their fellow local residents. Bob Wittman from the *Morning Call* came by at Joanie's request, interviewed the protesters, and wrote a fairly even-handed piece the next morning. Even the manager gave them a slight wave as he looked out the window.

That night, sitting in his drywalled cube at Tod's house, Ed went over the details of the day. The protest was far from glamorous, and by the end of nine hours, he realized that he had not spent more than five minutes thinking about his mother or anything else but the cause. Talking with people he otherwise never would have come into contact with almost made him want to paint again for the first time in years, and he wondered what exactly motivated that desire. The protest did not have the strange erotic allure of the Kinfolk's dreaming, but Ed was finding a different kind of feeling which he had no words yet to describe.

As the month flew by and the multiple boycotts they raised at Macy's and Wanamaker's failed to get one store chain to cancel an order, union members were beginning to panic. Management refused to budge on anything, and Freeman kept dropping the word "NAFTA" whenever things got too heated. The second Today's Man protest brought two hundred protesters. The shouts were not nearly as amicable this time and led to the police being called after the manager was not available. Even if she had been, she had no power to effect change in anything, since the corporate offices in another state made all buying decisions. Ed had never come so close to the feeling that he might be arrested and he was terrified at being asked to put his freedom on the line, even though he was ashamed to think back to everything that people in the labor movement had given up for the last hundred years, including their lives.

At the last minute, the union and management reached a deal with a contract only eighteen months long, rather than their usual three years. Both sides crowed to the *Morning Call* that they got exactly what they wanted. Joanie noted that management could claim that they were never wedded to the original offer, making them sound magnanimous to the general public. The union's field director claimed that by digging in, the union "won respect from the company," a point that no one in the union office really believed. A small notice buried within a larger paragraph pointed out that management agreed to the concessions only after the union okayed subcontracting jobs out to non-union factories, which the management swore they would not abuse. The only way to save the union was to be disunited. Joanie knew the difference between a paradox and a contradiction, although her father was so relieved at the new contract that she did not want to tell him.

CHAPTER EIGHT

"I have to say," Kevin said, "I find Tod's shaved head to be even more disturbing than the half Jesus."

Ed sighed, thinking of his mother and looking at the pages of *Gulliver's Travels* on the wall at Origen's. *Shnuwnh.* "I know. Before, I always thought there was a kind of ironic performance to the whole thing. Now he seems committed on a more fundamental level."

Neither are any wars so furious and bloody, or of so long a continuance, as those occasioned by difference in opinion, especially if it be in things indifferent.

"Let me ask you, honestly," said Ed. "Do you believe in Harmonic Energies?"

"In principle, or in Tod's principle?"

"Pick your poison."

"In principle, no. There's no harmony in the universe. Life's a big shitstorm of chaos and power, if you ask me. The ones who harness the power rule the chaos. Nothing harmonic in that, unless you get off on being oppressed."

"I've seen that porn," said Ed.

"No, you haven't. Trust me, your little Catholic head would explode with some Japanese shokushu goukan. I did a whole project on Hokusai's 'The Dream of the Fisherman's Wife.' Now, that shit will mess you up."

"I don't even want to know."

"Nope, you do not."

"Okay, so Tod's principle?"

"I don't know. Obviously, all this marketing rhetoric makes my balls want to crawl up back inside my body. Any time I hear someone talking about *paradigm shifts* or *thinking outside the box*, I think that somewhere, somehow, Jesus is being crucified again."

Ed smiled. He missed Kevin's committed irreverence. Even when they disagreed, Kevin somehow made him laugh about it.

"But then again," said Kevin, "it seems like there are worse things you can do with your time than starting a consulting firm to help people with conflict resolution."

"But this isn't one of your dad's couples therapy sessions. Tod's setting his sights way higher than that. 'Corporate Conflict Resolutions' sounds good on the adverts you are doing, but why set the sights on such empyrean heights?"

"The way he puts it," said Kevin, "is that this is the direction of our culture. We're heading faster and faster toward a corporatocracy. People are getting dispossessed and disaffected, and that's leading to things like the Compton brothers wanting to join up with a bunch of neo-Nazi assholes. Since this is inevitable, we have one of two ways of dealing with it. Complaining about it will just push the sides into more adversarial positions—"

"Thus bringing the apocalypse."

"Correctamundo. Or, we can try to come to a harmonious relationship with our new corporate overlords. The first way leads to *Blade Runner* and *A Clockwork Orange*, the second way is—slightly more hopeful."

"Do you buy that?"

"Oh, Lord, no. I'm an artist. Corporate CEOs and middle managers are somewhere down below Pol Pot in my moral universe, but that's *de rigueur* for my ilk. In your Dantean terms, they'll have to timeshare the circles in a rotation; they somehow manage to cover all seven of the deadly sins."

"All except for 'wrath.'"

"Maybe not in this country. Ask Latin America how they feel."

Ed frowned. "Point taken."

Kevin added another packet of sugar to his coffee, stirring.

"I miss you being around the house more often," said Kevin. "Seems like you're spending all your time with that union stuff and come back only to crash."

"It's probably just as well. Tod's getting pretty intense these days. To be honest, I'm not sure how you can work for him and his vision if you disagree with him so much."

"Ah," said Kevin. "Easter eggs and anamorphosis."

"That should be the title of Eva's next CD. And what, pray tell, are those?"

Kevin pulled out his sketchbook and showed Ed a mock-up of his last project, a full-page poster design that he had used for the shareholder meeting with the Pennsylvania Power & Light board of directors. The poster showed the PP&L building surrounded by a kind of Art Deco nimbus, the rays emanating from the building in a strange, crossed pattern. On the top of the building, shareholders and managers stood beaming as brightly as the rays from the building, all mixed together and unified. Ed had to admit, it all looked energetic and visionary.

"Nicely done. So, what's the anamorphosis?"

"Tilt the sketchbook to the right and look again."

Once Ed did so, turning the book on a forty-five-degree angle away from him, the rays actually spelled out a block letter message: *SKYSCRAPERS ARE THE DEVIL'S DICKS.* Ed burst out laughing. "How in hell did you get this past Tod?"

"He didn't see it, of course. People rarely look beyond what they're supposed to. I got the idea when I did the ersatz Holbein painting." He flipped to the copy of the Holbein painting he had pasted into his notebook during the snowstorm. "Ever notice the big blob in the foreground of all those worldly accoutrements?" He said this last in a mock French accent. He tilted the book, and Ed saw the skull for the first time. "A little memento mori to get your day going?"

"So, this is how you live with yourself, doing the devil's work?"

Ed mocked, flipping through Kevin's impressive sketchpad.

"Hey, Ed. Don't judge. You still live there, too. At least I can do my own work in my downtime. Sometimes you have to go down on Lucifer a little to get what you want. Sure, it might just be drawing a mustache on an image of the thug who's got his jackboot on your neck, but at least it feels good for a while."

Ed kept flipping and stopped at one image: a reproduction of the Greif symbol that looked just like the one at Adelaide Mills. "What's this?"

"Oh, Tod had me do that prototype when I was staying with you guys. He wanted a big one to hang in the performance space during the shit happens-ing. I figured he dug the griffin imagery because of his name. Egomaniac. He paid me for it, and I guess it auditioned me for the job."

A little farther back, Ed saw the sketch for Eva's second CD, which had come out the previous month. "Have you heard from Eva?" he asked.

Kevin told him about Eva's tour in support of "Cautiously Pessimistic." She was getting terrific reviews, the biggest one being a short blurb in *Rolling Stone*. "In the Country of Last Things" was charting in *Billboard*, so she was starting to tour small theaters throughout the East Coast. Ed could not believe that he actually knew someone who was successful at what she did. It seemed that so many of his friends and contemporaries in Generation X, as the media was calling them, were floundering, even those with college degrees. Serge and Tim were both working at a temp agency, doing itinerant filing and photocopying for anyone with a real job who could not make it that day. When Ed had seen them last, it had looked like they were back to their old habits. Felicia had moved back in with her parents and was taking time to find herself, she said. He hadn't heard from Ester in weeks since she quit her job at the Crisis Pregnancy Center. Lavinia had gone back to model-ing, but with a new twist. After the surgery, she decided not to have her teeth fixed or get dentures. Her mouth was permanently twisted in a rictus of jagged dental shards and black spaces in between. She saw it as her new self, as natural as her body had been to her before, and painters and photographers of a certain stripe paid well for her image.

CHAPTER NINE

Bill Clinton smiled from the television in a khaki suit and blue polka-dot tie. To Ed, he looked very pleased with himself. To Stan, he looked like the devil.

Today we have the chance to do what our parents did before us. We have the opportunity to remake the world. For this new era, our national security we now know will be determined as much by our ability to pull down foreign trade barriers as by our ability to breach distant ramparts.

"I don't know," said Stan. "Seems like that Ramzi Yousef was able to breach our distant ramparts pretty easily."

Twice before in this century, we have been forced to define our role in the world. After World War I we turned inward, building walls of protectionism around our Nation. The result was a Great Depression and ultimately another horrible World War. After the Second World War, we took a different course: We reached outward. Gifted leaders of both political parties built a new order based on collective security and expanded trade. They created a foundation of stability and created in the process the conditions which led to the explosion of the great American middle class, one of the true economic miracles in the whole history of civilization. Their statecraft stands to this day: the IMF and the World Bank, GATT, and NATO.

"Are you kidding me?" Stan shouted at the television. "What kind of history is this? The Great Depression was caused by *protectionism?*"

Some depressions might be, thought Ed.

"Well, there was Smoot–Hawley, dad. Not so great to the farmers."

"That was 1930, a *reaction* to the depression, not the cause. And it was the goddamn unions that gave us a middle class, not better trade."

"Dad," said Joanie.

"I'm sorry, little girl. But this is the best we got? If we had Harkin or Tsongas, this smug little neoliberal wouldn't be driving us off the cliff. Even Moonbeam Brown would've been better than this guy."

"The people just didn't give them the votes, dad. One hundred and two Democrats voted for NAFTA. They chose this world."

Stan grunted, listening again.

The cold war is over. The grim certitude of the contest with communism has been replaced by the exuberant uncertainty of international economic competition. And the great question of this day is how to ensure security for our people at a time when change is the only *constant.*

Ed thought back to Ester's claim that change was always good, and he could not help wondering if that was correct. Weren't some things worth preserving? Did we always need revisions and revolutions?

We cannot stop global change. We cannot repeal the international economic competition that is everywhere. We can only *harness the energy to our benefit. Now we must recognize that the* only *way for a wealthy nation to grow richer is to export, to simply find new customers for the products and services it makes.*

Stan started to shout at the television again, so Ed got up to go to the bathroom. He really liked Stan, but the shouting reminded him of being around Richie, and that level of passion made him nervous, even when he agreed with the person. He so much preferred feeling the way he did with the Kinfolk, and he felt a deep sense of nostalgia for that sense of coming together into a union outside of time. All of this constant analysis, all of this *history*, just felt so pointless. The ones in control always have been and always would be, he thought. Why bother trying to fight them? He had to find his peace outside that power. He also missed his intimacy with Ester, and it still hurt that she never would tell him what went wrong.

"Oh, Ed, you missed a good one," said Stan. "He just thanked Mickey Kantor for his 'laborious effort.' *Laborious*. Like that free trading Judas ever gave two shits about labor in this country. You can't get more tone deaf than that."

Clinton was still talking.

My fellow Americans, bit by bit all these things are creating the conditions of a sustained global expansion. As significant as they are, our goals must be more ambitious. The United States must seek nothing less than a new trading system that benefits all nations through robust commerce but that protects our middle class and gives other nations a chance to grow one, that lifts workers and the environment up without dragging people down, that seeks to ensure that our policies reflect our values.

Our agenda must, therefore, be far reaching. We are determining that dynamic trade cannot lead to environmental despoliation. We will seek new institutional arrangements to ensure that trade leaves the world cleaner than before. We will press for workers in all countries to secure rights that we now take for granted, to organize and earn a decent living. We will insist that expanded trade be fair to our businesses and to our regions.

"Oh, for chrissakes, turn it off. I can't listen to this anymore."

Joanie turned off the TV, and she and Ed went to her room.

"The die is cast," said Ed.

Joanie made a guttural sound. "God, I hate that phrase. Such wise fatalism for such a young boy."

"Hey! You're only three years older than me."

"People seem to forget that Julius Caesar completely defied the senate and the will of the people when he took his people into a horrifying war. Just because he won doesn't make what he did any less reprehensible from the point of view of democracy. He attacked the state, for heaven's sake, and helped start the whole godforsaken Roman Empire."

"History's written by the winners."

"Another cliché, spoken like an inevitability. Well done, Yoda. Yes, those in power manipulate the world and how we interpret it. It doesn't mean that it is just."

"Jesus, I'm sorry."

She sighed, sitting on the edge of her bed. "No, I'm sorry. This has been tough, Ed. Dad's unraveling, you can see that. He knows how bad this is for labor. Clinton's people have completely sold out the unions, and the Secretary of Labor, Robert Reich, speaking of fatalists, has been in bed with the free traders for years, thinking it was inevitable. These people have a theory, and they are undoing over a hundred years of labor history and selling out the promise of America we worked so hard to achieve. And they are betting all of our lives that it will work out in the end. Reich will be rationalizing this for the rest of his life."

Ed looked over at Joanie's computer, thinking of something Kevin had told him earlier. "Isn't it possible it will work out?"

"How so?"

"I don't know. Maybe this is a good thing for American workers. Let's face it, factory work is hard and boring. Maybe we'll have more time to focus on things like technology and creativity. Kevin uses the computer programs Photoshop and Illustrator to make these really interesting designs, and he was showing me something the other day called MOSAIC that blew my mind. It's called a 'web browser.' You use your computer and modem, but there are all these images and information. Even Central Catholic, my old high school, has a web site. Maybe the future is there, in the new technologies."

Joanie sighed. "Ed, do you know what a normal curve is?"

"The bell curve?"

"Yes. You went to that gifted school, so your IQ was at least 130. Nice for you. What really smart people seem to forget is that fifty percent of people have an IQ below 100. Are you going to be a mechanical engineer with an IQ of 90?"

"That's a little condescending, isn't it?"

"How so? That's realistic. I don't look down on the average person like you do. No amount of education is going to make that person the next Stephen Hawking or Bill Gates. That's just genetics. Don't think on the individual level. That's the first error of every bad philosopher and mystic charlatan, like your buddy, Tod. Think on the level of society. You're the president. The triumph of NAFTA and the rise of global free trade sets up the domino line that will eventually offshore all the manufacturing jobs in America because we're too fancy to do boring jobs. What are you going to do with all of those people when there are no jobs left that they can do, when it becomes cost effective to have child labor in Indonesian sweatshops making our things like it's the nineteenth century again, because Indonesia is the virtual equivalent of going South back then? You know, there are *moral* reasons why we should only support countries that have our environmental and labor standards. And what's going to happen to a working person's sense of self-worth, which someone like my dad has now, when he's bagging groceries at Food Lane at seventy years old because he has no way to retire? What is America going to look like thirty years from now?"

Ed had no answer, and he felt miserable that he had somehow started this conversation in the first place. Passionate people who had causes were exciting, but exhausting. He was hopeful that at least Tod's latest project would help Stan and the other workers feel better about the company and the contract they ended up with. Tod was right about one thing, he thought. Despite what Joanie said, that die was cast, and they might as well feel better about it.

CHAPTER TEN

Philos walked into the back room with a travel mug of coffee, his Eastpak slung across one shoulder. He greeted Ed, who gestured for Philos to join him. They exchanged Happy New Year's Eve greetings.

"How goes the book?" Ed asked.

"Almost finished," said Philos. "I'm heading on this evening. Ruth's already back in Toronto."

"Know where you're going, yet?"

"Oh, yes," Philos replied in his old cryptic way.

"Any spaces I should know about?"

"Tons. You really should get around some, Ed. Every city is a collection of fascinations that people have forgotten to see. Trout Hall is a gorgeous Georgian that goes back to the eighteenth century; it was just the summer home of the grandson of the founder of Allentown, and it is remarkable. The Neuweiler Brewery is so iconic—you'd know it if you saw it—although someone's running a pesticide company out of it now, which seems like a downgrade to me. Symphony Hall was pretty spectacular. That one goes back a hundred years. Teddy Roosevelt and Booker T. Washington gave speeches there; the Marx brothers performed there; even Sarah Bernhardt performed. The backstage folks had a ton of old promotional materials from the vaudeville and minstrel show days that'll give you chills."

"Jeez," said Ed. "And here I thought that Allentown was just my depressed little ol' hometown."

"History is everywhere, Ed. It is the air you breathe. It makes up your DNA. Most people just never notice it until it is too late."

"Sounds about right."

Philos checked his watch and put the lid on his travel mug. "I'm actually heading over to the old Hess building downtown to take a look before the grand opening of the new rooftop deck. A guy I know is going to give me a tour. I hear Tod is doing his first big gig there between Greif and the union. Care to join me to check it out first?"

CHAPTER ELEVEN

Some buildings carry history. Some buildings are part of history. Some buildings are masterworks of literature, every word planned and programmed down to the last semicolon. Some buildings are strips of newspaper type, tossed up and taped down in random configurations like a William Burroughs cut-up poem. Most buildings try to be masterworks but end up needing heavy revisions as time goes on and the gaping holes become evident. The Hess Brothers building was the text of America. The history of the rise and transformation of American entrepreneurialism could be seen for those who had eyes to see.

"It doesn't look that spectacular from the outside," said Ed. "Just your basic 1930s Art Moderne architecture."

True, said Philos, but look at your average person on the street. That woman over there. If you were to describe her in a novel, you'd be hard pressed to find the right adjectives. Most of us don't get dressed up for a South Street gothic parade. Most of us don't wear easy-to-interpret cultural signifiers like Manolo Blahniks or Chuck Taylors to give away some aspect of who we are, where the outside reveals the inside. The most you could say about that woman is that she is Hispanic, and she is wearing a brownish dress. And yet you know there's a history there. You know that she's been through things that you can't even imagine. Probably has a vocabulary that you could not even interpret—and I don't mean Spanish. The average building, too, is not usually such an iconic, ostentatious display as the PP&L building over there. In fact, there's a theory of architecture that suggests that the best architecture is the kind that blends in with the rest of the neighborhood organically, like an unassuming realist short story. Perhaps.

Hess's is not quite that realist narrative. In fact, the building you see now is really a facade of Indiana limestone added later to give it the illusion of being one thing, which, I suppose, suggests something else about the history of American entrepreneurialism as well. The original building, surrounded by nothing but a Hersh Hardware store and the lumberyards that would eventually help to construct this part of town, was built at 835 Hamilton Street in 1868 as the Black Bear Hotel, run by a bunch of white guys with thick handlebar mustaches, so I'm guessing that the potential Native American symbolism was inadvertent. The most logical reason for the name was that they wanted it to sound like some badass wild animal, but I like to think of the fact that the bear was the oldest worshiped deity in the world, perhaps going back to the Paleolithic period. They've found an original cave bear skull which had its own femurs stuck through its eye sockets, probably to ward off the evil eye. Seems like a nicely symbolic place to start our narrative. Of course, this was America, the land of lighting out for the territories and rechristening yourself whenever you've screwed up too much back home, so by 1890, perhaps to get past the butch patriarchal bluster, they were already rebranding the Black Bear Hotel to become the *Grand Central Hotel*. By an act of naming, they pulled the lines of force right around themselves. This was Allentown's Centrality, the vortex around which everything else would now define itself. And for the next one hundred years, that is pretty close to the truth.

In 1896, a thirty-two-year-old Jewish peddler from Perth Amboy, New Jersey with a slight hunchback, named Max Hess, attended a volunteer firefighter's convention in Easton, and he decided to follow up with a trip to Allentown, walking down this undeveloped part of Hamilton Street in the rather decidedly non-Jewish part of America occupied by the Pennsylvania

Dutch—not "Dutch" as in from the Netherlands, mind you, but Dutch as in the German word for Germans, the *Deutsch*. Hess had grown up in Germany, and he knew what he was dealing with; let's just say that Hitler didn't invent anti-Semitism. He had the primal vision that this would be the perfect place to offer honest dry goods at an evenhanded rate for a reasonable profit, and he went back to bring his brother Charles along for this endeavor. Charles resisted at first. He wanted to explore the promises of the grander theatrical potential offered in Atlantic City, which was just hitting its boom period, but he finally agreed to go along with his brother and their business partner, Solomon Hoffman. Unpack the symbolism of that name, if you like; it is one of those strange facts of history that reality sometimes writes a novel that is almost too obvious.

In February 1897, the brothers opened their fifty- by-one-hundred-and-twenty-five-foot store, Hess Brothers, in the Grand Central with anything but a small opening. The Allentown Band played John Philip Sousa's "Washington Post March," which was still as popular as when it was first introduced eight years earlier; you'd know it if you heard it. McKinley was in the White House, presiding over the recovery from the Panic of 1893, and people were ready to spend again. Hess knew something about American business even then, and the size of advertising in the local papers was a demand and a promise—you offer us your loyalty, and we will offer an experience that goes beyond what buying a sack of flour would seem to warrant. This was one thing that America did not invent, but certainly perfected—the concept that the perceived value of the thing could outweigh the actual value, and as long as the customer was happy with that mysterious addition, life would seem so much richer in the end—so much more *fun*. It was one thing the Soviets never got, and the Catholic Church certainly did: Spectacle feeds the gaps opened at the limits of civilization. With the massive success of Allentown industrialization in the silk mills, Bethlehem Steel, and Mack trucks, twentieth-century America gave Allentownians more free time, more pocket money, and more estrangement from the agrarian roots of the founding Dutch. When you are not forced to labor your entire adult life, the freedom of the extra time paradoxically limits the freedom of your fantasy life, and something has to fill those holes of meaning. Spectacle goes a long way.

Within two weeks, a large swath of Allentown's 35,000 residents visited the store, which hired a dozen more staff to its twenty-three salesmen, two office workers, window decorator, and night watchman. In three years, at the dawn of the twentieth century, they did what has become the centerpiece of American commerce in our era: They expanded. In 1900, they bought up the second floor and basement, installing an elevator along the way. In two more years, they swallowed the rest of the Grand Central Hotel, and the Hess Brothers department store was born. At the beginning of World War I, they bought up most of the neighboring properties to take up an entire city block. Soon the store employed over eight hundred people and expanded to two, then four hundred thousand square feet in the 1940s. The strange hybridity of the store was both a negative and a bit of its uniqueness. Because Hess Brothers slowly annexed the neighboring stores rather than starting off with one master plan, the store had a kind of hodge-podge quality rather than some grand vision. Adjoining buildings had walls hollowed out to allow customers to flow between them, making the store seem like it stretched for miles, with little grottos and oxbow discoveries to be found throughout the maze. The main showroom housed under its massive ceilings a forest of crystal chandeliers that dazzled the factory, mill, and mine workers with a bit of Manhattan splendor; the other parts of the store hinted at the mysteries that could not be contained in a single orderly plan.

The Hess brothers were as masterful at self-promotion as they were at spectacle. Max was the workhorse, who ran the day-to-day. Charles was a bit of a dandy, to put it mildly, and he channeled that desire for the glamor of Atlantic City into long trips across the pond to scope out the latest fashion trends on the Bois de Boulogne, sending back dispatches of desire that were dutifully published on the front page of the *Morning Call*. The French Room, Charles' creation, was an orgy of effete fantasies coming out of young men in the early twentieth century, and his communiqués from his trips through France read like some gossipy Vogue editor catering to a preposterous notion of beauty that was more a function of words than of the fashions themselves.

In 1922 the fifty-eight-year-old Max Hess, Sr. died suddenly, leaving his wife and son, Max Hess, Jr., suddenly without their ship's captain. The locals were shocked. Hess's department store had helped to put Allentown on the map, it was often asserted, and Max Hess was beloved by most of the community. As a resident of the area, Max Hess and Allentown were intimately symbiotic. They gave him millions, and he gave back a portion of the same, contributing greatly to the prosperity of your burgeoning little ol' hometown. He helped start the Jewish Community Center, the Allentown Public Library, and the first Reformed Jewish Temple, in addition to giving generously to hospitals and local charities. The *Morning Call*'s editorial obituary provided the hagiography: "His life is a romance of American opportunity and achievement. But it is more than that. It is an inspiration to good works. Max Hess performed to the utmost of his ability . . . His life is a model for community builders and Allentown can ill afford his loss." Hess embodied that early American ethos of the *noblesse oblige*, and the people loved him for it. Of course, unlike other nobles of the time like John Rockefeller, John Jacob Astor, and others paying at least mild obeisance to Andrew Carnegie's "Gospel of Wealth," he had the benefit of not having to scrape off his shoes the blood of those he had trod upon to get that money, so he could be so oblige-y. But that's another story.

Unlike some inheritors, Max Jr. synthesized the pragmatic business acumen of his father with the flamboyant theatricality of his uncle. He was the business world's P.T. Barnum, and he helped grow the company into one of the most famous department stores in America. From the time he became president in 1935 until he sold the company for $17 million cash in 1968, Max Jr. helped develop some of the most spectacular consumer experiences in the history of marketing. His merchandising motto was "Be the first, be the best, be entertaining." This drive was partly ambition, but he already was rich, famous, and beloved. It was also because, like his father, he believed in the community, not just as a place to excavate riches, although it was certainly that too. "There's gold downtown, waiting to be dug up," he reportedly said in 1965. "Nothing—absolutely nothing—pays like the heart of a city." He modernized the facade of the building to give it that unified look, adding the iconic eight-ton HESS sign with seven-foot-high letters blazing with 2,250 light bulbs and neon tubing that everyone

flocked to see. The store was known for its annual flower show, where flowers burst onto every free surface in the area and people like Zsa Zsa Gabor introduced the festivities, and its fashion show, where Hess would bring the biggest celebrities at the time to walk through the racks of merchandise and surprise the happy consumers with their auras. George Reeves (the original Superman), Johnny Carson, Rock Hudson, and a seven-year-old child star, Donny Osmond, all thrilled the working-class laborers and farm hands from the local and surrounding areas, and if you talk to any of the seniors around here like I have, they all get unironically misty about the glamor that Hess's brought to the area, which is odd to listen to in our postmodern times. I've heard stories about the year that Santa Claus arrived in a helicopter at Hamilton Street

during the Christmas celebration, while giant electric angels spread across the facade. I love this one: Apparently, Hess would send a fashion caravan with models and other displays to the area farms, factories, and mills because he wanted the local breadwinning men to know what their wives were bringing home, ostensibly, I assume, so that they would be more accommodating of the larger price tags. Nothing like that pre-feminist era thinking, don't you think? Speaking of nostalgia, you should hear the locals talk about the restaurant, the Patio, with its strawberry pie. It seems like everyone in the area either had a confirmation, graduation, or some special event there that might as well have been the witnessing of a UFO or someone being raised from the dead.

And yet it worked, like just about everything else Hess did. He was one of the first to do "clearance sales" to remove stale merchandise from last season. Hess's was the first store in America to import clothes from Russia and Japan, helping to feed the desire not only for the global, but for the "exotic," god help me for saying. But they also had their own shipping and receiving department, so they could send things beyond Allentown if they needed to. And, of course, there were the wily-but-not-so-nefarious tactics. I like this one. One person talked about how Hess used to send employees into competitors' stores, when they had a great sale on an item, with thousands of dollars to buy up all the bargains. Sounds counterintuitive, right? Why give them the business? But if those items were the lure, people would get angry at the store and go elsewhere—like Hess's, where he would just resell the merchandise at a higher rate anyway. There's a genius to that, somehow, that doesn't have the strong-arm tactics of other business leaders, like Bill Gates. At its height, the store's motto seemed hubristic, yet plausible: "You'll find the best of everything at Hess's." I like the way it does not even try to qualify that claim with the ineffable—literature, music, spirituality. No doubt, Hess thought, if it was something important, he would carry the best of it.

And, of course, the text continues. This great novel of America reached its peripeteia in 1968, when Max Hess, Jr. convinced a local developer and art collector, Philip I. Berman, to pay $17 million in cash to buy out his single, well-loved store. They say it took the Federal Reserve three days to drum up that much money in cash. Why exactly he sold the family business is a bit hazy. Did he know that he was sick and was going to die six months later, a year younger than his father? Did he want to leave a legacy to a family he knew was not as interested in developing the store to be the first, the best, and the most entertaining? Did he look at the absurdity of the offer, about $70 million today, realizing that while he loved nothing more than building the business his father and uncle had started into one of the most beloved institutions on the East Coast, he could not refuse cash in hand that outweighed the value of the thing itself? But why did Berman spend such an ungodly amount of money, when he did not seem to care in the least about retail merchandise?

Because Philip Berman had no intention of merely polishing the lovely object he had bought. He had plans for growth way beyond what the Hess brothers had envisioned. And this is one of the things I find most fascinating about their story. Max and Charles grew their business; Max Jr. thought it was enough. After they expanded to the full city block and added an eight-story annex, they concentrated on making the space the best it could be—for themselves, for their employees, and for their customers. You should hear how the people who worked for Hess talk about him—like he had been responsible for getting them out of Egypt. He told *Forbes* magazine in the fifties that he had a principle: "Strive for a specific goal." And unlike modern corporations, that goal was not merely growth as an end in itself to maximize profit. They had enough profit every year, so that was not the issue. There was a kind of steady state economy to the whole endeavor, where Hess realized that any other expansion would dilute what the family had achieved. Even when the suburban malls started to spring up, Hess did not want to expand, because if he did, he would have to cede control to the banks. Hess preferred to be the master of his own contribution to society.

Berman, however, wanted the brand, the name that he could exploit into a massive expansion. He immediately took out the "Brothers" and renamed the brand "Hess's," which is a weird possessive, if you think about it. Most of the older locals still call it Hess Brothers. The Hamilton Street building now was just one store in the empire Berman envisioned, and he had no emotional attachment to it or the community the way the Hesses had. He quickly removed the iconic sign during another downtown redevelopment deal, when he put up these horrid glass canopies that were meant to mimic an indoor mall but only ended up blocking out the light. He canceled the annual flower and fashion shows and the celebrity appearances, which were costly expenses not immediately on the black side of the books. Hess's primary function became expansion—buying up other chains and converting them to Hess's, including a hostile takeover of the Miller's Department Store chain based in Knoxville, Tennessee. Within a few years Berman expanded the brand into the ballooning suburban mall development, helping to bankrupt the local merchants as it spread into a thirty-eight-store multistate chain.

But, of course, that is never the end of such an expansion. In 1979, Allentown received its own imperial marker, Crown American, a developer of hotels and malls which bought Berman's chain unceremoniously and relegated it to a wholly-owned subsidiary of a company that saw the stores as just one of the many other assets it owned, and one which had better turn a massive consistent profit. By 1990, the chain had ballooned to seventy-nine stores, each of which was just one more cog in the grinding expansion of business. Of course, as with every empire before it, it had expanded so thin, like gold to airy thinness beat, that the merest breeze would shatter it. Just last year, the recession pushed them into the red just a little too much, so Crown American sold off forty-three of the stores. Rumor has it that the last thirty stores are about to be sold off, including this one, which is supposed to go to Bon-Ton, another corporate behemoth that oddly enough started with a couple of Jewish dry goods merchants a year after Max and Charles Hess started their little dry goods store. But that's another story. Some people are hopeful that Bon-Ton will save the flagship store, since they've been so successful in expanding their little operation over the last decade or so.

"What do you think?"

"I think that there's a point in every structure where once you've destroyed some aspect of its fundamental core, there's no going back to revise it."

"So where is Tod's event happening?"

"Do you see that giant addition that's been added to the top of the building, incongruously plonked up there like I.M. Pei's Louvre Pyramid? Not much of a realist story's organicism, is it? That's the Rooftop Garden, and that's the last hope for the old Hess Brothers building. It is quite an event that Tod's got planned. I can't imagine the union is too thrilled that they were just told that they were about to be out of a job, but the company's willing to drop so much coin for a symbolic gesture."

"Well, as you say, sometimes the spectacle is worth more than the actual value."

"Perhaps, perhaps."

Philos looked out the window of the café across the street from the Hess building, sipping his coffee while Ed called Ester to see if she wanted to come have a look. He saw two fire engines, the fire chief, and a UGI Corporation van parked a block down at Eighth and Hamilton, all standing in the middle of a cordoned-off area on the north side of the street. The fire chief came in to get a few cups of coffee to go. Philos listened to his conversation with a police officer who sat at the bar.

"Any idea what is going on down there?"

"Yeah, there's a water main break we're trying to get under control."

"Ah, jeez. Any idea what caused it?"

"Too early to be sure. There's been a lot of extreme temperatures lately, and that might be adding to some external corrosion on the pipes. That's usually the way it goes. My bet is that the goddamn Hess building settled against the main after they built that stupid addition up top. The main's old, too. Goes back to the 1950s. We've got to get this thing under control. We got word last night at 1 AM that the East Side and Huckleberry reservoirs dropped two feet in a half hour."

"That's not good?"

"No, not at all. They should be filling overnight."

"How bad?"

"Bad. We might've lost anywhere from three to seven million gallons of water so far. Can't be sure."

The officer whistled. "I don't get it. There's not water all over the streets. They're usually flooded, aren't they?"

"Well, that's part of the problem. This whole damn town is built on limestone, even the bedrock. Most of the state is, but there's a stretch from Allentown to Reading they call the 'Allentown formation,' which is particularly brutal. Unfortunately, limestone is really porous and has these pockets of air all over called 'voids.' Usually, you pour a good foundation wall and you're okay, but if you get any water in there, those voids open up into these crazy sinkholes that just go down and down and down into these measureless caverns. It's kind of like Swiss cheese under all these buildings and, of course, the center city is the highest concentration of known sinkholes. And if we're not seeing three million gallons on the street, that means it's going down. And it's not like these places were built with micropile holes."

"Never heard of 'em."

"Italians came up with it after Mussolini got most of their buildings bombed to hell. Foot-wide holes at least sixty feet into the bedrock with steel rods. They developed it as a way to save their old buildings that were falling apart. Most of the ones around here were built to last, but any more pressure on the foundation …"

"How bad could it be?"

"The whole street could collapse. But we're trying not to let that happen. We'll probably have to shut off the gas and electric for a while on the street."

Philos wondered if that was going to cause any interference with the grand opening that evening. He looked up at the rooftop garden and the thirty-foot-high glass walls that sloped on a sixty-degree angle, reaching towards the heights of the PP&L building across the street. Ed and Philos had been able to finish their tour there, and it was definitely a shock for them both. It was a spectacular addition, he had to admit, even if it did not fit with the Art Moderne facade below it. Perhaps they would eventually tear down the facade and put something else over the base to make it look right. Being in the addition itself was uncanny, as the foliage covered so much of the space that you almost forgot that you were in the middle of a city, except for the Tower Building next door, which reached always higher toward the heavens.

Ed came back from the payphone, looking shaken and confused. He towered above Philos in his black trench coat, his face squinting as though he were still listening to what Ester had to say. "Ester talked with her aunt this afternoon. Her aunt won't tell any details, but she's really upset by this visit she got yesterday from a guy named Philos. Maybe before you go, you should tell me why my mom and my signatures are in your big maroon book."

CHAPTER TWELVE

William Faulkner once wrote, "The past is never dead. It's not even past." Makes the past sound like a ghost haunting an old Mississippi plantation, lingering around, messing with the pots and pans, shouting out random antebellum slurs just to remind you of how guilty you are for the things you have. I wish that's what the past is for me, but we don't choose our fates, any more than we can ever give birth to ourselves. Ever notice that our births can only be described passively? *I was born*, not *I birthed myself.* We spend our lives fighting against the reality that we are all the function of a world and a time chosen for us. Our parents determine our lives the minute our fathers finish with our mothers—bring us into being, whether they wanted us or not. Our fates can only function within what's possible in that field of space and time, and sometimes our parents determine more than that. After my father died, I buried myself. In my work—the work your cousin saw a glimpse of; the work your aunt felt yesterday; the work I knew I had to do from the moment I found out what I wish I never knew. The trajectory of the work was clear, though the scope was not.

My father, Angelo King, was a great man. If we can judge greatness by the scope of one's achievements, he was certainly that. He was personally responsible for saving over ten thousand souls, and how many people can claim that outside of the old Christian missionaries who made deals with the kings of African tribes to convert the whole group, whether they knew it or not? Well, Angelo's convertees knew what they were doing, and they did it willingly. He was the best itinerant preacher in the postwar generation, when most of America had given up on itinerant preachers. They were all the rage going back to the Methodist circuit riders in the eighteenth century, when the frontier needed the occasional reminder of whose Manifest Destiny was at stake. They popped up to exploit the millenarian fears at the ends of the centuries, so there's no surprise that televangelists are becoming the new radio preachers from the Depression era, like Father Coughlin, who started off a New Dealer and ended up a supporter of Mussolini and Hitler. Amazing the lengths people will go for stability when they feel their houses are falling apart.

But my father bypassed all that, using charisma and cunning and an absolute belief in his mission. He hadn't started out that way. He didn't even start off Angelo. That was just the name he gave himself after Ellis Island butchered his name, Lysias Kazant-zakis, so badly that he figured he'd just rechristen himself when he moved alone with his cousin to the Little Italy section of Manhattan. At that time he was just thirteen years old. He liked Angelo because it's both a Greek and an Italian name, and he thought he could pass if he needed to in the somewhat enclavish world of new American immigrants. Besides, there was still a lot of animosity on both sides because of the Greco-Italian War. He was only twelve when that war broke out in Greece, and his father helped push the Italians back to Albania for a while; but when the Nazis invaded in 1941, my grandparents put the kids on a boat with a hope and a prayer. And while the Greek king went into exile in Egypt like some more famous exiles in the past, Angelo King came to America to give birth to himself.

Angelo scrabbled to get by. He claims he survived just by playing the ponies, but that seems shady, to say the least. I found out later that he delivered bootleg gin and cigarettes, ran numbers, and did any other marginal work he could until he could finally convince a recruitment officer that he was old enough to join the military. It wasn't that hard since the recruitment officers were in no mood to debate anyone who wanted to enlist. He paratrooped with the 82nd Airborne Division at Normandy, and when the war was over, he married a young woman two years older named Olah, my mom, who was working with the WACs in Paris. Perhaps there was an unconscious desire for reparations there. My mother was a Sephardic Jew, and Greece had just lost almost their entire Jewish population to the Holocaust. They couldn't go to his family in Athens, which was in the middle of a massive civil war, so they came back to America to blend into the postwar world of dishwashers and upward mobility. My mother worked as a seamstress at a tailor shop in the Lower East Side, and my father did janitorial work up at New York University, which was a lot smaller back then. I grew up in a blended religious household, and we attended Greek Orthodox services and took the subway to the Upper West Side to Shearith Israel for the High Holidays. They were two orthodoxies, but my parents made them work.

"Sounds like what the Kinfolk were trying to do."

There's a difference between embracing hybridity and pretending that differences don't exist. My parents were happy, but the one thing they wanted eluded them for years. By the time my father was thirty-one and my mother was thirty-three, they had all but given up on a child, and then my mother found she was pregnant with me. I came along, and the story is that I never screamed when I was born. Whether that was true or part of the mythology that grew up around me, I don't know. My father called me "the miracle boy" from that moment on, and he was so excited that he wanted to keep trying for another child. As the years went by, my mother got nervous, but he insisted on trying for a girl until my mom was in her early forties. The doctors warned my parents that she was getting too old, and yet when she died in childbirth with my stillborn brother, who was breach with the umbilical wrapped around his neck, my father was still shocked that the fates marked him for tragedy. He snapped for a while, and if I hadn't been smart enough to find my aunt Sarah's apartment up in Greenwich Village, I'm not sure what would have happened to me. There are a lot of ten-year-old boys that places like Manhattan swallow whole on a regular basis.

My father took off on a bus trip across America, and when he showed up again in three months, he had the fire in his eyes that suggested either a messiah or an antichrist—which really amounted to the same thing. My father had found Jesus, for real this time, and he concluded it was Jesus who punished him for marrying a Jew. The fact that Jesus was Jewish himself never bothered his interpretation, as it usually doesn't for most anti-Semitic Christians. But that's another story. He knew that to make reparations for his sins, he would have to help more people find their way to the Lord. My aunt Sarah was livid, but impotent, and my uncle Christopher joined my father and me on our tent revival tour of America—a tour that would last me the next eight years.

My father was sloppy at first, and he did not have the showmanship necessary to convert the kinds of numbers he wanted. He was earnest and clearly believed in his mission, and he made just enough money for us to keep moving from city to city. He preached about the revolution of the spirit and the power of revelation to cleanse the spirit of that which was corrupting it. These corruptions changed from town to town, the way St. Paul changed his metaphors of salvation depending on his audience. We got the whole notion of sin and redemption as debt and repayment, for example, from Paul's preaching to the merchants of Corinth. For my father, the metaphors often circled around the fear of mixing, of allowing the filth to corrupt the light.

Constant travel was hard at first, and I missed school desperately, but I found pleasures along the way. I loved my uncle Christopher almost as much as my father, and while my father prepared for his latest ministry, my uncle would spend hours teaching me both how to perform sleight of hand magic tricks and the strange intricacies of theology as he and my father understood it. They never used the whole text, I noticed, and kept coming back to the same passages—passages of hope, passages of wonder, passages of revelation.

I was twelve years old when I learned I could perform miracles. It was almost inadvertent, and it was lucky it came when it did, because my uncle had become terminally sick with stage four lung cancer, which I believe you know something about. He and my father had chain-smoked Lucky Strikes since the war, everywhere except in the tent, and by the time he found out, the cancer cells had metastasized to his lymph nodes and to his blood, so there was really no chance. He had only three months to live, at best. According to my father, this is what unleashed my abilities so that I became the true "miracle boy" he always said I was. My love for my uncle and my faith in Jesus allowed me to place hands on his body to alleviate the symptoms and undo some of the spread of the cancer. I had not power enough to cure the cancer completely, because I was too young, my father thought, but I could eliminate it from the most grossly infected parts before they metastasized again. My father and uncle Christopher would visit oncologists in the towns we visited, and they gave progress reports, confirming the places that I had healed and warning of new areas of his body that I would have to concentrate on.

After every faith healing episode, which I performed in front of the increasingly large crowds, I was exhausted and often would collapse onstage. This had a strange effect on the people, many of whom claimed to be cured of their diseases and ailments just by being in the presence of my miracles. It seemed that I had a calling, and I was proud that my love of my uncle could help so many people—thousands of people. My father collected signatures of everyone he converted to Jesus in the book you have seen, and these numbers grew into the hundreds in some towns as we continued the ministry. As the Vietnam War raged, our ministry boomed. People nowadays seem to forget that not everyone was a hippie back then, even though movies and the media make it seem that way. For every Whole Earth Catalogue reader, there were one hundred in the mainstream society who were terrified of violence, but more terrified of change. Even so, we recruited a number of hippies from the real happenings on which Tod was modeling his fiasco.

I'm not sure exactly when my father started to believe his lies, but when my uncle finally confessed to me that he did not have cancer and never had, my father seemed genuinely shocked that this was the truth. Even my uncle looked at him like he thought that my father was just refusing to break character, but my father looked almost like uncle Christopher was breaking his heart as much as he was breaking mine. Even when my uncle convinced my father that the cancer diagnosis had been a lie, my father pointed to his *Conversions* list to argue that it didn't matter if it was true or not. He had converted that many people to Christ, so if they didn't hurt anyone, what was the harm?

He didn't understand the depth of what we had done, and what he had done to me. For six years I had performed miracles, converting thousands in the process, and I believed it all. People fainted at my marvels; they bowed down at my visions. They felt the presence of the Lord. They would all swear to the miracle they had witnessed, and nothing could move their adamantine faith because of the holy light that many of them swore they could see emanating from my hands. And every second of it was a lie. I was culpable in the longest con of all, because these people turned their lives onto a track that would determine everything they did for the rest of their years. And I was responsible.

"But you had no say in that," said Ed. "You were a kid, for Christ's sake."

And so were you. You were four years old when I met you and your mother during our revival down at Jordan Park, down by the creek. You were four years old when your mom converted to evangelicalism, and you were four years old when you signed your name in our book, swearing your life to Jesus. Born again, just four years after your real birth. What choice did you have? And yet she still sent you to the Catholic Church with your cousin, because she had agreed to raise you that way. An invisible father sometimes has more influence than a breathing mother. As I said, we don't choose our fate. The human eye opened very late in evolution before it saw the sea of blood it required to exist. We needed redemption narratives from the animals—bison, bears, antelopes—who offered up their lives so that we could continue. Over time, this turned into a story about a man who had to be sacrificed so that we could live, so that we could continue to live the corrupt lives we wanted to with the promise of final redemption, rather than be a little bit kinder to the people who were right in front of us. And just like the human species, we all wake up at twelve or so to the person we are already, the person we've become, the person our families and our time and our country of our accidental birth have chosen for us, and we have to deal with that self as though we are dealing with some homeless dog we found in the streets.

"So how exactly are you dealing with your homeless dog? By writing travel books?"

"No, no. Travel writing pays my way, and gives an excuse to get to all the towns in my book for as long as I need to. My ministry is deconversion—to undo the influence I have had on these thousands and thousands of poor souls, who didn't know that they were making choices based on a lie. I go to each city in the book and find the people who I am responsible for, and while I do my research for my book, I meet with them all, one by one, and witness to them my story, like right now, in the hopes that they will see the light. Or the lack thereof."

"You are trying to unconvert them?"

"Well, that's often the byproduct. But you'd be surprised at how resilient people's beliefs are once they have faith in them. I just want them to know the truth—that the foundation of their faith is based on a lie."

"Which explains Ester's aunt."

"Yes, she took it pretty badly."

"How long is this project going to take?"

"Judging by my process so far, most of my life, if not the rest of it. A lot of people move around these days."

"But you are wasting your life away! What is the point? People can believe whatever they want. You aren't responsible for the sins of your father, are you? Wasn't that part of the point of Jesus?"

"One of the reasons we wanted Jesus's message so badly is because we wanted to believe that. But that's a lie, too. The Romans had it right. In their origin story, they were founded by a guy named Aeneas, who escaped from the Trojan War with his aging father strapped to his back. No wonder the Roman empire took to Christianity so fast. No one wanted it more. If you look closely, you'll see the ghost of my dead father hanging off my shoulders."

"Sounds pretty heartbreaking to me. Your whole life is an undoing. Don't you ever want a home and kids of your own?"

"Undoing is enough for some lives, especially when the scope of the sin is so large. But don't worry about me. After all, once you've been able to perform miracles, the real world looks kind of bland, anyway."

Ed watched Philos head down the street with his leather jacket and backpack, wondering how many times Philos had already told this same story, and whether he was highlighting certain details for Ed's benefit like some kind of inverted St. Paul. He had the same uncanny feeling that he had met Philos before, the same feeling as when he first saw him on Hamilton Street a year ago, but now he couldn't tell if it was from Philadelphia or from all the way back when he was four. As the twilight set upon them all, Philos turned the corner on 6th Street and returned back to the road. Ed walked into the Hess building.

CHAPTER THIRTEEN

At the south front of the Rooftop Garden, dwarfed under the thirty-foot glass wall, Tod Griffon stood looking down on the street below. He watched Ed enter the building again, and he glanced over at the four fire engines down at the street corner. From up here, they did not look like ants, like they would from the top of the Tower Building; they looked like someone's Matchbox cars and Legos, going through a simulation of life. Something about the perspective made the whole thing look like theater that had nothing to do with Tod. He wondered if people with power always saw the world this way. He stood between the two massive sculptures that Kevin had forged for the event, both suspended from the steel support ribs of the glass canopy: to the left, a ten-foot solid steel Greif logo of the griffin in the futurist G; to the right, a six-foot, hollow-cored aluminum logo of Harmonic Energies, the parallel lines across eternity, which would be his brand's new traveling symbol. He thought for the first time in well over a year about his poor dead kid, and he wondered vaguely where Ester was these days. As twilight descended, he could see himself reflected in the glass wall, which was like a mirror with the night outside. He straightened the lapels of his Perry Ellis suit and ran his hand over the stubbleless side of his scalp. It was strange, he thought, how he had had to shave his head at first. After all these months, now it seemed like he was just getting bald. Just like the old man, he thought, grimacing.

Through the reflection, he surveyed the newly added glass atrium enclosing the entire south side of the Hess building. From the street, it looked like one quarter of a cylinder. The whole atrium was a horticultural EPCOT. Plants from all over the globe were imported and placed into geographical zones to give the customers the feeling that they were traveling to exotic locations without ever leaving home. In the farthest corner, surrounded by exhaust fans, two particularly exotic plants lived: from Borneo, a spectacular three-foot orange *rafflesia arnoldii*, or corpse flower, which smelled like rotting flesh; next to that, the *hydnora africana*, which stank of feces to attract dung beetles and carrion beetles, its natural pollinators. The *hydnora africana* did not use photosynthesis, but instead mostly fed on the roots of other plants. These plants were for the decadent connoisseur, the kind of person who also liked to consume puffer fish and Japanese pornography. Tod marveled at such bizarre species and again wondered how exactly evolution worked. They said that Lamarck's version, where the species adapted to the environment with an almost conscious intent, had been disproven, but how did you evolve the ability to smell like shit so that you'd get what you needed? That possibility must be a genetic option for all species, an option that just might randomly appear but in most cases was not genetically selected for. That would explain the New York City subway system, he thought with a snarky grin.

In the center of the space, the cleared meeting area was in the shape of a Mercator projection map of the world, with Europe dead center and Africa roughly the size of Greenland. For special events like tonight, Africa could be removed to provide a spacious dance floor.

From behind him, Tod saw Kevin get off the elevator some eighty feet away. He waited until Kevin got close enough, and he started to laugh.

"There's the clever little son of a bitch," said Tod, turning.

Kevin paused and raised an eyebrow, wondering if he was in on the joke.

"You know, I might never have noticed the latest one if I wasn't standing here at this angle when they hung your promotional poster." Tod pointed to the poster Kevin had painted in the manner of Viktor Deni, but with a union worker smiling and shaking hands with someone who looked a whole lot like the CEO of Greif. "'CORPORATIONS R KILLERS'? Really, Prince? It wasn't ironic enough to use a Soviet propaganda style?"

"Um," Kevin said, impishly. "Would you believe me if I said I don't know what you're talking about?"

"Don't worry, I'm not mad. No one will notice, anyway. They haven't yet. No one really pays that much attention to art these days, and certainly not advertising. I just don't understand the need for the vitriol."

"It's not vitriol. It's not like I'm even a communist or anything. It's just my coping strategy for selling out."

"Selling out? Oh, please. What does that even mean, anymore? This isn't the 1960s and you're not the Rolling Stones going on a tour sponsored by Budweiser. You're just a semi-talented smartass who can't look at himself in the mirror because you are laboring under some antiquated notion of authenticity, which is funny, considering your version of what is authentic consists largely of staying completely ironic about everything. Makes it a rather strange form of the genuine, I'd say."

"Oh, I'm the only one who likes irony? You can't really believe in this nonsense, can you?"

"Of course, I can."

"You don't really think some dinner and dancing is going to make up for what the company did to those workers, do you? They are going to remember. You can't repair the past."

"Of course you can repair the past," Tod beamed with self-satisfaction. "I did it with you."

Kevin looked at him, cautious. "What do you mean?"

Tod smiled with what he thought was warmth. "After the happening, I visited the lawyer down in Philly. Not only did my great-great uncle Whoever have some money, but he had a lot of it—a whole lot of it squirreled away in a safety deposit box way back during what he no doubt referred to as the War of Northern Aggression. It appears the Griffons were not always the lovable white trash scamps that they became. In fact, they owned quite a lot of land back in Virginia, and they required a lot of workers who would work for less than pennies, if you know what I mean. Cheapest labor there is, except for the moral costs, of course. The North came down and swiped four hundred thousand acres of land from the losers, remember, and the Griffons were getting out while the getting was good to avoid repercussions, stashing away a stack of cash and jewelry with the hopes of coming back one day when the South rose again. So here I am, looking at a pile of ill-gotten doubloons and no way to make reparations. The Griffons kept no records of the slaves they owned, and they spent so much time acting like they weren't part of the antebellum culture after they fled to Pennsylvania that most of the family forgot that any of them ever had the money in the first place."

"So that's where you got the money to start Harmonic Energies?"

"No, that was my old marketing money. The inheritance is where I got the money to buy you." Kevin raised an eyebrow. "Ed told me about your mother's side of the family, though I could tell you were black right away. I figured that since you were struggling so much, I could help you out and make reparations for my family's past."

Kevin vibrated.

"So much talk these days," said Tod, "about how should we make good on the promise of 'forty acres and a mule.' Should we give cash payments? Should we take the money from their descendants and redistribute the wealth? Should we invest in inner city schools to help, *structurally*?" He said this last word with unnecessary irony, Kevin thought. "Well, I actually did something. I found the balance."

"Forty acres," Kevin fumed, "was part of Sherman's decree that was supposed to give up the entire coastline of Georgia, stretching thirty miles inland, to freed slaves, where no white people could live. Which, of course, Andrew Johnson overturned as soon as he took office, the little fucker. And even that could not have repaired twelve million Africans sold over three hundred years. What, you think that by giving me a job, you are going to pay reparations to make up for our African Holocaust?"

"I can't answer for anyone else. I can only answer for my family's history. It's a step in the right direction, don't you think so?"

Kevin turned to him, squaring his shoulders. "No, I don't fucking think so! It's almost worse, because you think your little gesture wipes the slate clean. You can't Wite-Out history. You can't *repair* slavery. The only thing you can do to make it right is to make it never to have happened. And I don't think that's within the capabilities of you or your buzzing little Harmonic Energies. You can't fix the past. The best you can hope for is to live with your shame."

Tod shrugged. "I guess we'll just have to agree to disagree."

Kevin had a vision of throttling Tod to the ground and splitting that cracker's egg across the dance floor, but he stayed back, trying to find the moral high ground. His chest heaved. "I'm out of here."

"Oh, no," said Tod. "I'd like you to stay. I think it is a strong symbol to have the two representatives of Harmonic Energies be a white man and a black man, coming together for a common good. Like Paul McCartney and Stevie Wonder. Besides, it is in your contract, any violation of which will require you to return your back pay from this year."

Kevin looked down, calculating furiously and despairingly how long that would take to pay back with money from Lowes.

"Look on the bright side, Kevin," said Tod. "You are doing good work, and you are helping people to be happier with their lot in life. You could be doing worse than that, don't you think? Hell, you could be convincing them that your pissy irony as a way of life is the way to live."

Three hours later, Tod sat at the head table, looking over the mass of people flooding the circular banquet tables. Over half of the Hanover Township Greif plant was there, including all of the union representatives, both in the plant and at the Amalgamated Clothing and Textile Workers Union. At the head table, flanking the podium like the wings of an eagle, stretched the factions of either side of the tensions. To the right of the podium sat representatives of management, including half of the board and the CEO, Nate Freeman. To the left sat the union representation, including Aaron Blumenfeld, Stan, and Ed, who sat in Joanie's chair. She was home with an asthma attack, waiting to hear how things went. She hated when she had asthma attacks, since it was literally her body's overreaction to something in the environment that was not really a threat. She preferred things she could fight face to face. Tod sat on the right side, talking with Nate and going over the finer points of their rhetorical tactic. Tod was proud that Nate was using almost his entire marketing strategy, and he was excited to hear his words booming out of this intimidating man throughout the atrium. Nate wore a $3,000 double-breasted Armani suit with a blood red power tie, which Tod had warned him against since the plant did not make Armani. But there was only so far that Freeman would stoop.

Kevin stood by the long atrium window, looking down onto the six fire engines out on Hamilton Street. He had just spoken with Eva, who had had him near tears, laughing at her account of her reception in Mobile, Alabama. She made it sound like a wacky adventure, but the details were laced with the terror of her near escape. No selling of merch out in the lobby on that one. Kevin had hoped she would return sooner than she was intending. Aside from her Tranny Adventures South off the Mason-Dixon Line, as she referred to them, she was killing the tour in general, and her manager was extending it across the urban archipelago from Mobile to the West Coast, where she would no doubt find smoother acceptance—New Orleans, Austin, Sante Fe, Denver (where, the manager had promised, the Boulder crowd "will absolutely adore you"), then straight to Cali, where she planned to work the coast for a while. "All that Ring of Fire heat," she said.

"I can't wait."

The dinner was winding down and Nate Freeman stood, gathered his cards and headed toward the podium, where a warm light bathed him in a golden mandorla that softened his usual hawk-like features. He placed the note cards on the ledge and stretched his hands on either side of the lectern. He did not make a sound, but some collective intuition tamed the crowd's voices as the assembled throng quieted each other to a silent hush. Nate did not clear his throat.

"Ladies and Gentlemen, welcome to our auspicious night—a night of forgiveness, a night of harmony, a night of redemption." Tod smiled at Nate. He had written the line, and he liked keeping his own brand reinforced to help grow it. "We gather here tonight at a momentous turning point in history. At midnight, the North American Free Trade Agreement goes into law, and when it does so, it will begin to usher in the new millennium. Six years away? Yes, but imagine, if you can, the brave new world we are constructing for the next thousand years. For almost two years now, we've been hearing the doomsayers' gloomy prognostications about NAFTA being the beginning of the end of American manufacturing—that somehow, by being more open, we'll all close down. That is a contradiction that I refuse to believe. As our Labor Secretary Robert Reich said back in July, the overall increase in demand for U.S. products will make American manufacturing grow substantially, and continuing to lower all trade borders will raise the standard of living and the total number of jobs, just as it did after World War II.

"After one hundred years of labor struggles in America, we are finally getting to the point where unions will no longer be needed. And by that, I mean that in every substantive way, unions have changed the face of America as much as the right to incorporate has. There are no Triangle Shirtwaist factories anymore; children are not on the line, not that we want them to be, for heaven's sake. The eight-hour workday; the five-day week; OSHA standards; retirement benefits—labor has won, and in hindsight, they had the right to win those moral battles. Hell, you even won the right to move from a pension system to a 401(k), so even you all are in the stock market with the rest of us." A titter rose among the five hundred assembled guests. "That means that your retirement depends on the same corporations labor used to have to fight. But no more. We are all part of the same system now.

"Never let it be forgotten that corporations are people, as the Supreme Court mandated all the way back 1819, and later offered the same personhood protections the Fourteenth Amendment gave to newly freed slaves. But that sounds so dry. What could that mean, 'corporations are people'? That sounds so unintuitive. Are we going to be playing racquetball at the country club with Greif anytime soon? Well, no. But the robber baron days are also over. No one owns the corporation but individual people, just like you, just like me. Everyone up here on the dais is part of the same new world. Your 401(k) makes you part owner of hundreds of corporations, including Greif and our parent, Genesco, and other workers in other factories who really own the corporation that you work for. Every corporation is the sum total of those workers' lives. For the first time in history, you all have a say in what makes your company thrive. And that is what we all want now—to thrive in a place of international global commerce, in which the rising tide, as John F. Kennedy once said, will lift all of our boats."

Tod smiled again. He was proud of that last one. Kennedy had been talking about a dam project, he knew, that had nothing to do with trickle-down economics. But saying the name Kennedy to union folk was like saying the name "Jesus" in the Hail Mary, and they all unconsciously bowed their heads a little.

"Our futures shall all rise together or fall together. There will be no more oppositions, no more strikes, no more anger. We are one, always looking for the common ground. So, I say again, let us all raise a glass to celebrate our new world, in which we no longer need unions, because we are finally all united."

The room was quiet for a second until Tod began the applause, which snaked down the management side and out into the tables, through the Rooftop Garden, finally mooring to the ground at the table on the other side of the dais, where Stan and the others sat gaping. The workers applauded Tod's words in Nate's mouth, which Ed had to admit sounded good, even if he could read the substance beyond the surface. But could over five hundred people really not hear the words that were right in front of them? Could they be so easily swayed?

Nate gave some final words, encouraging them all to start to dance on the African dance floor surrounded by Madagascar orchids, lavender, and Hottentot sugarbush. He sat down next to Tod, who exulted at his first major triumph. He and Nate shook hands, and Stan stared across at Tod like he was trying to stab him with his eyes. As most of the workers made their way to the dance floor, Nate and the board members slouched toward the elevators. Apparently, they were not staying until the ball dropped. Ed walked in their direction to use the restrooms while the music shifted from Dvořák's *Symphony No. 9* to a medley of hits from the past year: Billy Ray Cyrus's "Achy Breaky Heart," Charles & Eddie's "Would I Lie to You?" and Janet Jackson's "The Best Things in Life are Free." Ed prayed silently for an ice pick to shove into his eardrums while wondering about the choice of songs. Were they random, or was it the equivalent of making a mix tape for a woman with carefully coded messages in the song titles? Everything was text, right?

Ed saw something in his peripheral vision. He looked across the room and saw Kevin at the atrium window. Suddenly Kevin looked up from at least eight fire engines staggered around the corner of 8th and Hamilton Streets and mouthed the word, "Run!" As he said this, the east side of the room suddenly shifted, like a fast elevator coming to a quick stop, as the lights and music in the room all went black. Hundreds of dancers tipped in mid-move, a heaving gasp arising from the horde. Ed and Kevin stared at each other and Kevin looked down to the street again. The ground was beginning to split, pulling the surrounding street asphalt into a ten-foot collapse and releasing a geyser from under the surface that shot up twenty-five feet into the air. Far below them, something in the old Hess building crashed deep into the earth and the floor of the atrium started to pitch, sloping to the North, and the partygoers continued to stare at each other in silent horror as the lowing howl of the building's structure started to buckle and groan like some harpooned leviathan wailing for its absent mother. Anyone who happened to be under the ground at that moment would have seen the eighty-foot cavernous hole that had opened below the south side's foundation wall, which finally lost the strength to distribute its weight across the void and crashed into the earth's gaping maw, making the building's facade cleave from the face of the structure and collapse like an avalanching mountain. Panes of glass cracked in webbing above their heads as the girders started to shift. The large Greif logo broke from one of the support girders, crashing down onto the left side of the table, right where Ed had been sitting, and collapsed sideways, smashing Stan's leg into thousands of shards and pinning it to the tilting floor. The last Ed saw of Stan was his face contorted in a howl of pain, screeching before his final heart attack as he went into shock, while Kevin was sucked out of the shattered window into the vortex of the night. Ed sprinted towards the exit several feet away from where he stood, making it to the stairwell first, while the dancers ran panicking into one another, trying to find their loved ones for comfort while looking for a way out. As the door closed behind him, everything in the room atomized into a spray of fissile panic, everyone looking individually for a way out of this garden, running in random patterns into one another in a pandemonium of chaotic ecstasy. Some lone guests made it to the stairwell with Ed while the glass shattered in sheets from the atrium's rib cage and the steel girders buckled, snapped, and twisted their tangled bine-stems, scoring the sky like the strings of broken lyres, raining down millions of glass shards that pierced their skin in an agony of scorching pain like fireballs from the sky.

The din of screams and grunts and the horrifying sound of human bodies crushed underfoot as everyone trampled their way to the exits followed Ed into the blackness of the stairwell, where he leapt down five steps at a time into the unknown. As he crashed to the bottom of the well, he twisted his right ankle and the white flash of pain exploding behind his eye sockets seemed to light up the bar of the security door to the outside, although that must have been an illusion. He burst outside into the open night air as the countdown to the New Year began to the splatter of bodies dropping onto the pavement twenty feet to his left, sounding like uncooked chicken breasts being thrown against a brick wall. Ed did not look back and ran limping across 9th Street, hobbling along the base of the PP&L Tower Building towards Linden Street, each step flashing blinding pain in his eyes. Behind him he could hear the monstrous Hess building, patch-quilted over the century to accommodate the growth of the American dream, pitching south into the monstrous sinkhole opening across the entire width of Hamilton Street, pulling everything down into the cavernous void underground. Its collapse was announced by giant shards of shattered glass and toppling masonry, blasted bricks and leaping bodies, the totality flowing like a waterfall and crashing down to the collapsing street below. The hole snaked along Hamilton Street, pulling everything in its wake three blocks down to 6th and Hamilton, where a crack started to cleave the Sovereign Building's face in two.

As Ed made it to Linden Street, he came to a throng of spectators armed with cameras who had flowed out to the street from their New Year's Eve parties to see what all the commotion was about. Ed felt emboldened by their stillness and turned hobbling to see the last of the building's structure imploding, falling down, deep below the calm telluric plain. He paused for a moment, scanning the epic scene that was beyond poetry, beyond words, and where the Hess building was, he saw nothing now but a flat curvilinear limitless horizon that spoke of . . . that spoke . . . of what? Trying to think, yet not thinking. Beyond thought, he would imagine, as if there were some fundamental reality beyond words, some transcendent being of which he was but a function like some passive vessel, a sense organ of the divine. The thought comforted him, and for a moment the terror, the deadening empty meaningless space between past and future, between here and there, the shimmerless static still point of existence stopped leaping fore and aft and he understood, if only for a moment, that this center of infinite nothingness was always there, and always would be: neither limitless possibility, neither the peace which passeth understanding, but rather the more infinite, more insubstantial, more profound

And in that silence, he saw that there was no peace, there was no gentleness, there was no mother waiting in the paradise he had lost. There was only this   in the center of it all. And again and again and again. The gas line exploded, and the calm gave way to the shattering moment like the inconsequential movement of six billion ants across an inconsequential ant heap, moving not where, but moving, an enduring phantom, a pulsing horde of throbbing meaningless life, each individual reaching his only possible apotheosis in the final understanding, the culmination of his pitiless three-score-and-ten. His mind raced again with no sense of a continuous self, as if consciousness were created anew at every slice of time, consciousness the cause of itself, out of the sheer unending oblivion. His mind reeled at the horizon, the dead metaphor, and the more dead, yet dying, being of the Being that he imagined, the trivialized roads that stretched through a million superfluous poems as though a mere road could give grandeur to the wretched horde of raving harridans called temporality, and he searched the cold impersonal immutable chaos for a metaphor to give direction, meaning, and solicitude to the no longer only intuitively apprehended nihilation that was the flat line of existence—not even dead, just *not*—and he found the only image to express this knowledge, this understanding that was not even allowed to be called an epiphany, and he did not write it down, but made a mental silence, an unnote, for there was none of the kind of paper available that he would have needed.

CHAPTER FOURTEEN

And Phil Berman, who bought the regional company from Max Hess, Jr. in 1968 and built it into a 38-store multistate chain before he retired in 1985, seemed almost indifferent. "When I sold it, I left it," Berman said from his Allentown office yesterday.

- The Morning Call, August 2, 1994

The next morning, the *Morning Call* ran a spectacular series of pieces on the devastation. No one could have seen this coming, the mayor guaranteed, although he reminded reporters to remind residents that most insurance companies in Pennsylvania did not automatically include sinkhole coverage unless specifically requested. Engineers could not decide immediately what the cause of the collapse was, whether the sinkhole or the water main break came first. "Insurance adjusters and attorneys will have the final say," ran the piece with quietly ironic understatement. What they agreed upon was that the non-local architectural firm that had designed the Rooftop Garden addition had not anticipated what the extra load would do to the foundations of the old building, especially in a town built on such porous limestone voids. All was not lost, however, as the damage to the four buildings on the east side of N. 7th Street "were slated for razing before the sinkhole to create Century Square, part of the downtown renewal program." So there was a positive to this tragedy, the mayor assured. Allentown was set to rise again.

Over four hundred people perished in the disaster, the paper reported, including the entire union delegation and half of the workforce. The CEO, Nathanial Freeman, who had just barely exited before the building's collapse, assured shareholders that factory production would continue as before, and they were looking to hire new employees starting on Monday. The company had been planning to downsize their labor force anyway, so they would be hiring back only a percentage of the people they had lost.

By the time the fires were finally extinguished, over one third of the building had collapsed deep below the ground; one third was smashed from above; and one third remained, hulking its exposed girth like a rotting beached blue whale. Implosion of the remainder of the building would begin after the city was able to determine just how deep the void went. Engineers had already begun filling the hole with a grout compound to test the depth, but there seemed to be no end in sight so far. A lottery was going to be held for residents who wanted to compete for the right to push the button to ignite the explosives. This was expected to raise several hundred thousand dollars to help in area renewal.

CHAPTER FIFTEEN

Greif Calls It Quits
650 Will Lose Jobs Apparel Maker To Shut Down By Spring
November 05, 1994 | by MICHAEL HERNAN, *The Morning Call*

Apparel maker Greif Cos., hammered by tough competition and a steady drop in sales and profits, will shut down by spring and lay off 650 area workers. "We're actively exploring alternatives to continue the Greif line through another company, but it will not be in Allentown," said Kevin Gwin, a Genesco spokesman. Greif's Shippensburg plant, which employs 164 people, also will close, Gwin said. A Greif plant in Verona, Va., closed this summer, cutting more than 500 jobs. Founded more than a century ago, Greif came to the Lehigh Valley from Baltimore in 1982 when it was merged with Phoenix Clothes of Allentown. A bitter fight with its union cost the company several big orders, and the company lost several valuable licenses, including Ralph Lauren.

"Although our (apparel) operations contributed $105 million in sales in fiscal 1994, the capital now invested in the apparel business can be more productively employed in our footwear operations," Genesco's president and chief executive said in a statement yesterday. Genesco said it will take a $92.5 million charge in the third quarter to cover the cost of the restructuring.

PART IV
ALLENTOWN
APRIL 20, 2003

During the summer at Oxford University, John Donne's ghost provides no valedictions. De Quincey's specter whispers no confessions. And Shelley's spirit seems not only bound, but gagged, to boot. Exeter College, one of thirty-nine colleges of Oxford, where I was staying, was responsible for educating Edward Burne-Jones, Tolkien, and William Morris. Perhaps they haunted in regular session.

Summer session was for foreigners financing revisions and renovations. There were twenty-eight of us at Oxford on scholarship—the brightest of the fourteen universities in Pennsylvania's State System of Higher Education—handpicked to learn about "English Art and Architecture from Stonehenge to the Present" and the role of "Women in Medieval and Renaissance England" so that we could inspect the actual architecture of the actual Tower in which the actual Anne Boleyn was actually beheaded. From Edinboro University in northwest Pennsylvania to Cheyney in the southeast, we represented Pennsylvania's rich diversities and hailed from various socioeconomic backgrounds—working-class to lower-middle-class, white and black. Most of us watched Jeremy Brett's BBC production of *Sherlock Holmes* on PBS, arguing that it was clearly the best adaptation to date, and all of us could quote the entirety of every episode of *Monty Python's Flying Circus*. Our bibliophilism was so pronounced that we would usually file directly into the local bookstore in whatever -wold, -shire, or -bury we found ourselves in, so that we would have the book about Salisbury Cathedral before seeing the cathedral itself.

We also bought postcards. My mother would have been proud if I had sent home postcards.

I had returned to college out at Kutztown University the year after the Hess building implosion. I double majored in literature and history, with a focus on labor history, and I finally made it to Europe with the benefit of thoughtful benefactors and supporters of public education. Our entire speech was a string of shibboleths to the locals. When we were fairly sure that no one was listening, Jon and I would practice terrible British accents, years before poor Madonna was struck with the same affliction. He deviated-septumed his way through a vaudeville John Lennon, while I squawked more or less like I should be begging for a ha'penny on the streets of Manchester or proffering a licked-clean bowl to Mr. Bumble while asking for "more." Karen had an infectious staccato laugh and a western Pennsylvania screech about two octaves too high for an episode of *Masterpiece Theater*, and I kept having nightmares and aural hallucinations of what that voice would sound like echoing through the Bodleian Library's marble chambers.

The second weekend, four of us took the shuttle to London to stay at immoderately priced YMCA lodgings in the North End, which consisted of a large, irregularly shaped cinder block room with four cots, iron wardrobes, and a single spigot in the center for showering. Karen and Kathy—or was it Cathy with a "C"?—wanted to get to the Tate Gallery to see if Millais's drowning *Ophelia* really looked like their friend Beth in real life, but they first wanted to go down to Piccadilly Circus to meet some other people. Jon, as the only one who had been to England before, wanted to look up some friends in the West End. I also wanted to get to the Tate to see Dalí's *Métamorphose de Narcisse*, but first I was hoping to visit Westminster Cathedral, Parliament, Buckingham Palace, the National Gallery, and the British Museum. I still loved architecture, and every space I visited reminded me of what Philos had said about the palimpsest of history, which in Europe goes down, down, down into the depths of the earth. Everywhere you walked in England, you could feel the presence of the past haunting like a benevolent banshee, unlike the illusory blank slate of an American plain.

We decided to breakfast in the second story of Shakespeare's Head, a pub where Jon joked about Shylock serving us while we ate bangers and mash among puce felt wallpaper and fading reproductions of Hans Holbein the Elder. Afterwards, we came out onto Fouberts Place and Carnaby Street, which we walked down briefly, trying to imagine The Who, The Kinks, and Pretty Things shopping at the Soho Jag T-Shirt Centre and Soccer Hooligan Shop. We tried to find our way to Piccadilly Circus, which should have only been a half-mile away. No one seemed to know the way, and we were mocked merrily by a Cockney Hare Krishna who kept slapping his thigh, John Wayne drawling, "Pardner, I sho 'nuff don't know." Someone finally pointed us in the right direction.

We made it down Regent Street, finally dumping out onto Piccadilly, which was formed in 1819 by the intersection of five roads. In the center of the Circus is the famous statue of Eros, dedicated to the Victorian philanthropist, the Earl of Shaftesbury. I almost did not recognize Eros from the pictures I had seen. Depending on the angle, the statue becomes eclipsed by gargantuan electric billboards, giving Eros a McDonalds, TDK, and Coca-Cola nimbus. Even unlit, during the day, the signs made it difficult for us to discern our friends. The Circus was already bustling, and you could easily see why many considered this area to be the center of London.

I turned from the spectacle to read about it in my travel guide.

I had known about Piccadilly before, but it was not until now that I learned that although everyone called it the Eros statue, Eros wasn't the Greek god of love at all, and the statue wasn't really a statue. He was originally intended to be Anteros, the god of requited love, and literally translated as "love returned." Anteros was Eros's brother, and he was given to his brother so they could play together, because love needed a counter-love to exist. They renamed the statue after the Angel of Christian Charity to appease the somewhat scandalized public, because that was the closest approximation to the Greek god of selfless love. The fountain now claimed to be a symbol for Christian Charity, even though everyone thought it was Love, and the statue itself was made of aluminum. In the mid-nineteenth century, aluminum was a metal both singular and novel.

One of my mother's favorite recurring stories: When she and my father were dating, she dragged him to see *Love's Labour's Lost* on a Friday night after they had worked all day on the line at Phoenix Clothes. He fell asleep. They never returned.

And so, manufacturing left, as no one could have predicted—not to Mexico, but to Asia. America had been revised, and Walmart was now the largest employer in the country. The Internet propped us up for a while, until the bubble burst on Pets.com and other can't-lose innovations, right around the time that everyone thought that planes were going to fall out of the sky and nuclear power plants were going to melt down because the number of digits in the years in computer programs were not enough. The millennium came, and the world did not end, although it certainly felt that way one September morning in the first year of the next thousand. But that's not the point of the apocalypse. The world was always already ending, and history was a catalogue of horrors you wouldn't believe. To destroy the world completely would be redundant. The idea of the apocalypse reminded us of this basic truth.

Last year, Joanie and I went to the Leonardo da Vinci exhibit at the Metropolitan Museum of Art while we were in New York for our seventh anniversary. We lined up in the freezing weather like we wanted to get on a Disney ride, waiting for over two hours to come within ten feet of da Mazing da Vinci. I knew it would be crowded, but I had no idea it would be *that* packed. At one point I found myself wedged in a corner next to a four-by-six-inch palimpsest of horse sketches, and I looked at the people around me, thinking that I recognized these same faces from the Dalí exhibit the year before. Something told them to come out. Something told them that this was Art, and it was their duty to look, to analyze, to appreciate. And they knew that whatever else happened, whatever else they did not comprehend, Leonardo da Vinci was Art. They tried their best to understand. Happily, the horse palimpsest had a description next to it, telling the viewer that this was one of the most important papers in all of da Vinci's work: They should feel lucky that it was on (rare) exhibit. They looked like they felt lucky. I remember how on our way out of the series of rooms, we first had to pass the gift shop and then the Goya room, which was filled floor to ceiling with eight images that made Joanie and me stop and gape. At the center of the display was a work on loan from the Prado, *Saturn Devouring His Son*, showing the titan eating one of his children to avoid the prophecy of his eventual destruction by his own offspring. Goya had painted this on the walls of his dining room, and this moved and perplexed me in equal measure. Most people were still too busy situating their packages and putting away their credit cards to look up. I'm still glad that Joanie made me stop, even if we both had seen the other paintings before.

We also found a much smaller exhibit containing photographs of WPA murals from across the country. Since the murals were permanent fixtures, often meant to adorn the factories of which they became a part, this traveling exhibit showed twenty-three images of old factories, ones still operating or ones long gone. I was also held in arrest for some time by Ernest Fiene's 1938 painting, *The History of the Needlecraft Industry*. The mural had been commissioned by the International Ladies Garment Workers Union and included a detail of the Triangle Shirtwaist Company fire in 1911, when one hundred and forty-six workers, largely Jewish and Italian immigrant women, burned to death because the owners had barred the doors to the stairways and exits to prevent the workers from taking unauthorized breaks. This was a common practice at the time.

"I gave up on art a long time ago," I thought, remembering another time I had said those same words.

The other week, we saw *Dead Poets Society* on cable again, and I had to watch it all the way through, as I always do. I know that Diane Brightfoy uses it in her English class, which she now teaches down the hall from me at William Allen High School, where I teach honors U.S. History to juniors and seniors along with a special class on Pennsylvania history. I always have a great class where I point out how curious it is that we have a steroided-up canary as a mascot, since the canary was used in coal mines to see if there was a gas leak. If there was, our muscle-bound mascot would die, a signal for the miners to escape. That always puts a damper on the football games, and some parents have complained. They claim some local mythic nonsense about a canary being brave enough to fly into a hurricane. But I've got history on my side, and I've never been much of a booster. I use essays from Philos King's book from his ever-growing *Individual Vision* series, which is up to sixteen volumes. Every time I read the chapter on Allentown, I feel his presence sitting across from me, across from the Hess building. His final version of the story contained the historical epilogue it needed, documenting Greif's eventual relocation of its mill abroad. I have subscribed ahead of time for all the future books in the series to be sent to me as they come out.

I've meditated about my longstanding fascination with *Dead Poets Society* from time to time, and I think I figured out what much of the allure is. Robin Williams's character, Mr. Keating, obvious Jesus figure that he was, was bringing the Word of the words to the highly educated spawn of the bourgeoisie. There is fascination in this conceit, I think, because of the romantic notion that the poor old rich folk can't make life choices on their own to become poets, artists, actors, and whathaveyous. You see—sniff, sniff—they are being forced against their wills—sniff, sniff—to become lawyers and investment bankers. But their lives will be poor—so much poorer!—than the lives of those of us who can appreciate a line of the poetry of Walt Whitman.

This motif is profound, no matter how false. Or if not profound, it at least has legs. I am not sure exactly why it continues to function and who keeps perpetuating it. Is it merely the sour grapes consolation myth of the working class? Who exactly is paying for those million-dollar Rothkos at auction? The Salvation Army? And who is filling up those seats to all four nights of Wagner's *Der Ring des Nibelungen* at the Met? It probably isn't people who find "$500 a week" to be a better description of their income than their entertainment budget.

We finally got that opportunity last year, after saving up for over two years. We pooled resources from Joanie's public relations job at the union and my teaching gig, the salary of which the local parents still liked to complain about, but which was still just solidly middle class, thanks to the NEA. We went to Vienna for the first time to watch all four nights of the genius' great play cycle. We went on the New Year, and it was the first time since her father's death that we made it out of the house on that date. By the fourth night's opera, *Götterdämmerung*, I was pretty opera'd out, even though I loved vibrating next to Joanie's rapturous face. The long dark passages of old Norse myths made little sense to me at first, although I was of course as thrilled as anyone to hear the "Ride of the Valkyries" and picture the scene from *Apocalypse Now,* where Robert Duvall's character, Lieutenant Colonel Bill Kilgore—no subtlety to that name symbolism—guns down a Vietcong-controlled area of the river because he wants to go surfing, and "Charlie don't surf." Wagner's opera is far more literally apocalyptic, and in the *Götterdämmerung*, the "Twilight of the Gods," there is the remarkable passing of Wotan, father of the gods, as the massive infighting and intrigue between the gods and their offspring destroy Valhalla and all the gods in a spectacular conflagration. According to the libretto, the cycle was a hybrid of many different sagas and traditions—the Old Norse *Edda*, the

Völsunga saga, and the old twelfth-century German poem, *Nibelungenlied*—that merged in Wagner's vision of the end of all things, both mortal and divine. Last night, I came across an essay from George Bernard Shaw, who interpreted the cycle as an allegory for the final collapse of the internal contractions of capitalism. I don't know if this was what Wagner intended, but it helped make sense of a whole lot of Teutonic sound and fury. In Vienna, I looked at my wife, who looked at the singers on stage, and her gaze seemed to disappear into the performance and spectacle laid out in front of her. I smiled at how happy she was, and I knew that if we ever had a boy, his name would be Anteros.

Joanie exulted.

CREDITS

Page 5: Caroline Cunningham, https://carolineryancunningham.com

Page 13: Love and Rockets, "Mirror People"

Page 14: Daniel Modell

Page 15: Joy Division, "Love Will Tear Us Apart"

Page 18: Robyn Hitchcock, "Superman"

Page 22: Jag9889, https://commons.wikimedia.org/wiki/File:
Lower_Trenton_Bridge_20091103-jag9889.jpg

Page 36: Pantera, "Cowboys from Hell"

Page 39: Morrissey, "Ordinary Boys"

Page 44: The Goldcoast Singers, "Plastic Jesus"

Page 109: Frank H. Jump (Fading Ad Blog),
https://www.fadingad.com/fadingadblog/2012/10/20/adelaide-
silk-mills-allentown-pa

Page 121: Radiohead, "Creep"

Page 204: Morning Call file photos, https://www.mcall.com/
2017/04/20/pictures-historic-photos-of-hesss-department-store

ABOUT THE AUTHOR

SCOTT DIMOVITZ has taught writing and contemporary literature at New York University and Regis University. He has twice won the Bennett Harris Humorous Writing Award, which meant quite a lot to him at the time. While he grew up in the Pennsylvania working-class world depicted in the novel, he now lives in Denver, Colorado among piles of books, guitars, and many half-graded student essays.